Barbara Delinsky is... "one of this generation's most gifted writers of contemporary fiction."
—*Affaire de Coeur*

"(An author) of sensitivity and style."
—*Publishers Weekly*

"Kelsey Roberts will take you on a fun, fanciful and fascinating journey. If you're looking for romance and intrigue with an interesting twist, you won't want to miss her."
—*New York Times* bestselling author Nora Roberts

"Ms. Roberts writes an intriguing blend of suspense, passion, humor and warmth. She'll keep you hooked!"
—*Rendezvous*

D0192265

BARBARA DELINSKY

was born and raised in suburban Boston. She worked as a researcher, photographer and reporter before turning to writing full-time in 1980. With more than fifty novels to her credit, she is truly one of the shining stars of contemporary romance fiction. This talented writer has received numerous awards and honors, and her involving stories have made her a *New York Times* bestselling author. There are over twelve million copies of her books in print worldwide—a testament to Barbara's universal appeal.

KELSEY ROBERTS

had her first book, *Legal Tender*, published by the Harlequin Intrigue line in 1993, and since then has produced twenty-three novels that always garner award nominations for her talents in writing romantic suspense. Before turning to writing as a full-time career, Kelsey worked as a paralegal, a profession that provides wonderful fodder for the types of stories she enjoys writing. She makes her home outside Annapolis, Maryland, with her college professor husband and three-year-old daughter.

BARBARA DELINSKY

Father of the Bride

KELSEY ROBERTS

Handsome as Sin

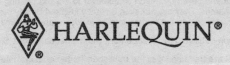

HARLEQUIN®

TORONTO • NEW YORK • LONDON
AMSTERDAM • PARIS • SYDNEY • HAMBURG
STOCKHOLM • ATHENS • TOKYO • MILAN • MADRID
PRAGUE • WARSAW • BUDAPEST • AUCKLAND

ISBN 0-373-83453-5

HARLEQUIN SPECIAL Vol. 1

Copyright © 2001 by Harlequin Books S.A.

The publisher acknowledges the copyright holders of the individual works as follows:

FATHER OF THE BRIDE
Copyright © 1991 by Barbara Delinsky

HANDSOME AS SIN
Copyright © 1995 by Rhonda Harding Pollero

CONTENTS

Father of the Bride

Barbara Delinsky

Chapter One

TWENTY-FIVE YEARS was a long time not to have gone home. Russell Shaw thought about that on Monday afternoon as his plane winged south toward St. Louis. He had been eighteen when he left. He had lived more of his life away from St. Louis than in it. But he had left part of his heart there, which made twenty-five years a long time indeed.

The view out the plane window told him nothing. He might well have been on his way to Chicago or Denver or San Francisco, each of which he had visited professionally in the course of those twenty-five years. Despite the brilliance of the late afternoon sun to the west, the carpet of clouds beneath the aircraft hid the distinguishing features that would have branded the landscape home. But Russ didn't need the reminder. There was no possible way he could forget where he was headed and why. For one thing, there was a faint ache in the part of his heart that he thought had long since healed. For another, there was a vague knot in his stomach—excitement, nervousness, downright fear; he guessed a little of each. And finally, there was the letter in his hand.

He opened it along folds that had become soft with wear over the past few weeks. The paper was white, thick and rich-feeling in keeping with the embossed

DIANE SARAH BAUER at its top. The ink was blue, again with a rich feel to it, and the script was confident and feminine—rightly so for a young woman who had been raised in high society, had a good job and a fledgling business of her own and was in love with a man she adored.

Love made people confident. Russ knew. He remembered those days so long ago when he himself had been on top of the world. Love could conquer all, he'd thought then. Love could hold people together regardless of how incongruous their upbringings, how disparate their bank balances or how angry their parents were about the union.

He had learned the hard way that love couldn't do all that, but he prayed to God that Diane would fare better than he had. She certainly had more going for her. She had maturity on her side, and she had the support of her family, if he had correctly read between the lines of her letter.

> We're being married at Saint Benedict's, on Saturday afternoon at two. It's going to be a big wedding. Between my grandmother's friends and my mother's friends, and Nick and my friends and Nick's family, there may be four hundred people there. But they're all wonderful. You'll like them, I know you will.

He supposed he would, at least as far as Nick's people went. He had already met Nick—once, with Diane in New York—and liked him. Nick was from a large Italian family, and though the Granatellis weren't at all impoverished, the Hill, a historic ethnic neighborhood, was a far cry from Frontenac, the finely manicured, grandly built enclave of St. Louisians of the Bauer ilk. Russ could identify with the Granatellis. He had been from the wrong side of the tracks himself. He would be able to talk with them easily.

Actually, he would be able to talk with the rest of the guests easily, too. He had come a long way since leaving St. Louis. The Connecticut private school of which he was headmaster had, in addition to its many scholarship students, a healthy share of the upper crust's sons and daughters. Russ had learned how to deal with the wealthy, and how to do it with grace. In contrast to the eighteen-year-old boy who had left St. Louis with a broken heart and a single satchel containing all his belongings, he was a man of considerable social skills. He was counting on those skills to stand him in good stead over the next five days, through the inevitable confrontation with Gertrude Hoffmann—and the inevitable one with Cynthia.

The prospect of seeing Cynthia gnawed at him. Because of that, he had thought long and hard about the wisdom of returning to St. Louis. He had a satisfying life in Connecticut. He didn't need pain from the past. Nor did he want his presence to spark anything— tension, an argument, words of resentment, however brief—that would hurt Diane. This was her time. He wanted it to be perfect for her.

For that reason, he should have stayed away. But for the same reason, he was coming. Diane had asked him to, had handwritten her request. Russ read that part of her letter for the umpteenth time:

> Had Matthew been here, he would have given me away. But he died before Nick and I even reconciled. Mom has asked Matthew's brother to do the honors, and though Ray was always wonderful to me, it isn't the same. This is one of the most important days of my life. I want it to be perfect, which is why, more than anything, I want you to give me away. You're my father. I know that coming back may be difficult for you, but if you can possibly see your way clear to do it, I'd be so, so happy.

Russ believed her. In the dozen or so meetings that he'd had with Diane over the past six years—dinners, first in Boston, when she had been at Radcliffe, then in New York after her stint abroad—he had come to know her for her sincerity. While not the confrontational type, she let her feelings be known through the look in her eye, the set of her mouth, the tone of her voice. Her wariness at their first meeting had been obvious to him, as had her subsequent warming. The last few times they'd met, she had greeted him with a hug. A hug. A warm, genuine, happy-to-see-him hug.

Each time he thought of that, Russ choked up. He suspected he would walk barefoot over hot coals if Diane asked him to. Of course, she wouldn't. She had never asked a thing of him. Until now. So how could he possibly deny her this request?

The clouds had begun to thin out, breaking at spots as the plane began its descent. Russ folded the letter and replaced it in the breast pocket of his blazer, near his heart. He wasn't sure if he deserved the honor of walking Diane down the aisle; wasn't sure if he deserved Diane at all. The last time he had done anything of a practical nature for her had been when she was three months old, on a night he'd relived hundreds of times since. Having made his decision to leave St. Louis, he had bathed the baby and gotten her ready for bed. He remembered how small she was, how neatly, trustingly, she curled against him. He remembered her sweet smell, her smooth skin, the tiny noises she made as she sucked on her thumb in the crib. He remembered turning off the light and feeling himself thrust into the dark, then being caught up for a brief, bright time in Cynthia's arms, before slipping out into the deepest darkness he'd ever known.

"This is the captain again." A voice with a distinct Midwest twang filtered through the airplane. "At this time we are beginning our final descent into St. Louis. Weather conditions at Lambert Field are partly sunny, with the temperature a warm seventy-six degrees. Air traffic permitting, we should be on the ground in just about twelve minutes. I'd like to take this opportunity to thank you all for flying with us today and to wish you a pleasant stay in St. Louis."

The easygoing timbre of the man's voice snapped Russ from past to present, darkness to light, sorrow to joy—and he *was* here on a mission of joy. His daughter, his only child, was getting married. Sure, he was meeting with a former colleague, a man now teaching at Washington University. But that meeting was incidental to the occasion of Diane's wedding.

As the plane dropped lower, the knot in his stomach became more pronounced. His apprehension had nothing to do with flying, he knew, and everything to do with returning to St. Louis. He hadn't thought he would ever come back. His mother had died before he left, and his father, a wanderer in the best of circumstances, had set out for parts unknown soon after Russ joined the Army. Not that Russ would have come back to St. Louis after Vietnam even had his father remained. Memory would have made living there as much of a hell as the war had been.

So he had gone directly to Washington, D.C., where he had enrolled at Georgetown under the GI Bill. Four years later, with a history degree in his pocket, he had taken a teaching job in Connecticut and made a life for himself that was sufficiently far removed from St. Louis.

That didn't mean he hadn't thought about Cynthia, or Diane, or the life they might have had together. Particularly in those early days at Hollings, when he'd had a modest but reputable salary that would have supported them, he had thought of them often. But he had made a decision, and he couldn't go back. There was nothing to go back to. Cynthia had returned to the Hoffmann family fold and had their marriage annulled. Then she'd married Matthew Bauer, who had adopted Diane and proceeded to raise her as his own.

All that was what Russ had intended. As clearly as he knew the words on the letter in his breast pocket, he remembered the words in another letter, one he himself had written twenty-five years before. He had agonized over every sentence, every phrase, wanting to minimize Cynthia's hurt and make her understand why he was doing what he was.

This is the only way, Cyn. If I leave, they'll take you back, and if they take you back, you'll have all the things you and the baby should have. I can't give them to you. I thought I could, but I can't. I can take two jobs and work forever and still come up short. It's not fair that you should have to live this way.

"Excuse me, sir?" the flight attendant said. "We're preparing to land. Would you raise your seat back, please?"

With an apologetic smile, Russ pressed the button to return the seat to its upright position, then looked out the window again. At the sight of the skyline coming up on the right, his heart began to thud. The Gateway Arch identified the city—he remembered the excitement when its construction was complete—but otherwise he might well have been approaching a foreign land. He had never viewed St. Louis from the air before, true. But twenty-five years of growth had dramatically altered the city as he remembered it from the ground. Tall, gleaming buildings had sprouted where low ones had once been. Some shone with glass; others were more muted with stone. Some were square, some round, some terraced, some sleek.

Russ didn't know why he should be surprised. He had been in many a cosmopolitan area over the years, and he knew that St. Louis was as cosmopolitan as any. Having been a subscriber to the *Post Dispatch* for years, he also knew the specifics of what went on inside those new buildings. Somehow, though, seeing the city now, in contrast to the way it had stood for so long in his memory, served to emphasize just how much time had passed.

He had changed, too, he knew. He had grown taller and broader. He had also come by crow's-feet at the corners of his eyes and his once dark hair was shot with strands of silver, but he wasn't ashamed of either of those things. Given that he hadn't gained an ounce since graduation from high school—and that he ran upward of thirty miles a week—he thought he'd aged well.

He knew Cynthia had. The pictures that appeared in the paper from time to time told him so. She had grown into a beautiful woman whose clothes, hair, behavior were all eminently flattering and socially correct. No doubt Gertrude Hoffmann was pleased.

He wondered if the old lady knew he was coming. Surely Cynthia did, since he had received a formal wedding invitation from her with his name and address written in calligraphy on the front. He had no sooner returned the reply card with his acceptance than he had received Diane's personal note asking him to give her away. He wondered what Cynthia thought of that. He wondered what *Gertrude* thought of that, the old battle-ax.

The plane touched down with a small jolt. To gather his composure he closed his eyes for a minute and conjured up an image of his home in Connecticut and the life that he found so rewarding. When the plane finally pulled up to the gate, he rose with the other passengers, took his carryon from the overhead compartment and slowly made his way up the aisle.

The terminal was filled with welcoming committees. Families, friends, business associates, lovers—Russ's imagination touched on the possibilities as he passed by the expectant groups. Diane had offered to meet him, but he hadn't wanted her to fight through late afternoon traffic for him. Besides, he was renting a car.

Though both arguments were valid, there was another that he hadn't wanted to voice in his last letter to her. From the start he had known that returning to St. Louis would be an emotional experience for him. He wanted a little time alone to merge past with present, a little time to gather himself, because more than anything he wanted to come across as being self-assured and strong. He wanted Diane to be proud of who and what he was. He wanted Cynthia to be proud, too. He was the father of the bride—the father of a beautiful, personable, privileged bride—and it behooved him to fit the role. He had a point to prove. Based on little more than his home address, Gertrude Hoffmann had deemed him unworthy of her daughter's love years before. He was going to take pride in showing her how sadly she had underestimated his ability to rise in the world.

As had been true of the rest of the trip, his luggage came through without a hitch. So did the rental car his travel agent had reserved for him. With surprising speed he hit the interstate, intent on going straight to his hotel as he always did when he traveled, to shower away the fatigue of the flight. There wasn't any fatigue this time, though, or if there was, it was buried beneath excitement. Without quite making a conscious decision to do so, he found himself driving directly downtown, actually appreciating the traffic, which was slow enough to allow him to study his surroundings.

The Arch was as impressive as ever, as was the Old Cathedral, but those were mere jumping-off points for Market Street. He passed the Old Courthouse, which he remembered, and Kiener Mall, which he didn't. Farther on he passed the City Hall, but he didn't pull over until he reached Aloe Plaza. He had always loved the sculpted fountain there, had spent hours as a boy studying the bronze figures that commemorated the joining of the Mississippi and Missouri rivers. Male and female, they had symbolized in his mind happiness, freedom and love. He remembered spending hours sitting in sight of that fountain with Cynthia, holding her hand, watching the play of the water. He remembered touching her stomach as they sat there, feeling the tightening of her muscles, the movement of the baby inside. Given what had happened to his marriage, he should have been disillusioned watching the water's spray now, but he wasn't. Good had come out of his marriage in the form of Diane. For the sake of her existence alone, the pain had been worthwhile.

With an odd mix of reluctance and curiosity, he looked across the street toward Union Station. He'd spent his last night there in St. Louis, slouched on a hard bench, waiting to take the dawn train out of town. At the time he was sure it would prove to be the most miserable night of his life, but that was before he had suffered through basic training without sight or sound of Cynthia. And before he'd been sent overseas.

Union Station was no longer a railroad station. Russ had kept abreast of its conversion into a complex of shops, restaurants and a hotel, and given his memories, he wasn't sorry for the change. The less there was to remind him of that sad and lonely night, the better.

Driving slowly on, he turned down one street and up another. None of the reading he'd done over the years had prepared him for so many alterations. What wasn't new was refurbished, and what wasn't refurbished had been carefully preserved. He was impressed. St. Louis had done well for itself.

He drove on a bit longer, gradually losing himself in his thoughts. He passed a restaurant that hadn't been there twenty-five years before, and one that had—not that he'd ever eaten in it. He hadn't been able to afford such places. Pizza and a movie had been his limit, but Cynthia had never minded. She'd been incredible that way. Raised with a silver spoon in her mouth, she had been willing to give it all up just to be with him. They'd be sitting in his secondhand Ford, sharing a pack of Lorna Doones and a milk shake, curled against each other in the dingy shadow of the soda shop because they couldn't go to her parents' estate or to his father's hovel, and she'd make him feel like a million bucks. He had loved her so much. *So much.*

The traffic eased. Though more than an hour remained before dusk, with the low slant of the sun and the exodus of the working set, it felt like evening. Turning west at last, Russ headed for Clayton. He had chosen to stay in the suburb for its proximity both to the university, where he would be visiting his colleague, and to Cynthia's home, where the wedding reception was being held. He had chosen the Seven Gables Inn not only for its New England connection but for its small size and its reputation for charm and warmth. He didn't think he could stand a large, impersonal hotel. Not this trip. Not when he was feeling more exposed than he had in years.

The inn proved to be brighter than the Nathaniel Hawthorne house Russ had visited in Salem. The personnel were upbeat, as well. His suite had a European flavor but was distinctly homey. A decorative headboard and footboard set off the large bed, which was covered by a quilt of a dusty blue design, picking up the color of the floral wallpaper and the café curtains. The artwork was gentle—dancers, a landscape. Cut flowers stood in a vase on a small round table, alongside a basket of fresh fruit.

After tossing his blazer on the bed, unbuttoning his shirt cuffs and turning them back, Russ picked up an apple and took a bite. Idly he ambled to the window, which overlooked the front of the inn, and opened it to let in the evening air.

Before he had taken more than a single short breath, he went very still. From behind the wheel of a pale gray Lincoln that had pulled up to the curb across the way, emerged a stunning woman. She was of average height—five foot six, Russ knew for a fact—and more slender than he remembered. What he didn't remember was the air she exuded. With the sleek linen suit she wore, the prim knot of her long, honeyed hair, the confidence of her carriage and the sober look on her face, she was all business.

Russ wished he could be, too, but the sight of Cynthia made his mouth go dry. She had been his whole world once. He had measured his days by the time he spent with her. She had been his warmth, his laughter, his hope. He had wanted nothing more in life than to take care of her and make her happy.

He hadn't done that.

Unable to move, he watched her cross the street and disappear under the awning of the inn. His heart beat loudly—the same way it had the very first time he'd set eyes on her in the soda shop twenty-six years before; the same way it had the very first time he'd taken her out, then kissed her, then touched her; the same way it had the very first time they'd made love. His heart always beat that way when he saw pictures of her in the paper, as though she were still his and simply on loan to another life for a time.

If that was so, their lives were about to collide. In a matter of minutes there was a knock on his door. Russ turned quickly and stared in its direction until the knock came again. Swallowing, he drew himself up to his full six-foot-three height, took a slow, deep, bolstering breath and went to open the door.

Chapter Two

CYN HOFFMANN and Rusty Shaw had been classmates for years, but it wasn't until late August, just prior to the start of their senior year in high school, that they looked at each other and were lost. For as long as she lived, Cynthia would remember the day she had gone into the soda shop with a group of her friends and seen him. He had been working behind the counter, fixing milk shakes and banana splits, when she ordered a lime rickey. His eyes had been brown and bottomless, his jaw straight and shadowed by the kind of beard that few of his classmates could boast. But his smile was what had done it, sending waves of awareness all the way to her toes.

She had returned to the soda shop the next afternoon, and the next. Each time she came with one less friend, until she was finally alone at the counter ordering the lime rickey she barely tasted for the excitement of being near Rusty.

He was tall and good-looking, a serious athlete, a fine student. Had he been part of her social set, she would have been drawn to him sooner. But he lived with his father in a part of town that Cyn had never stepped foot in, and he kept to himself.

That ended when he and Cyn started to talk. From the very first, they connected. If anything, their differences made the conversations they had more exciting. They became a party of two—Rusty and Cyn, Cyn and Rusty—letting other friends wander off while they talked and laughed, while they shared their thoughts, then their dreams.

The first time he kissed her, Cyn thought she would explode. She had been kissed before, but she'd never felt the heat. With Rusty, she felt it. She felt it ten times over. Simply looking at him stirred her, but when he touched his mouth to hers, everything inside her sizzled. And that was just the start. When the soda shop proved limiting, they found different places to meet, different places to park his creaky old Ford. Kisses evolved into touches that grew bolder and more intimate. Then came the day when they needed to be closer still, when her skirt was pushed up and his jeans opened. Cyn was a virgin, and Russ not much more than that, but what they lacked in experience they more than made up for in love. She felt no pain that first time, she adored him so, and each time was better, then better, until they could no more have done without making love to each other than they could have gone without air.

By the time spring arrived, marriage seemed the only acceptable course of action. They had both been admitted to college, Rusty on a basketball scholarship, and they figured that with the scholarship and a little help from Cynthia's family, they could survive.

Gertrude Hoffmann didn't see things quite that way. She had envisioned Cynthia taking the year off to make her society debut. Everyone who was anyone in St. Louis society made her debut. But a married debutante was unacceptable. *Rusty Shaw* was unacceptable. He came from nowhere, was going nowhere. He was no proper match for her daughter.

But Cyn adored him. Everything about him excited her, from his intelligence to his liberalism to the way he turned her on with just a look. He worshiped her in ways the other boys she knew were too self-centered to do. She couldn't envision a life without him. So within days of their high school graduation, young and idealistic enough to believe that Cyn's parents would come around once their marriage was fact, they eloped.

Cyn's parents didn't come around. To the contrary, they cut her off without a cent, which meant there would be neither the grand coming-out parties nor college. Cyn was quite happy to do without the debut, and while she was sorry to be missing college, she would take Russ over college any day. What did bother her was that he had to put his own college plans on hold. He couldn't support a wife on his scholarship money, and his father couldn't help them at all.

Determined to make it, they came up with a plan whereby they would both work for several years and save every spare cent. Then Russ would reapply for his scholarship and return to school part-time. It would take him longer that way, they knew, but they could make it. And they might have, if Cyn hadn't become pregnant. The baby was born nine months after their marriage. They were both eighteen at the time.

Through the months leading up to Diane's birth,

then the weeks following it, they struggled to make things work. But the cards were stacked against them. Not only were they not able to make much money, but what they did make they needed to live on, which left nothing to save. Shortly before Diane's birth, Cyn had to stop working, which meant less money to pay an increasing number of bills. Their dreams grew more and more distant.

But those dreams did remain, at least in Cynthia's mind. They helped carry her through the fatigue and the worry. She clung to them, convinced that if she and Russ loved each other enough, things would get better.

Then, when Diane was three months old, Russ left and took Cynthia's dreams with him. Her grief was unspeakable. Only Diane kept her going in those first lonely days. In time, there was her mother, and then Matthew Bauer, but it was ages before Cynthia could look back on those months with Russ without starting to cry.

Now he was back, and she thought she was prepared. She had been gearing herself up for seeing him ever since his name had appeared on Diane's wedding list, and she honestly thought she was ready. She was long over the anger and hurt of his leaving, long over mourning the dreams they had shared. She had assumed she would simply see him on Saturday, with hundreds of people around to remind her of who she was and where she belonged. She had hoped to say hello to him, shake hands, even smile. Then, without so much as a twinge, turn right back to the life that had been so good to her.

She hadn't counted on his looking so tall and broad-shouldered, and so strikingly handsome that her heart constricted. She hadn't counted on the years disappearing in the space of an instant—on being yanked back to the soda shop and the moment his deep, brown eyes first met hers, then being spun ahead to that awful, awful morning when she awoke to find her world had fallen apart. She hadn't counted on feeling bereft again.

For a minute she was unable to speak. In her shock, Russ found the wherewithal to rise above his own emotional tangle. Allowing himself a trace of the pleasure that he'd always felt looking at her, he smiled. "You're looking well, Cyn, really well."

She wanted to say the same to him, but words wouldn't come. His appearance stunned her. Oh, he had been handsome—gorgeous in that tall, dark, athletic way—when they'd been younger, and the physical details weren't so different. But he had something else now. He had confidence, poise. He had presence.

But then, so did she, she reminded herself. At least, she was supposed to. She was Mrs. Matthew Bauer, chairwoman of dozens of charity events over the years, and Gertrude Hoffmann's daughter. More immediately, she was the mother of the bride, on the verge of pulling off the most elegant wedding St. Louis had seen in years. It wouldn't do for her to fall apart—or freeze up—at the sight of the father of the bride, regardless of how long it had been since she'd seen him last.

"How are you, Russ?" she said in a voice that

should have been stronger. But she wasn't about to quibble. She was grateful for any voice at all.

"I'm fine."

Because it was familiar and comfortable—and because St. Louis wasn't his home anymore—she lapsed into the role of hostess. "How was your flight?"

"Smooth."

"And the room here is all right?"

"Very nice."

She glanced at his hand. "Am I coming at a bad time?"

He lobbed the apple onto the plate by the fruit basket and wiped one palm on the other. "Nope." Then he dropped his hands and stood there, unsure of what she wanted, unsure of what *he* wanted. There was so much they could say, or so little. He didn't know which way it would go, but he did know that it wouldn't go anywhere if they stayed at the door. "Want to come in?"

What Cynthia wanted was to hightail it back to Frontenac, where the house and the gardens and the help made things safe and secure. But running wouldn't accomplish anything. She had come with a purpose. Stepping over the threshold, she let Russ close the door. When he gestured her toward a chair, though, she shook her head. She didn't think she could play at relaxing, not with Russ, not seeing him for the first time in so long.

Lips pressed together, she went to the window. Keeping her back to him, which made things easier, she said, "I feel badly about this, because I know you've come a long way, but Diane shouldn't have done what she did.''

"Shouldn't have invited me to the wedding?" Russ asked.

"Shouldn't have asked you to give her away. I didn't know about it until earlier today. I told her she'd have to call you, but she said it was too late, that you were already on your way.'' She turned to face him. Her jaw was firm, and he caught a flare of defiance in her eyes. "If Matthew were alive, he would have walked her down the aisle. He raised her. He loved her. He was her father in all but the biological sense. Since he isn't here, his brother is filling in.''

Russ didn't miss the criticism of him implicit in Cynthia's praise of Matthew. One part of him felt he deserved it; one part wanted to object. Both parts yielded to the more immediate concern. "That would be Ray. Diane mentioned you'd asked him. She didn't mention that there would be trouble if you told him I'd be here.''

"Not trouble," Cynthia explained patiently. "It's a question of what's appropriate and what isn't. Matthew was here, you weren't. *Ray* was here, you weren't. For you to show up at this late date wanting to suddenly take over your fatherly duties is a little silly, don't you think?''

Once, Russ could overlook the criticism. Twice was harder. "Actually," he said, "I don't think it's silly at all. Given the circumstances, I think it makes a whole lot of sense.''

"What circumstances?''

"My relationship with Diane. It's not a question of suddenly taking over my fatherly duties. We've been in touch for six years now."

"Yes," Cynthia acknowledged.

"Against your wishes?" he asked. He had often wondered about that, but he hadn't ever been able to ask. Diane made as much of a point not to discuss Cynthia as he did. It was hard enough forging a relationship between father and daughter without opening a Pandora's box of other issues.

"I knew Diane was seeing you. She's an adult. She can do what she wants."

"But you don't approve?"

"It's not my place to approve or disapprove."

"Come on, Cyn, that's a cop-out," Russ chided, but with a sad, gentle tone that took the sting from his words. "You're Diane's mother. Just because she's an adult doesn't mean you opt out of feeling where she's concerned. I'm asking whether you wanted her to see me. My guess is you didn't, since you'd already told her I was dead."

Cynthia quickly raised a hand. "I didn't tell her that. I never told her that."

"Someone did. She was sure it was true. After I contacted her the first time, she was so skeptical that before she would see me again, she flew down to Washington to look for my name on the Vietnam War Memorial. Did you know that?"

Cynthia dropped her gaze to the carpeted floor. She'd known it. She couldn't have *helped* but know it. Diane had been livid. It had taken hours of talking, hours of explaining thoughts and feelings, before her daughter had calmed down. "My mother was the one who said you were dead," she told Russ now.

"But you didn't deny it."

"No."

"That was wrong."

"So Diane told me in no uncertain terms."

"Did she tell her grandmother, too?"

"In gentler terms. Diane has always been more independent of Gertrude than I was. She isn't threatened by her. They're close in some ways, but in others Diane keeps her distance. Somehow she manages to find compassion for the woman."

"I never could," Russ scoffed, "and I'll be damned if I'll do it now. How could she tell my own daughter that I was dead?"

Cynthia wished she could sound as indignant as Russ. But since she hadn't refuted the story, she wasn't much better than her mother. "It was a comfortable scenario for her. Her friends all knew about our marriage. They all knew that I'd been estranged from the family. My mother had an easier time saying you went off to war than that you'd deserted me." More dryly, she added, "No one deserts a Hoffmann. We're too valuable."

If Russ hadn't been so embroiled in his own anger, he might have heard the self-effacing note. But he'd been stewing about his alleged death for years. "Your mother hated me. From the beginning, she thought I was good for nothing. All she had to do to prove her point was to say that I ran away."

"The war was more honorable." Cynthia frowned, running through the same arguments she had that night six years before with Diane. "My mother is a proud woman. What she did and said with regard to you was more by way of saving face than anything else. She had let it be known to her friends that I'd done a stupid thing in marrying you. Once she knew I was coming back home, she wanted me to look a little less stupid. Mind you, she didn't broadcast your death around town. She didn't dare, lest she be caught in a lie by someone who knew you weren't dead at all. She just let it quietly slip when certain people asked."

"Like Diane," Russ said, tempering his anger. "Didn't she ask about me when she was little?"

Cynthia looked him in the eye. "She thought Matthew was her father. He had legally adopted her. She had his name. It wasn't until she was eight that I told her the truth."

"But what did you say, if not that I was dead?"

"I said you'd had to leave us. That was general enough."

But Russ knew children, particularly the intelligent kind, of which Diane had clearly been one. "Didn't she ask where I went?"

"I told her you went to war."

"But the war was over by the time she was eight."

"My mother told her you had died."

"Didn't she ask *you* about that? At her age, she'd have had all sorts of questions about death. What did you tell her?"

"I was vague. I never specifically said you were dead."

"But you didn't deny it."

With accusation in her eyes, she answered, "I wasn't in much of a position to be making denials, particularly about something coming from my mother. In case you've forgotten, I was destitute. I'd been kicked out of my house, totally disowned. The only money I had to my name was the little you'd earned. Do you know that I stayed in our apartment for a whole month after you left?" The memory brought tears to her eyes.

Russ's anger faded at the sight of those tears. "I told you to go home."

"I wanted *you*, not home!" she cried, uncaring of the emotion she displayed. Clearly he thought she had simply returned to the lap of luxury, with no harm done. He should know some of what she had suffered. "I kept hoping you'd change your mind and come back. I loved you. You loved me. I was sure we could make it if we just stuck things out long enough. Then my money ran out, and I had no choice but to crawl back to my mother."

"She didn't keep you crawling for long."

"And that's to her credit," Cynthia countered with renewed strength. "She accepted us back. She let bygones be bygones. She took care of everything at a time when I was totally shattered. If she had wanted to say you had drunk yourself to death in an alley, I'd probably have let her."

"Would you have let her say that to Diane?"

Cynthia was slower in answering. She wanted to hurt Russ because he'd hurt her, but she had never been a vengeful person. With quiet resignation, she said, "No. I wouldn't have let her say that. I couldn't have. It implied you were a bum. I wouldn't have let Diane think ill of you that way."

Russ recognized the admission as the first hint that Cynthia didn't hate him completely. "Thank you," he said, his voice as quiet as hers.

In the silence that followed, he found his eyes roaming her face, reacquainting themselves with the features he had once known so well. Her skin was smooth, as dewy as it had been when she was eighteen, and though he was sure she wore makeup, it was light and finely applied. Time hadn't changed the sculpted quality of her face. Nor had it changed the softness of her lips, the pale green of her eyes or the rich, honeyed sheen of her hair. He remembered when that hair had surrounded him, forming a veil around their kisses. Except for a few wispy bangs, it was anchored in a knot now. He wondered how long it was.

"I think—" she began, then cleared her throat and began again. "I think I'll sit down after all." Her knees weren't as steady as she wanted them to be— Russ's scrutiny had always done that to her—and there was still the matter of the wedding to decide. Slipping into the chair that he had offered her earlier, she crossed her legs, folded her hands in her lap and looked up with what she hoped was restored composure. "About your relationship with Diane—"

"I'm not giving her up," Russ vowed. "I'm not walking away. I did that once, because I felt I had no choice, but I can't do it again. She's my daughter. Anyone looking at the two of us together can see that."

Cynthia would be the last one to argue. She remembered how painful it had been, particularly in those first hard years, to look at Diane and see the resemblance. In time that resemblance took a back seat to Diane's vibrant personality. Still, there were odd moments when a look or a gesture would conjure up Russ again.

"I've never denied that she was your daughter, and I'm not asking you to give her up. I'm simply asking that you let my brother-in-law walk her down the aisle."

"Why is that so important to you?"

"Diane has always been close to him—and to his daughter, Lisa, who's the maid of honor. Ray was good to us over the years, particularly after Matthew died. I felt it was an honor he should be given. Besides, I've already asked him. To take back the invitation would be a slap in the face."

"Not if you explained the situation."

"I'd rather not do that."

"Explain the situation? Or take back the invitation?"

"Either."

Russ sank into the chair opposite her. He sat forward with his elbows on his knees and laced his fingers in the gap between. "I can buy the problem about taking back the invitation. But I'm not sure I understand why explaining the situation is so difficult. If Ray is fond of Diane, he should want what she wants." An unpleasant idea intruded on that thought. "Are you dating him?"

"Of course not. He's my brother-in-law, and he's married."

"Are you dating someone else?"

"I don't think that's relevant here."

Russ knew it wasn't, but since he had broached the topic, he wasn't backing down. He wanted to know what to expect on Saturday. "I'm curious."

"You gave up your right to curiosity the night you walked out on me," Cynthia said more sharply than she'd planned. Seeing Russ had stirred up old feelings, the most immediate of which was anger at his desertion. She hadn't realized the feeling was still so strong.

He turned his hands over and studied them. In a grim voice, he said, "I didn't walk out on you. Not the way you make it sound."

"You left. I had a three-month-old baby, a one-room apartment with someone else's furnishings in it and two hundred dollars in my bag."

"That was more than I had." He had taken only the train fare, wanting to leave everything else for her.

"But I couldn't work. You could. You were supposed to take care of me."

"On *what?*" He raised his eyes. "I had a high school diploma and no skills. I was working two jobs, neither of which would get me to first base, and when I wasn't working, I was helping you with the baby. I was exhausted and scared and disgusted with myself that I couldn't do better. So I left. You can criticize me for that, but it wasn't a decision I made lightly. I agonized. I went through the alternatives again and again, trying to find a way to make it work. But it was a vicious circle. Without a college education, I couldn't earn good money, but I couldn't get the college education because I wasn't earning good enough money to stop working and study." He raked a hand through his hair. "Don't you think I wanted to stay? I adored the baby, and you—you were the light of my life! I wanted to give you so much, but I wasn't going to be able to give you a damn thing the way we were going. All I was doing was sentencing you to a life of hard labor. That tore me apart. So I sent you back home."

"Without asking whether I wanted to go," Cynthia challenged, but the challenge fizzled with Russ's immediate acknowledgment.

"Of course you didn't want to go. I knew that. I knew that as long as I hung around, you'd be right there with me. But your mother wouldn't accept me, and because of that, she wouldn't accept you or the baby. And because of that, you were suffering in ways you didn't deserve. We were living in poverty, for God's sake."

"I didn't think it was so bad."

"You would have after a year, or two or three. You would have thought back to what you'd grown up with and begun to wonder where you were going. You'd have hated me by then."

"No—"

"Yes." He was determined to make her understand why he had left her that fateful night. "I saw it happen with my parents. My mother kept thinking things would get better, but they never did. Poverty eats at relationships like nothing else can. By the time she died, she couldn't stand the sight of my father.''

''But we loved each other!''

''So did my parents when they first married. I thought our situation was different because of your family. I thought that if I could support myself with my scholarship and they could support you until I graduated, we'd do fine. I assumed too much.''

''We both assumed it,'' Cynthia argued. She didn't like Russ playing the martyr, when they had made their decisions together.

''Well, we assumed wrong. We were bucking the tide, Cyn. There was no way we were going to keep from drowning at the rate we were going. I was dragging you under. I had to leave.''

''So you disappeared.''

He let out a breath and sat back. ''I joined the army. It was the only thing I could afford.''

''You never wrote me.''

''I figured you were back home and that there would only be trouble if mail arrived from me.''

He was right, she knew, but she wasn't conceding the point aloud. For years she had been haunted by the fact that he had never tried to contact her after he'd gone. ''You could have written to Diane.''

''She was too young to read, and by the time she was old enough, you were married to Bauer.''

''You could have written to her then. You could have contacted her. You could have let her know that her father cared.''

''Would that have made life easier for her?''

"Yes!" Cynthia exclaimed, but the expression on her face that followed gave her away.

"It wouldn't have," Russ chided. "She had a wonderful life. She had you and Bauer. She had dancing lessons and private school and big birthday parties on the lawn of your home. She even had a horse of her own."

"You didn't know that then."

"I did. The Bauers were society. The *Post Dispatch* covered most everything you did."

"You read the *Post Dispatch?*" she asked in surprise. She knew he'd been living in Connecticut for years. She couldn't believe that the *Post Dispatch* was sold on newsstands there.

"I've subscribed to the thing since the day I was discharged from the army. It was the only way I could keep up with what you were doing."

Cynthia felt a small ache in the pit of her stomach. For years she'd assumed that Russ had pushed her into his past and gone on with his life. Believing that had made it easier for her to do the same. Now, knowing that he'd never forgotten her, she felt a rush of things that spelled trouble. To ward it off, she ignored his statement. Rather, out of sheer curiosity, she asked, "What made you finally contact Diane?"

"I read about her graduation from high school and knew she was going to Radcliffe. College seemed the right time to contact her."

"When she was away from me?"

Cynthia had always been quick. That was one of the things Russ had loved about her. She hadn't played sweet and dumb, like the other girls. She put two and two together, often guessing his thoughts before he expressed them. Apparently she hadn't changed.

"I didn't know what you'd told her," he explained. "I didn't know how you felt about me yourself. It seemed easier to wait until she was out of the house. That way I wouldn't have to deal with your feelings, too."

"But you waited until her sophomore year."

"Freshman year is tough for kids, with all that's new and different. I wanted to give her a chance to settle in and realize she wasn't going to flunk out before I threw her a major loop." He arched a brow. "Aside from not believing me, she wasn't terribly thrown."

"She has a level head on her shoulders." *She got that from you,* Cynthia wanted to say, but resisted.

"She's a great girl. You did a good job, Cyn."

The compliment was from the heart. Cynthia sensed that, and it touched her more than she wanted to be touched. Lowering her eyes, she twisted the ring on her finger. Actually, there were three rings, two simple gold bands flanking a central one studded with diamonds and sapphires—wedding bands and an engagement ring that Matthew had given her. Looking at them reminded her who had helped raise Diane into the great girl she was.

Eyes still lowered, she said, "I would really prefer to have Ray give her away."

Russ had felt she was beginning to soften and was immediately disappointed. "If you're ashamed of me," he burst out, leaning forward again, "there's no need. I have a Ph.D., a prestigious position and a fine reputation. I know how to talk, how to act, even how to waltz. I've already made arrangements with the shop Nick is using to be fitted for a morning coat, striped pants and the rest tomorrow, so I'll look as dignified as any man there, and if it's a matter of the amount of money in my bank account—"

"That's not it," she cut in.

"Then what is? Is Ray particularly fragile?"

"Not at all."

His eyes hardened. "Then it is me. My existence. That's it, isn't it? You have your place in society, and you don't want it threatened. You don't want people reminded that you married beneath yourself and that Diane's father deserted her. There'll be people there who don't know I ever existed, and you want to keep it that way."

"That's not it!" she cried. But her composure was starting to crumble—not so much because of what he was saying as because of the look in his eyes. The hardness was new. He had never looked at her that way before. In the past there had been nothing but gentleness, understanding and adoration. Irrational though it was, given that they were nothing to each other anymore, what she saw now hurt her nearly as much as his disappearance had twenty-five years before.

Rising to her feet with a surge of feeling, she cried, "It's me. *Me.* Seeing you hurts *me!* I've spent months planning every detail of this wedding because I want the day to be perfect, so I've been excited, but tense, too. When Diane put your name on her list, I knew

I'd have trouble, but I told myself I could handle it. I'm grown-up. I'm rational. I'm past pettiness.'' She shook her head. ''But your walking her down the aisle is too much.''

''I'm her *father*, for God's sake, and a wedding is a milestone.''

''So is going off to kindergarten, but were you there for that? Or for her first horse show? Or her first ballet recital?''

''I couldn't be there then,'' he said more quietly as he looked up at her. ''I've already told you why.''

But Cynthia wasn't thinking of his reasons. She was reliving the agony of losing him. ''You weren't there when I ran out of money. You weren't there when I knew what I had to do but was terrified of doing it. You weren't there when I thought I was pregnant again.''

The air was still. ''Pregnant?''

''Yes, pregnant.''

''With another baby of *ours*?''

''Who else's baby would I have had?'' she cried. ''All the signs were there. I was sure I was pregnant. I didn't know whether to be happy or sad, so all I was was scared to death!''

In hindsight, Russ felt all those things for her, plus a helplessness in the here and now. ''I didn't know.''

''Of course you didn't know. You were too busy playing soldier and convincing yourself that you'd done the honorable thing.''

His eyes went wide in disbelief. ''Playing soldier? I was *miserable*.''

''But you didn't come back!''

"I couldn't!"

"But I needed you!"

Hearing the words, seeing the look in her eyes that said she had felt betrayed, Russ understood that this airing of their emotions had been inevitable. But they were going in circles, and it was painful. He didn't know how much more he could take.

Cynthia was wondering the very same thing about herself. She hadn't planned to fall apart. It was fine to say that she'd been under pressure of late, but that didn't excuse what she was doing or saying. There was no point in lashing out about what was long since over and done.

"About the wedding," she began with a sigh, only to stop when he rose abruptly from his chair and crossed to the bed. The muscles of his shoulders flexed when he reached into the blazer that lay there. Her gaze fell to his pants, stylish twill ones that broadcast the tightness of his bottom and the length of his legs. She had always loved those legs—strong and well formed without being grossly muscular, and, though hairy, not so much a thick, wiry kind of hair as a wispier, smoother kind. She remembered sitting naked beside him, running her hands up and down those legs—

"Before you say anything else about the wedding, Cyn, I think you should read this."

Her eyes shot to the folded paper he held. She took it and lowered it to her lap, which gave her the excuse to drop her head, the only way she could hide the color she was sure stained her cheeks. The feel of the paper was familiar. Even before she opened it and saw the name embossed at the top, she knew it to be a piece of the stationery she had ordered for Diane six months before, at the same time she'd ordered the wedding invitations that had long since been mailed.

She read the entire letter. It was a chatty one, telling Russ in the lightest tone, almost tongue in cheek, about the parties and dinners of the past few months, then about plans for the wedding itself. The tone grew introspective when she related her feelings for Nick, her excitement about the marriage, her hopes for the future. The tone grew softer and more beseeching when she asked Russ to give her away.

Without raising her eyes, Cynthia held the letter for a minute longer before refolding it. She knew why Russ had let her read it. More than anything he might have said, it spoke of the relationship that had grown between Diane and him in the past six years. It made another point, too, one that was directly relevant to the issue of the wedding. Diane had asked Russ to walk her down the aisle. The idea had come from her. Clearly it was something Diane very much wanted.

The fact that Cynthia didn't want it was suddenly irrelevant. So much of what she had done in life— including returning to her mother's after Russ had left—had been done for Diane. Given her druthers, Cynthia would probably have gone off in search of him. But Diane had needed care and protection, and Cynthia had been determined to give her both. She loved her daughter. She wanted her to be happy. That would never change.

She passed the letter back to Russ, but for a moment she didn't let go. Quietly, thoughtfully, with her eyes focused on the spot where his large hand closed over the paper, she said, "When Diane was little, I spoiled her terribly. She was so undemanding, it was easy to do that. She rarely asked for anything she didn't really want, and when I gave her whatever it was, she thanked me forever. Despite all she had growing up, she never took things for granted. I know she couldn't possibly have remembered how strapped we were during the first three months of her life, but there were times when I wondered whether it somehow registered on her subconscious."

Dropping her hand from the letter, she dared raised her eyes for a final moment. "I'll talk with Ray," she said. Without another word, she left the room.

Chapter Three

BY THE TIME RUSS ARRIVED at the Bauer home at nine-thirty the next morning, he was already well into his day. He had awoken at six, taken a forty-minute run along a course that the hotel management had recommended, and returned to shower. After putting down a full breakfast at Bernard's, a restaurant at the inn, he set off in the car to see those things he hadn't seen the day before—namely, the neighborhood where he'd grown up.

He found a mixed bag. The schools he had gone to looked exactly as he remembered them, as did the library and the supermarket, but the soda shop had been converted into a video store, and the house he had called home had been razed.

Cruising down one street and up another, his eyes darting left to right in recognition of familiar landmarks, he gathered memories. Some were of the days before he had met Cyn; most were of the days after. They had had such good times together. The simple act of walking down a street with her had been a joy. He remembered the way she had leaned into him, wrapped her arm around his waist, matched her step to his. Mostly he remembered the way she had looked up at him with happy, trusting eyes. She had made him feel invincible, a grave error on his part. If he had been more realistic, he might have been able to prevent the pain.

Hundreds of times he had wondered what would have happened if he and Cynthia had known before they eloped what Cynthia's mother would do. He supposed they would have waited, gone to college, stolen time together. He supposed that when he finally got his degree and was gainfully employed, when he'd finally been able to support Cynthia without Gertrude's help, they would have married. Then again, in the ensuing years Cynthia might have been swept up into the whirl of society and left him behind. That thought had terrified him.

The irony of it, he realized as he headed for Frontenac, was that that early fear had come to pass with Cynthia's marriage to Matthew Bauer. In addition to being older, Bauer had been everything Russ wasn't. He'd been educated. Cultured. Wealthy. He'd been a perfect match for Cynthia, as society matches went. Had he made her happy?

If happiness was judged by the beauty of one's home, the answer had to be yes. Russ had known the Bauers lived in an elegant area, but he wasn't quite prepared for the extent of the elegance when he turned onto their street and found their drive. It was flanked by two brick gateposts covered with ivy, as was the gatekeeper's cottage just inside. Since the black wrought-iron gates were open, he passed through and proceeded slowly up the drive.

That slow procession was an education in and of itself. The drive was pebbled, perfectly edged and newly replenished, if the light gray of the stones was any indication. Lush green lawns rolled away from the drive on either side, ending in a stand of maples and birches on the left and an apple orchard on the right. Ahead was a collection of trees and shrubs that he was sure a landscape architect had been paid a bundle to create. Likewise, he was sure, the upkeep cost a bundle. Russ could see no fewer than three gardeners working—one mowing the lawn in the distance, two others trimming the greenery in front of the house.

The house itself was brick and ivy-covered, as the gatekeeper's had been, but that was where the similarity ended. This one was Georgian and large, with no fewer than twenty windows blinking back those rays of the sun that made it through the trees.

Russ lived in an area where ivy-covered brick was common. His own house had its share. But his own house was modest compared to this one—not that anything here was gaudy, he had to admit. It was impeccably kept, from the neatly painted black gutters to the shiny black shutters to the clean, bluestone walk and the polished brass numbers on one of the front columns. The house was clearly ready for a wedding. Russ felt good for Diane. And for Cynthia.

The drive branched to form a circle before the front door. Russ pulled to the right, parked halfway around and turned off the ignition. He had told Diane he would be there, so he was, though he had second thoughts about the visit. The words that had passed between Cynthia and him were still fresh and stinging. He wished he had had time to put them into perspective.

Diane. Think of Diane. She's all that matters this week, he told himself. Still, it was Cynthia he thought of as he climbed from the car and approached the house. He wondered whether Bauer had owned the place before she met him, whether she had lent a hand in shaping the landscaping, whether she remembered that she and Russ had always talked about owning a place in the woods.

The brass knocker was as polished as the numbers. He rapped twice, then waited. After a minute the door was opened by a young black woman, who, wearing a simple linen sheath, low heels and pearls, was as elegant as the house.

"Dr. Shaw?" she asked, then stood back with a smile to gesture him in. "Of course you're Dr. Shaw. The resemblance between you and Diane is marked." She extended her hand. "Diane told me you were coming. I'm Mandy Johnson, Mrs. Bauer's social secretary."

"Social secretary," Russ echoed, shaking the woman's hand. He had assumed a housekeeper, a cook and cleaning people, but not a social secretary.

"Actually," Mandy explained, "I'm here to help out with the wedding. Usually I work for Mrs. Hoffmann."

Russ found that even more surprising. His limited experience with Gertrude Hoffmann had taught him she was something of a bigot. If the young woman before him was for real, he was impressed. He was about to ask how long she had worked for Gertrude when a shout drew his attention to the top of the winding stairs.

"Russ!"

Diane came trotting down, ran to him and threw her arms around his neck. He hugged her tightly for a minute, then held her back for a speculative once-over. From the crown of her straight, dark blond hair to the tips of her white ballet flats, she was a beauty. His gaze lingered on her sundress. He recognized the pattern as a staple among girls at his school. "Laura Ashley?" he teased.

She laughed. "I know, I know. Totally out of character. If I were in New York, I'd be wearing either jeans or silk, but this is St. Louis, and St. Louis is Grandmother's turf. I'm going over to see her later."

"Ah," Russ said sagely. Mandy Johnson had quietly disappeared, leaving Diane and him alone. "You look great, Laura Ashley and all."

She grinned. "Thanks. You, too. I like the shirt. I've never seen you in anything but a tie and jacket before."

He was wearing a soft, oversize white jersey, tucked into a pair of snug-fitting chinos, and deck shoes without socks. "Even stuffy old professors have to relax sometimes."

"Stuffy?" she asked dubiously, and followed it up with a mocking "*Old?* If you looked any younger, they'd never believe you were my father."

"I was a child dad."

Chuckling, she gave him a final squeeze before releasing her hold on his neck. "Want some breakfast?"

"Already had some."

"How about coffee?"

"Yeah, that'd be nice—but only if it's made."

Slipping her arm through his, she guided him through the front hall and down a side corridor. "It's always made around here. Mrs. Fritz sees to that."

"Mrs. Fritz is the cook, I take it?"

"You take right." They entered the kitchen, where a small, round woman was kneading what Russ guessed to be bread dough. "Mrs. Fritz, say hello to Dr. Shaw."

The cook scowled. In a voice heavy with German intonation, she said, "How do you do, Dr. Shaw. I must make excuses for Miss Bauer once again. I have told her many, many times not to bring her guests through the kitchen. If you would like something to eat, I will be glad to serve you in the dining room."

Undaunted by the woman's reprimand, Diane dropped Russ's arm and made for the coffee maker. "No need to wait on us. We're just having coffee. You make a great cup, Mrs. Fritz." She filled two mugs with the dark brew—remembering that Russ took his black—and motioned him toward a side, screened door. Moments later she was placing the mugs on the table and settling into a white, cushioned wicker chair.

"Beautiful setting," Russ observed. The patio was of flagstone and huge. In addition to the six chairs at the table, there were occasional wicker armchairs and lounges scattered among large potted plants. Beds of brightly colored flowers bordered the flagstone, broken only by broad stone steps that led to the lawn. Set into one side of that lawn was a gleaming turquoise pool. Balancing it on the other side was a rose garden in vivid red bloom. The remainder of the lawn was an expanse of lavish green, undulating gently into the distance, where a gazebo fronted a graceful grove of willows.

"Take a good look," Diane said with a sigh. "This is the last time you'll see it like this for a while. The tent people start bringing things tomorrow. By the time they've set up fifty-plus tables, four hundred chairs and a dance floor, the place won't look half as peaceful."

"It'll still be spectacular." He took his eyes from the view to study Diane. "How's Nick?"

She grinned. "Great."

"Are you excited?"

"Very. And nervous. There are so many things to think about. Mandy has been a godsend. So has Tammy—she's a party planner and, boy, she's earned her money with this one. If it isn't the caterer on the phone, it's the florist or the photographer or the videographer or the dressmaker or the jeweler or the stationer. I swear, if I'd realized what was involved with an extravaganza like this, I would have eloped. Up until the very day the invitations went out, I was considering it. If it hadn't been for my grandmother..." Her voice trailed off.

Russ raised the mug to his mouth and took a drink. The brew was satisfying—Diane had been right about that—but the true satisfaction came with the company. Having spent so many years alone and out of touch, he was stunned each time he saw her to realize Diane was his. "You're doing this for Gertrude, then?"

"In part. She loves productions." Diane sent him an apologetic look. "I know you never had cause to feel kindly toward her, but she's mellowed over the years. In some regards, she's a lonely old lady. She has lots of friends, but at the end of each day she has no one to go home to but the hired help. It's sad."

Russ couldn't feel too badly for the woman. "I'm surprised she doesn't live here with your mother and you."

Diane nearly choked on her coffee. With a hand on her chest, she said, "Are you kidding? I may have said she's mellowed, but that doesn't mean she's a peach. If she were here, she'd be driving everyone crazy. As it is, she's going to antagonize the photographer and the videographer when she insists they be hidden behind flowers and latticework at the wedding ceremony." She snorted. "I really *should* have eloped."

"No," Russ said. "That wouldn't have been right."

"You did."

"We had no other choice. If we'd told your grandmother what we wanted to do, she wouldn't have allowed us to get married at all. Then we wouldn't have had you, and that would have been awful."

Diane stared at him for a minute before breaking into the gentlest, sincerest of smiles. "I'm so glad you're here. I don't care if she's furious—"

"Your mother?"

"My grandmother."

"Is your mother angry?" Russ was anxious to

know. He wondered how much of her feelings Cynthia shared with Diane.

"She was yesterday afternoon. She was quieter when she came in last night." Diane dropped her gaze to her coffee. "I'm sorry about that. I didn't think she'd actually go over to see you. Was it very uncomfortable?"

"Not as bad as it might have been. Was *she* uncomfortable?"

"A little, I think." Her eyes returned to his. "That's why it's good you came on Monday. She has the whole week to get used to seeing you so she doesn't start to hyperventilate on the day of the wedding."

"Hyperventilate?" he quipped. "Your mother?" Cool, composed Cynthia Hoffmann? It was an intriguing thought. "Why in the world would she hyperventilate?"

"Because you're handsome enough in a shirt and chinos or a blazer and tie. In formal wear you'll be a killer."

Russ grinned. "Are all daughters good for their fathers' egos, or is mine just unusually biased?"

"Maybe I'm making up for lost time," she said with a softness that brought a lump to his throat.

He curved a hand around her neck. "You and me both." Leaning forward, he kissed her cheek. He barely had time to draw back when Diane's gaze shot past him. He caught looks of surprise, then pleasure, then unsureness on her face before he glanced around.

Cynthia had just come past the side of the house. The sight of her brought him to his feet and at the

same time took his breath away. She had been running—at least that was what it looked like to Russ,
who had run with enough people over the years to
recognize the symptoms. Though she was standing
stock-still now, she was breathing hard. She wore top-
of-the-line running shoes that looked well used, a pair
of brief, teal green nylon shorts and a matching sin-
glet. Her hair cascaded from a high ponytail, from
which had escaped loose, honey-colored wisps. Along
with her bangs, they framed her face, several catching
in the rivulets of sweat that trickled down her cheeks.
Those cheeks were flushed with heat, but the eyes that
were glued to Russ had a shocked look in them.

"Hey, Mom," Diane called, "perfect timing. We
were just having coffee. Come join us."

Russ had begun to breathe again, but barely. Fully
dressed, as she'd been last night, Cynthia had looked
spectacular. She looked even more spectacular wearing so little. Her limbs were slim, well toned and
lightly tanned, and if twenty-five years had added
scars, liver spots or cellulite, he couldn't see any.

Aware of a quickening inside, he forced himself to
inhale. The breath escaped in a shaky whoosh. "This
woman can't be your mother, Diane. She's not old
enough."

"She's my mom, all right, but she puts me to
shame. She's so *fit* it's *disgusting*."

"Since when has she been running?"

"Since forever. I can't remember a time when she
didn't. She says it clears her head."

Russ knew that for a fact, but any benefit he had
derived from his own morning run was gone. His

head was filled with images of the last time he'd seen Cynthia so undressed, and his body was responding accordingly. Unable to sit down while she was standing there, yet more fearful by the minute that his arousal would be noticed, he didn't know what to do. He was relieved when Mrs. Fritz created a distraction by barreling out of the kitchen with a slam of the screen door.

Every bit as relieved as Russ, Cynthia took the towel the woman handed her and covered her face. She hadn't been prepared to find Russ there. She wasn't ready to see him again so soon. She hadn't begun to analyze the feelings that had kept her awake for a good part of the night. But because she had been awake so late, she had slept later than usual, which was why she had gone running later than usual, which was why he had caught her in such a state. Not that he wasn't seeing anything he hadn't seen before. Russ had seen her naked and sweaty—just as she had seen him aroused. But neither condition was appropriate at the moment.

After mopping at her neck and arms, she took the glass of ice water from Mrs. Fritz and drained it before handing it back. "Coffee, ma'am?" the cook asked.

"No, thanks," Cynthia murmured. She waited until the woman had gone back into the kitchen before turning to Russ. The towel hung from her hands, the only shield she had against the exposure she felt. "I'm sorry," she said softly. Her breathing may have slowed, but her body still hummed. "If I'd known you were coming, I wouldn't have barged in this way.''

"It's your house," Russ said as softly. He couldn't take his eyes from her, but that was nothing new. "You can barge in whenever you want. I'm the intruder. I just wanted to stop by and say hi to Diane. And make sure you're all right.''

"I'm all right.''

She didn't look it. She looked as paralyzed as he felt. No, he realized, *paralyzed* was the wrong word. *Mesmerized* was more like it. From day one in the soda shop, they had been captivated by each other to the extent that the rest of the world had fallen away, leaving only the two of them, drawn closer and closer. He decided now that the attraction was caused by something chemical, a magnetic response neither of them could control. He didn't imagine she wanted to be drawn to him any more than he did to her.

But Cynthia wasn't thinking about the soda shop or chemical attractions or magnetic responses just then. She had a more immediate quandary. She knew she should excuse herself and go inside, but she couldn't make herself leave. Nor could she continue to stand there. Needing more protection than the towel offered, she crossed the patio and slipped into a seat all the way across the table from Russ. With the towel draped around her neck so that its ends covered her breasts, she felt better.

Russ, too, sat. "Your house is wonderful, Cyn. Was it Matthew's before you married?''

"No. We bought it fresh. The woman who had

owned it for years passed away right around the time we were looking. It needed a lot of work.''

The little Russ had seen of the inside of the house was in wonderful condition, though he assumed it had been redecorated more than once since they'd bought it. ''Did you have to do much with the grounds?''

''Uh-huh. Nearly everything had been neglected. Some things came back with just a little pruning. Others had to be replaced.''

''Your landscape architect was brilliant.''

''I didn't use a landscape architect. The ones I talked with wanted to do all kinds of lovely little things that would have given a prissy look to the place. I wanted the grounds to be lush, which, believe it or not, is easier to achieve. So I directed everything myself.''

Russ was impressed, though not surprised. He had always known Cynthia could do whatever she set her mind to—and it had nothing to do with money or the confidence of the wealthy. She was a hard worker. Whether learning how to cook, keeping their tiny apartment neat and clean, caring for the baby or caring for him, what she did she did well.

''You must have designed everything with this occasion in mind,'' he commented. ''It's a beautiful setting for a wedding. Now, if the sun cooperates—''

''It will,'' she said with a quick smile. ''It always cooperates for weddings.''

Russ's own smile was slower and filled with reflective amazement. ''You were always so positive. I don't think I've ever met anyone as positive as you. When we were in school, you used to study your butt off for exams, but by the time you closed your books, you were sure you'd do well, and you always did. When we were looking for an apartment, you were sure we could find something we could afford, and we did. When we were looking for jobs, you were sure we could find ones close enough so we could meet every day for lunch, and we did.'' He remembered those lunches. From the affectionate look on Cynthia's face, he guessed she did, too.

''Brown paper sacks,'' she mused. ''Peanut butter and jelly sandwiches, cream cheese and olive sandwiches or tuna sandwiches—two for you, one for me. Potato chips that were usually crushed in transit. An apple. And a thermos of chocolate milk.''

''Bosco and milk,'' he added with a grin. ''Remember that?''

She grinned back and nodded. ''I always told you it would stay mixed, and it did.''

''You also told me there was no rush to get to the hospital after your water broke. We were so damned laid-back that by the time we got there, you were fully dilated.'' He turned to Diane. ''You were nearly born in the front seat—'' He stopped at the sight of her eyes, which were bright with tears. ''What's wrong?'' he asked, instantly alarmed.

She smiled through the tears, which remained unshed. ''Nothing. It's just so weird seeing you two together.'' Her gaze flipped to Cynthia, then back. ''It kind of brings things full circle. On the eve of my wedding. That's poetic, don't you think?''

What Cynthia thought was that Diane was a gem. Some daughters might have been angry at their mothers for having made them wait so long for such an occasion. Diane merely seemed delighted that it had come, which went to prove what Cynthia had told Russ in his hotel room. Diane had never been a demanding child. Whatever she received she appreciated. She was so, so special that way.

Russ must have thought the same thing, because before Cynthia could brace herself, he hooked an elbow around Diane's neck and drew her face to his shoulder. Cynthia felt a sharp jolt inside, then a tilting sensation near her heart. This was a first for her, too—seeing father and daughter together as adults—and it affected her more deeply than she would have imagined. Russ's ease with Diane, his spontaneity, his obvious affection—he would have been a wonderful father if he had been around. She supposed the relationship was better late than never. Still, for her daughter, she felt a loss.

Marginally aware that the loss she felt was for herself, as well, she rose from her chair and started for the house.

"Cyn?"

"I have to shower," she called back. Ignoring the creak of wicker behind her, she continued on to the screen door, but before she could do more than draw it open, Russ was by her side.

"Wait." His voice was low and close. "There's something I have to ask you."

She kept her eyes on the floor, not that that helped. She didn't have to raise them to be aware of his height. It seemed he always towered over her. When they'd been eighteen, part of the towering had been in her mind. She had been in awe of him for the hardships of his upbringing and the person he was in spite of it, and she'd been in love. In theory, she was over both the awe and the love, but he was still tall. She wanted desperately to believe that it was nothing more than a physical fact.

"I'm really a mess," she told him. "I don't feel comfortable sitting out here like this."

"I've seen you looking worse."

"When we were kids. Things are different now."

"You don't have to stand on ceremony with me. I'm family."

She did raise her eyes then to meet his. "Not to me. Our marriage was annulled years ago."

Russ saw the hurt and sorrow on her face and was as surprised by their strength as he had been the night before. He would have expected her to have put the past behind her. After all, she'd gone on to marry well.

"That's...kind of what I wanted to ask you," he said quietly.

Her eyes widened. "About the annulment? Are you thinking of marrying again?"

"No, no. But one of the priests who'll be assisting at Diane's wedding is an old friend."

"Jackie Flynn," she breathed, then watched the corner of his mouth turn up.

"Better known on the basketball court as the Dunkin' Dubliner."

"I wouldn't try that one now, if I were you. He's Father John to his friends."

"Father John," Russ repeated in a properly subdued tone. "I wrote him that I was coming in for the wedding, and he suggested I call, which I did this morning. He's invited us to be his guests for dinner at the Ritz."

"Us?"

"That's what he said."

"*His* guests?"

"That's what he said."

"At the *Ritz?*"

Russ shrugged.

"That's *appalling,*" she cried. "I can think of far more appropriate ways for the church to spend its money."

"That's what *I* said."

"What did he say then?"

"That we'd both made such generous contributions to the church in honor of Diane's wedding that it was the least he could do. And that the Ritz-Carlton is new in town and he wanted to eat there—and that, in fact, he wouldn't be paying a cent because he was making good on a bet he'd made with the manager."

"The rogue," Cynthia muttered, but fondly.

"That's just what I called him. So what do you say? Are you free tonight?"

"Yes, but—"

"He suggested we pick him up at the rectory at seven. Any problem?"

"No, but—"

"Good," Russ said with a sigh. "He really had his heart set on this. I wasn't looking forward to disappointing him."

"But you were the one who was his friend," Cynthia protested. She questioned the wisdom of spending any unnecessary time with Russ. Something told her that only heartache would come of it. "You'll want to talk over old times. Wouldn't it be better if the two of you went alone?"

"He said something about discussing the wedding."

"I've already discussed the wedding with him."

"He wants to discuss it with *us*."

She squeezed her eyes shut. Russ was being persistent, and she didn't know how to handle it.

"I know what you're thinking," he said in a soft, private voice, "and believe me, there's a part of me that agrees."

"That we shouldn't go?" she asked without opening her eyes.

"That we shouldn't test fate by sharing the same table." As it was, he was testing fate by leaning close enough to discover that Cynthia's scent was as sweet and alluring as ever. In an attempt to lessen the torment, he straightened and took a small step back. "But he's a priest. What better buffer could we find?"

She thought about the word *buffer* as she opened her eyes to his. *Referee* might have been a more appropriate word, if being together was going to cause the kind of heated discussion they'd had the night before. Or *chaperon*, if she didn't get used to seeing him fast. She could understand that there would be an awareness of the time of their first reunion, since sexuality had played a major role in their relationship. But that first reunion was over. This was the second.

Tonight would be the third. The awareness had to die down. It *had* to.

So she thought positively. "Okay. What time should I be ready?"

"Six forty-five?"

She nodded. "I'll see you then."

Chapter Four

CYNTHIA SPENT most of the day trying to find a way to get out of dinner. But though she had deliberately left her evenings early in the wedding week free for the inevitable flurry of last-minute arrangements, there were surprisingly few. She was in daily touch with the florist and the caterer, both of whom were skilled at their jobs and perfectly calm. Tammy Farentino had been in touch with the string quartet and the band to make sure they understood exactly when and what Cynthia wanted them to play; she had also touched base with the tablecloth person, the limousine service, the photographer and the videographer. Mandy Johnson had picked up the leather-bound book that Cynthia had ordered for guests to sign on entering the church, and she'd met with the calligrapher, who was busily writing table numbers on place cards as per the seating arrangement Cynthia and Diane had finalized the weekend before. Diane was in near-daily contact with each of her attendants and had been to the bridal shop for last-minute fittings. There was a small matter of picking up the gold rosebud earrings she would be giving to each of those attendants as a gift, but that was it.

So Tuesday evening found Cynthia sitting nervously on the Louis XVI-style settee at the far end of the living room. She was wearing a simple dress of apricot-colored silk and she clutched a patterned shawl, both drawn from her closet for their dignity. After the way Russ had seen her that morning, she felt compelled to repolish her image.

The bell rang at six-forty, which didn't surprise Cynthia a bit. Russ had always been prompt to the point of being early, which was why she had been on the settee since six-thirty. She rose so quickly her heart beat double time, so she forced herself to stand still for a good ten seconds, breathing slowly in and out. When she felt she had regained a modicum of composure, she started for the door.

Robert beat her to it. He was the butler, tall and lean, with those straight lines accentuated by perfect posture and the dark gray vest and trousers he wore.

"Mrs. Bauer, please?"

Cynthia arrived at the foyer. To the butler, in a soft murmur, she said, "Thank you, Robert." He nodded to her, then to Russ, before turning and, back straight, walking toward the kitchen.

"He's a dignified-looking man," Russ remarked.

"He's Mrs. Fritz's husband."

Russ would never have paired them. "You're kidding."

"No. They've been with us for years. Robert serves not only as butler but as chauffeur, courier and handyman. He's also the keeper of the rose garden."

Russ arched a brow. "A true master of versatility."

Cynthia arched a brow right back. "You could say that."

He smiled. "I'd rather say nice things about you. You look beautiful."

She said a soft thank-you, all the while reminding herself that compliments were a dime a dozen, that Russ's was nothing special and that the rapid thump-thump of her heart was left over from the anticipation that had built while she'd waited for him to arrive. Without quite planning it, though, she heard herself say, "You look terrific yourself." Her expression grew bemused as she took in his navy summer suit, crisp white shirt and paisley tie.

"What?"

"You look so—" she raised her eyes to his face "—so grown-up."

He grinned. "I am grown-up."

"I know, but the picture I carried in my mind all these years was of you at eighteen. To suddenly see you at forty-three is strange."

She gave a tiny frown, but it held the same bemusement of moments before. "I don't think I've ever seen you in a suit."

"I'd never owned one when we were together."

"It looks..." she struggled to find the right word, only to go with the simple and eloquent "...great."

His grin grew lopsided. "Thanks." He actually looked slightly embarrassed, but endearingly so. He had never been at all cocky. She remembered the way he used to blush when she said personal, intimate things, and the way she had loved it when he did. Though he wasn't quite blushing now, she loved the expression on his face nonetheless, particularly in light of the very sophisticated way the rest of him looked. She felt she had connected once again with the boy he had been—which was only right, since part of her felt like the girl she had been, young and starry-eyed and excited by the thought of being with Russ.

Memory. That was all it was, she told herself. Forcing her eyes from his, she glanced at the slim gold watch on her wrist. "Would you like a drink before we leave?"

"No, thanks. I have a feeling John will be offering us something at the rectory. Our reservations aren't until eight. Are you all set to go?"

Taking a small evening bag from the antique table by the door, she nodded. Moments later she was tucked into Russ's car and they were on their way.

The rectory was a modest stone house behind the church. John Flynn was waiting for them, but the look on his face wasn't as easygoing as Cynthia had come to expect from the man. He did produce a smile and a warm handclasp for her, and when he turned to Russ, there was mischief in his eyes and genuine affection in the bear hug he gave.

"Gee, Russ, it's good to see you!" he said, then repeated the words with several hearty shoulder slaps. But his smile faded soon afterward, and his gaze moved from Russ's face to Cynthia and back. "I was so looking forward to tonight, but it appears the Ritz will have to wait—for me, at least. I received a call twenty minutes ago from one of my parishioners. There's been a serious accident."

"Oh, dear," Cynthia said, wondering which of his parishioners it was and whether she knew the person. She knew many of the people who lived in the area.

Father John was aware of that. She guessed that if he wanted her to know who'd been hurt, he would tell her. "An automobile accident?"

"No, it was a construction accident. A fluky thing, from the little I was told, but my source was quite upset. I promised I would be at the hospital as soon as possible. I tried calling the house to save you the trip here, but you had already left, and I didn't want to be on my way without speaking with you myself." He looked at Russ. "I'm sorry. I feel terrible standing you up."

Russ knew what it was to have emergencies. "Don't apologize, John. More than once in the past year I've been called from an evening engagement to see to an emergency at one of the dorms. Certain jobs demand that you be on call. Yours is one of those jobs. I'm only sorry we'll miss this chance to talk."

"We'll have to reschedule, that's all," John said. "And in the meanwhile, you two will go on to the Ritz tonight as my guests."

Cynthia came to attention. "Oh, no, Father John, we couldn't possibly do that."

"But it's all arranged," he insisted. "The manager owes me. I've already talked with him. He's expecting you."

Russ was feeling as uncomfortable as Cynthia. "Why don't we just rereserve. Are you free tomorrow night?"

The priest shook his head. "Not tomorrow or Thursday night, either, since I believe we all have a wedding rehearsal, then dinner at Granatelli's Restaurant." To Cynthia he said, "And you're not going to want to go out the night before the wedding."

"I don't dare," she said apologetically. "Annie D'Angelo will be at the house, along with who knows how many more of the bridesmaids. Diane may be nervous. I feel I should be available in case she needs me."

"So you'll go to the Ritz tonight," John instructed, "and you'll report back to me on how it is." He turned to Russ. "Can we talk at the rehearsal dinner?"

"Sure thing."

"I still don't think we should go without you," Cynthia said. The thought of being alone with Russ was making her stomach jump. "What good is a bet if you can't collect on it."

"I'm collecting," John told her.

"But for *you*."

"I'm a priest. Given the vows I took, the Ritz is a little too much, don't you think? Besides," he added with a mischievous gleam, "that bet had to do with the Blues. I've got another one going on the Cardinals that's a sure winner, too." He put an arm around each of them and, becoming more serious, turned them back toward the car. "My evening is apt to be difficult. It'll give me great pleasure thinking of you at dinner. Would you deny me that pleasure?"

"That's blackmail," Cynthia chided, but fondly.

As fondly, Russ added, "I can see that the old Jackie Flynn is alive and well behind that Roman collar of yours."

With an unrepentant grin, John dropped his arms

to open the car door for Cynthia. "The good Lord understands that even the most pious of men aren't saints."

Cynthia slid into the passenger seat. "What fun will it be for us without you?"

John shut the door and leaned down to the open window. "You'll make your fun. I seem to recall a time when you guys didn't want *anyone* around."

"Those days are long gone," she said with a wisp of sadness, then, before he could add anything, covered his hand with hers. "We'll be thinking of you tonight. I hope everything turns out well."

"So do I," he said, and looked at Russ. "Thursday night?"

"You got it." Russ started the car and drove off. He hadn't gone more than a block when he realized what the Dunkin' Dubliner had done and what it meant. He'd passed Russ the ball and was expecting him to take it down the court. But damn, it was a long time since Russ had played the game, and the stakes were *so high*.

Silence reigned for another block, by which time he was desperate to know what Cynthia was thinking. So he said, "That's too bad. I was looking forward to talking with John. I wonder who's been hurt."

Cynthia's thoughts had been on the so-grown-up man by her side and the evening ahead. At Russ's reminder, she felt instant guilt. Some poor soul was struggling for his life while she was debating the pros and cons of showing up at St. Louis's new Ritz-Carlton on the arm of her onetime husband. Turning her gaze to the window and away from Russ's too-imposing presence, she shrugged. "A fluky accident, he said. That's scary. I always used to worry that something fluky would happen to Diane." She reconsidered the words. "I used to worry that something *not fluky* would happen to her, too." Reconsidering yet again, she finally admitted, "I used to worry, period. There are times when I still do. She may be twenty-five and off on her own, but if I let myself think about her in New York City, I go a little nuts. I'm glad she'll have Nick with her from now on."

"Don't tell her that. She'll say she's perfectly capable of taking care of herself."

"Still, I worry. Not all the time. Only when I think."

Russ was about to say that was a mother's prerogative, when he shot her a glance. She was diligently keeping her head angled toward the window, but her profile was lovely enough to drive the words from his mind. Long after he returned his eyes to the road, he saw that profile, and felt increasingly confused. He was looking forward to the evening. He was looking forward to it too much.

"Cyn, if you'd rather not go to dinner...I mean, if being with me is going to make you uncomfortable, I can take you back home."

She lowered her eyes. Uncomfortable? Was that what she was feeling? She didn't think so. She didn't think it was possible for her to feel uncomfortable with Russ for long. He was too easy to be with, too accommodating, too interesting. When they'd been seniors in high school, she had wanted to know all about his life and his classes and his extracurricular activities. Twenty-five years later, she wanted to know the very same things.

There was danger, of course. He still turned her on. She could feel the pull even though—it stunned her to realize—he hadn't touched her once, not once, since that last night twenty-five years before when they'd made love. They hadn't shaken hands last night at his hotel. He hadn't so much as touched her arm to stop her from leaving the patio that morning or, when he'd picked her up tonight, laid a hand on her waist to guide her to the car.

"Cyn?"

The pull was still there. His voice touched all the places his hands hadn't, and his eyes touched more. But she could handle it. She was *determined* to handle it. With all that had been going on in preparation for the wedding, she deserved a quiet, private dinner, and who more appropriate to have that quiet, private dinner with than the father of the bride? Besides, she was curious. She had gotten glimpses of what Russ had done with his life. She wanted to hear more.

"I can handle it," she sighed, more to herself than to him.

The sigh hit him the wrong way. "Don't do me any favors," he muttered.

She shot him a surprised look. "Why do you say that?"

"Because I'm not so hard up for company that I can't eat alone."

"I said I'd come."

His eyes clung to the road and his hands to the

wheel. "But you sound like it's the last thing you want, and if that's so, I'd *rather* eat alone."

"Maybe you'd rather eat alone, anyway. You sound like you're looking for an out."

"I'm not. I think you are."

She faced him more fully. "Why would I want an out?"

"Because you're uncomfortable with me."

"Did I say I was?"

"No, but you wouldn't. You're trained not to say things like that."

"Where you're concerned I'll say anything I want!"

He scowled. "Right, and maybe that's why we shouldn't go to dinner together. "You're angry at me for something that happened twenty-five years ago. You couldn't keep it in last night, and you probably won't be able to tonight."

"Because it still hurts!"

"Twenty-five years later?"

"Yes!"

"You should be over it."

"I thought I was, but seeing you brings it back."

"It shouldn't, damn it," he said, feeling angry. "Twenty-five years is too long a time for something like that to linger."

"Twenty-five years is *nothing* when people feel things like we did! Do you mean to tell me you didn't feel a thing after the night you left? That you didn't ever think of us over the years and feel a sense of loss? That you didn't ever wake up in the middle of the night with a longing so intense that you'd have turned a cold shower hot?'' As soon as the words were out, Cynthia was appalled. But it was too late to take them back, and she wasn't sure she would have, anyway. She was being honest. No one could condemn her for that. ''If you can truly say that you got over us—'' she snapped her fingers ''—like that, something was wrong, very wrong with the way we were then. Was it all a sham?''

Her words echoed in the car for the longest time before Russ could react. When he did, it was with carefully controlled movements, pulling the vehicle to the side of the road, letting the engine idle. He dropped his hands to his lap and stared at the center of the steering wheel. An air bag was packed there. In case of an accident, it would inflate and save his life—and he would want it to. But that hadn't always been so.

''It wasn't a sham,'' he said quietly. ''What we had was the most beautiful thing I've ever known. There were times when the loss I felt was nearly unbearable. There were times during the war when I honestly didn't give a damn whether I made it home or not. Someone was watching out for me there, because I sure as hell wasn't. When I got back in one piece, I decided I owed that Someone for what He had done. So I worked harder in school, and after that at work, than I might have done otherwise. I had no one to do it for. You were lost to me—by my own hand—and if you think you were the only one lying awake at night, you're dead wrong. There were nights I wanted you so bad I swear I almost flew back here.''

His lower lip came out to cover the upper one.

Slowly it slipped down again. "You're right. Twenty-five years isn't long at all with feelings that strong. When I suggested it was, I was trying to deny things I've been feeling myself since I saw you last night." He hesitated, unsure of how much to say. But one of the most beautiful things about his relationship with Cynthia had been its openness. They had poured out their hearts and souls to each other. There was nothing they hadn't shared—except his decision to leave. In terms of forthrightness, he owed her one. So he confessed, "Everything's come back. I didn't plan on it happening. I didn't want it to. But it's there."

Cynthia sat much as he did, with her hands in her lap and her eyes straight ahead. She wanted to look at him but didn't dare. His words alone had a powerful effect on her. "Maybe it's memory. Maybe what we're feeling now is just the memory of what we felt then."

"Maybe."

"Maybe it's just a residual from things that went unresolved after you left."

"Maybe."

"Maybe it's not what we really feel—I mean, what you and I feel as the individuals we are today. Maybe it's all for old times' sake."

"Maybe." He raised his eyes to the windshield. "So how do we handle it?"

"I don't know." Still staring straight ahead, she threw the question back at him. "You were always the sensible one. How do we handle it?"

He thought hard, trying to separate what his mind recommended from what his heart did, only to realize there wasn't much difference between the two. "I think we have to talk. We have to get to know each other as we are now. We have to put reality between us and the past. Could be that once we get to know each other, we'll find a comfortable middle ground to stand on."

"Somewhere between attraction and antagonism?"

"Right."

"Do you think that's possible?"

"Yes. We're neither of us antagonistic people."

"About the other," she said in a smaller voice, because she could still feel it, could still feel the pull.

Russ didn't have to ask what she meant. He could feel it, too. Slowly he turned his head, and the sight of her heightened the feeling. He had dreamed about her over the years, and come morning had always pushed her image from his mind. But she was here. With him. After all those years of dreams.

"I think it still exists," he said in a voice so low she might not have heard if there had been any noise outside the car. But it was a lazy June evening. Traffic was light. The only noise was the whisper of cool air coming from the vents, and that coolness wasn't nearly enough to take the edge off his heat. "Look at me, Cyn."

After a moment's reluctance, she turned her head. What she saw in his eyes reflected what she was feeling inside, and it nearly broke her apart. She held her breath when he raised his hand. It hovered for a minute before ever so lightly touching her cheek, then curving around her neck. His thumb brushed her mouth.

"It still exists," he said, hoarsely this time.

"I know," she whispered.

"But we're adults now. We can resist it."

"We have to. I don't think I can bear the pain again."

"But what about the glory?" He was thinking about the way she had always taken him out of himself and elevated him to a plane where everything was breathtakingly beautiful. "Wouldn't you like a taste of that again?"

"Oh, God." She was being drawn in by his smoky eyes, his sandy voice, the spray of silver in his hair— and the silver hadn't been there before, which shot the theory of memory turning them on. She wanted him to kiss her, wanted it more than anything in the world at that moment.

It was her turn to raise a hand, then hesitate. Then she put her fingertips on his lips, moved them over his cheek to his temple, then back by his ear.

He drew in a shuddering breath and trapped her hand on his neck. "Don't tempt me, Cyn. Don't tell me it's okay. I haven't changed much where you're concerned. I never could resist when you touched me. Given the choice, I'd take you back to my hotel room right now and to hell with dinner. But I don't think that's wise."

One part of Cynthia wondered. That part would opt for the hotel room, too, on the premise that what was building between them simply had to be released to be gone. The other part was worried it wouldn't ever be gone, and she didn't know what she'd do then.

Retrieving her hand and anchoring it on her lap,

she said, "You're right. Let's go to dinner." The words were rushed, she knew. Russ had to know she was torn. But he didn't say anything more. She was infinitely grateful when he put the car in gear and moved off.

"TELL ME ABOUT YOUR LIFE," Russ said. Having arrived at the Ritz in advance of their reservations, they were having drinks at the bar.

Cynthia took a slow sip of her martini. She felt much safer now that they were out of the confines of the car and surrounded by other people. "That's a tall order. Where should I start?"

"At the beginning." He wanted to know all the things the newspaper hadn't covered. "When I left."

She ran her thumb along the rim of the glass. "At the time I thought that was the end, not the beginning. I was so happy with you, then you were gone. I was sure life would go totally downhill from there."

Russ knew there would be pain in what she had to say, but he needed to know. What had happened after he left was all part of who she was now. "What did your mother say when you showed up at her door?"

"I called first. I didn't have the courage to show up without knowing whether she would let me in. If she rejected me after you had—"

"I didn't reject you."

"That's what it felt like to me at the time," Cynthia argued, then purposefully gentled her voice. She didn't want to be angry at Russ. All she wanted was to make him understand. "I was feeling very vulnerable. So I called her." She stopped then, remembering back to that sticky July day and the phone booth that had looked so dirty next to Diane's baby-soft skin.

"What did you say to her?" Russ asked quietly.

She sighed. "Actually nothing. I started to cry. She got the message. I managed to tell her where I was. She was there in ten minutes."

"You should have called her sooner."

Cynthia shook her head. "I couldn't. It took that month alone before I could face her."

Russ took a swallow of Scotch and jiggled the ice in his glass for a minute before he said, "I wanted you to go home, because I knew she would take care of you, but I was worried that she would make things impossible for you in the process."

"Like drilling my stupidity into me?"

"Yeah."

"She didn't. She didn't say a word about that. She really did play her cards perfectly. I was heartbroken that you'd left, and she could see that. She made things so easy for me at home that when I finally came out of my blue funk, I was ready to be the kind of daughter she wanted."

Russ wondered who had taken care of Diane while Cynthia had been in her "blue funk." She had been totally devoted to the baby when he'd been around. "I suppose you weaned Diane to a bottle pretty quickly, huh?"

"I nursed her until her first birthday."

He was inordinately pleased by that fact. As an afterthought, he grinned. "What did Gertrude think of that?"

Cynthia's mouth twitched. "What do you think she thought?"

"That it was a vulgar practice fitting only for peasants."

"That's pretty much it." Her eyes grew serious. "But what she thought didn't matter when it came to Diane. Diane was mine. I took care of her. She was the only peace of mind I had in those days."

The pain was there again. Russ wondered if they'd ever be able to escape it. "When did you meet Matthew?"

"When I was little, long before I met you. He was sixteen years older than me, but he moved in the same circles as my family. I was with Diane at the club one day—she was eighteen months old—and he and I started to talk. We were engaged two months later and married seven months after that."

"Why the seven-month wait? Was it so that Diane could get used to him?"

Cynthia shook her head. "They took to each other right from the start." She turned her glass on its cocktail napkin. "My mother wanted to do everything she had been denied the first time. There were engagement parties and postengagement parties and showers and prewedding dinners. She was in her glory."

"Were you?" he asked. He knew it was a loaded question, but the answer mattered.

She raised her eyes to his. "Was I in my glory? No. Did I enjoy myself? Yes. I never rejected my world when I married you. That world, thanks to my mother, rejected me. But I'd been raised with those people. I fitted back in. There were—are—many of them I really like. Sure, I had to deal with some shallow people, but there are shallow people at every level. I surrounded myself with the ones who weren't. They're the ones who work with me on fund-raisers for the art museum and the cancer society. They're the ones who helped me raise money for the homeless long before it became fashionable to do so.'' She gave a slow, sure shake of her head. "I make no apologies for what I did then or at any time since.''

For a minute Russ couldn't think of a thing to say. He wanted to criticize her for taking the pleasure she had. After all, while she had been lifting canapés from silver trays, he had been slogging through rice paddies. But she was eloquent in her defense of the life she had lived. If she had made the best of the circumstances, using her position in society to benefit worthy causes, he couldn't find fault. He had to respect her for acting on her beliefs.

"Excuse me? Dr. Shaw?''

Russ swung his head around, and he found himself confronting a familiar-looking man. In a matter of seconds he placed him—the father of one of his students. With a smile, he rose from the bar stool and extended his hand. "It's odd seeing people out of context. I've only seen you in Connecticut, my own neck of the woods. But Chris is very definitely from St. Louis. How are you, Mr. Mason?''

"Very well, thanks, and the feeling's mutual. I've been sitting over there with my friends watching you, wondering if you were who I thought. I didn't expect to see you so far from home.''

"I'm here for a wedding,'' Russ said. "Do you

know Cynthia Bauer? Cyn, this is Phillip Mason. He's the father of one of my more promising sophomores.''

Cynthia smiled and let the man take her hand. "We've been introduced before, I believe." She frowned, trying to remember exactly when and where. "Don't you sit with the Grahams at Powell Hall?"

"You have a good memory," Mason commented. "Powell Hall it was. And aren't you the one putting on the wedding?"

"That's right."

Releasing her hand, he pointed a thumb at Russ. "So what's his connection?"

With a serenity that stunned Russ, she said, "He's the father of the bride."

It wasn't a secret exactly. But someone like Phillip Mason, who had known Cynthia only as Mrs. Matthew Bauer and Diane as Diane Bauer, wouldn't necessarily know the truth. Indeed, the look on his face was priceless. His eyes lighted in surprise one minute, then grew perplexed the next, and when he opened his mouth to say something polite, nothing came out.

Russ, who was counting on the man to give a significant contribution to his school's Annual Fund that year, took pity on him. "Cynthia was my child bride. Diane was born shortly before we separated."

"I hadn't realized," Mason murmured. To Cynthia, he added, "I simply assumed Diane was Matthew's."

"Most people do," she said kindly.

Russ was reassured by her tone. So, apparently, was Phillip Mason, because he grew confident again. "She is one lucky young lady to have this man as her father. For years he's been one of Hollings's best teachers, and now he's proving to be a top-notch headmaster. You can tell her I said that.'' He turned to Russ. ''Will you be in town long?''

''Only until Sunday.''

''If you're free, we'd love to have you out at the house.''

''That might be difficult. It's a short trip with a lot to do, but thanks for offering. Has Chris left for the Southwest yet?'' He had been trying to remember what the younger Mason was doing for the summer. With more than three hundred students enrolled at the school, it was hard to know about each, but Russ did recall something about an archeological dig in Arizona.

''Next Tuesday. He's looking forward to it.''

''Will you give him my best and wish him a wonderful trip for me?''

''I certainly will.'' Mason slapped him on the back. ''You have a good summer, and congratulations to you both—'' he broadened his gaze to include Cynthia ''—on your daughter's wedding.''

''Thank you,'' Cynthia said. As the man walked away, she couldn't help but consider the irony of being in one of St. Louis's newest and poshest hotels with Russell Shaw and having *him* be the one recognized. Not that it bothered her. To the contrary. She felt a glimmer of pride. Apparently he had made quite something of his life. She wanted to know more.

''TELL ME ABOUT *YOUR* LIFE,'' she said. They were seated at a pleasantly private table, but the privacy wasn't bothering Cynthia. They had already been visited by the manager, the maître d', the wine steward, the waiter and the busboy. She was grateful for the momentary respite, during which she was hoping to learn something about the father of her daughter.

"That's a tall order," he drawled, echoing her earlier words. "Where should I start?"

"With your discharge from the army."

"What do you already know?" He wasn't the arrogant type. The last thing he wanted to do was to repeat old information.

"Only that you're Dr. Shaw and that you're headmaster at the Hollings Academy in Connecticut."

He would have thought she'd know more. Diane certainly did. He felt vaguely hurt that she hadn't been curious over the years. God knew he had been about her. "In a nutshell, I got my B.A. from Georgetown and went to teach history at Hollings. Over the years, I picked up an M.A., then a Ph.D. I was named headmaster last year."

She didn't seem at all daunted by his curtness. Her eyes were wide and expectant. "Go on."

"With what?"

"Why you chose teaching, why history, why Hollings, how you came to be headmaster, whether you like the job."

"I can't answer those in order."

"Why not?"

"Because they sound like they'd be a chronological succession, but they're not. I chose history because it fascinates me."

"It always did," she said, remembering. "You were good at it."

"Because it fascinated me. So I was getting ready to graduate with a degree in it, and the most obvious thing to do was to teach, but I was feeling unsettled. Homeless. Insecure. I had gone straight from the army to Georgetown, and for the first time in six years I didn't know where I was going. Then I heard about the opening at Hollings and went to visit the place. That was it. I was sold."

"What's it like?"

His mood softened as he thought of the school. "Green, very green. And warm. It's like a college campus in miniature, with tree-lined walks connecting one old stone building to the next. There's a feeling of history to it. And a sense of caring. When I first went there, it was all boys. More than half of them board, which means the school has to take the place of parents and family. And it does. More than anything, I think that was what appealed to me—the caring, the camaraderie between students and students, students and faculty. Hollings gave me a family. It also gave me a place to stay."

"You had an apartment on campus?"

"It was a two-room job in one of the dorms. It was furnished, so I didn't have to buy anything, and I got extra money by being a dorm parent."

"Was it hard work?"

"Not if you like kids, and I like kids."

"I never knew that," Cynthia said with a bemused look.

"Neither did I while I knew you. We were kids ourselves."

"When did you find out?"

"When I was at Georgetown. I took part in a volunteer project with inner-city kids. Those kids were tough, but they were great. Obviously the kids at Hollings were different, but they were great, too."

"So you stayed on. Did you take time off when you did your degree work?"

He shook his head. "I did it evenings and summers."

"That must have been hard."

He shrugged. "I didn't have anything else to do with my free time."

"Didn't you date?" she asked. He was such a strikingly handsome man. She couldn't believe that single women would come within range of him and not look twice.

"Some."

"Were there many female teachers?"

"Some. More now, since we've gone coed."

"When did that happen?"

Russ told her, then, when another question came, answered that, too. With the natural flow of her curiosity, he found himself relaxing. Their waiter brought rolls, then salads, and through it Cynthia was enrapt with piecing together a picture of his life. More than once, basking in her enthusiasm, he was taken back to their days together. Enthusiasm had been a mainstay of her personality then. He was relieved that that hadn't changed.

They were interrupted again, twice actually, when acquaintances of Cynthia's approached their table. Though Russ would have been happier without the intrusions, Cynthia was so apologetic each time that he couldn't be angry. Besides, she always picked up where they'd left off, letting him know that her interest was real, and in that, making him feel ten feet tall.

That was pretty much the way he ended the evening. By the time he returned Cynthia to her elegant, ivy-covered house, he felt just as high as he had after spending an hour with her at the soda shop—and as horny. Sitting across from her at an intimate table for two for the better part of three hours, watching the graceful shift of her hands, the gentle movement of her mouth, the curves of her shoulders and breasts, had taken its toll. His blood was hot and racing.

Cynthia was suffering a similar fate. As Russ walked her to her door, her heart was beating far faster than she wanted. After stepping inside, she turned back, hesitantly, to look up at him. "Thank you, Russ," she said softly. "It's been a really nice evening."

"I thought so, too." He wanted to kiss her but didn't dare. One kiss wouldn't be enough. It would never be enough when the lips involved were Cynthia's and his. But neither of them was ready for more. Too much shaky ground remained between them. Still, he couldn't bear the thought of waiting two days, until the wedding rehearsal on Thursday, to see her. It would be a waste of precious time. "I'm having breakfast with Diane and Nick tomorrow. Join us?"

Cynthia would have liked that if she trusted herself, but she didn't where Russ was concerned. She was feeling overwhelmed by things she hadn't felt in years. She needed time to think.

Doing her best not to drown in his gaze, she said, "I'd better not. I have an early meeting with Tammy, and besides, you haven't had much time with them. I don't want to take away from that."

"You wouldn't be taking away. You'd be adding."

"I'd better not."

"I'd really like it if you came."

But she shook her head. She had to be firm, had to act with her mind rather than her heart. She couldn't afford to be hurt the way she'd been hurt before. A second time she might not recover.

Chapter Five

RUSS KNEW ALL ABOUT ACTING from the mind rather than the heart. Over the years he had given lectures aplenty on the subject to his students and knew all the words to use. He had acted with his mind on the night he'd walked away from Cynthia—and when he'd joined the army, when he'd enrolled at Georgetown, when he'd taken a job at Hollings. Acting with one's mind meant considering every angle of a situation and making the most sensible decision. It meant acting deliberately rather than on impulse.

He thought he had done that when he refrained from kissing Cynthia good-night at her door. They weren't ready for a deeper involvement. The potential for warped judgment was too great. They were seeing each other for the first time in twenty-five years, a highly charged situation on its own. Add to that the emotion of their daughter's wedding and the highly charged situation increased in voltage. They were prime candidates for making a mistake.

So his mind said.

His heart said that it wouldn't be making a mistake at all but correcting one made long before.

His body pretty much echoed that conviction, with reverberations that lingered through the night and into the morning. When he arrived at the house to pick up

Diane, he looked out for Cynthia, but she was nowhere in sight. She had a meeting with Tammy, she'd said. So he looked for her again when he brought Diane back after a thoroughly enjoyable breakfast with Nick.

"Think your mother's home yet?" he asked in a nonchalant way when he didn't see her wandering about.

"I doubt it," Diane said. "She had a list of things to do." She grew cautious. "Is everything all right?"

"Fine. I was going to offer to help, that's all."

"Aren't you spending the day with your professor friend?"

He nodded. "But I'll be free by four. I'm feeling a little fraudulent, accepting the title of father of the bride without doing any of the work. Haven't you got anything for me to do?"

"You're a guest. You don't have to work."

"I'm the father of the bride, and I *want* to work."

"Most everything's arranged for. Mom is good at that."

"Efficient."

"Very."

Frustrated by the fact, he frowned. "It's a bad habit to get into, Diane. Take my advice. When it comes to Nick, be helpless sometimes. Men like that."

She gave him a lopsided grin. "Modern women aren't helpless. For that matter, traditional women aren't helpless, either. They just pretend to be for the sake of their men. Nick isn't like that. He loves my independence."

"He loves everything about you," Russ corrected.

Seeing them together over breakfast had reinforced his first impression of Nick. His daughter would be in kind, caring, capable hands—and he didn't give a damn about Diane's talk of independence. A man needed to be needed.

That thought stuck in his mind throughout the day, dallying there along with thoughts of Cynthia. He met with Evan Waldman, who had taught at Hollings before moving to St. Louis, but no matter how engrossing their talk, at the slightest break in the conversation Russ's mind wandered. On his drive back to the hotel later that day, he actually took a detour past Cynthia's. But he didn't stop. He hadn't been invited, didn't think he was needed, refused to make a fool of himself.

It was a matter of mind versus heart again. He stuck with his mind's decision through a dinner he barely ate, until loneliness eroded his resolve. This time, when he drove to Cynthia's, he pulled right up to the door and parked.

Robert answered with a genteel, "Good evening, sir."

"How are you tonight, Robert?"

"Just fine, thank you, sir."

"Is Mrs. Bauer in?"

"I believe so. If you'll come in and have a seat—" he showed him into the living room "—I'll let her know you're here."

"Thank you." Russ lowered himself to the settee but sat on its edge, his elbows on his knees. He shouldn't have come. She was going to be annoyed.

As it happened, Cynthia wasn't at all annoyed. To

the contrary. If she had been able to wish for one thing, it would have been to see him just then. With a tired smile she leaned against the living room arch. "Hi."

He got quickly to his feet. "Hi." His eyes scanned her face. "What's wrong?"

She scrunched up her nose and took a deep breath. "Ooooh, it's been a bit of a rough day."

"Last-minute glitches?"

"In a way." She wrapped her arms around her waist. "You know the accident Father John mentioned last night?"

Russ nodded.

"The boy who was injured is the son of one of my friends."

He came closer. "I'm sorry, Cyn. I didn't know. Diane didn't say anything this morning."

"She didn't know. *We* didn't know. They kept things quiet until midday."

Tucking his hands in the pockets of his slacks, he came closer still. "What happened?"

"The boy's father—my friend's husband—is a developer. He got Jimmy a summer job working at one of his building sites. Scaffolding collapsed. Jimmy fell."

"How badly hurt is he?"

"They still don't know for sure. He's in a coma." Her eyes teared. "He's twenty years old with a whole life ahead of him if only he wakes up…and they were worrying about telling me, because they didn't want to put a damper on Diane's wedding week." She pressed a hand to her upper lip, which had begun to tremble.

Thinking only that he'd finally found a way to help, Russ reached out and drew her to him. "Good friends do things like that."

Against his shirt, she murmured, "I've been at the hospital for most of the afternoon. There isn't anything they can do but wait. They're positively distraught."

Russ knew that Cynthia was, too. He rubbed her back, willing her to relax against him. When she did, he rewarded her with a kiss by her ear. "I'm sure it meant a lot to them that you were there."

"I wouldn't have been anywhere else." She moaned. "They kept talking about having to miss the wedding and mess up the seating arrangement. Can you believe that? For God's sake, I'd redo the arrangement ten times over if it would make Jimmy better."

"I'm sure you would," he said, and continued to hold her. She felt so right in his arms. She always had, but now even more so. He had missed the way she nestled against him. He hadn't realized how much. Through a tight throat, he whispered, "Want to take a walk?"

She didn't lift her head. "Now?"

"Yes, now."

"It'll be getting dark soon."

"We still have an hour. Better still, how about a run?"

"A run?"

"Have you had one today?"

"Early this morning." She sighed. "Feels like an aeon ago."

"Then put on your gear, we'll go back to my hotel while I change, and I'll show you the route I've been taking."

She drew her head back. "You've been taking?"

"I run, too." He gave her a little nudge and stepped back. "Go on. It'll make you feel better."

What made Cynthia feel better was the realization that, on top of everything else that drew them together, they had this in common. She did feel like running, but she wouldn't have done it alone so late. Russ's company was a gift.

Less than thirty minutes later, they were running side by side. He tempered his pace to one he felt would be comfortable for her, then picked up a little when he saw that she could handle more. When he felt they'd hit stride, he asked, "How're you doin'?"

"Great," she said, breathing easily. "Feels good."

"It always does."

"Especially when you're down. That call shook me today."

"I could see that."

She ran on a bit before saying, "Life is so fragile. Things can be fine one day and shattered the next."

"Was that how it was with Matthew?"

"Uh-huh." Matthew's heart had been the culprit. It had ticked fine on Monday and stopped cold on Tuesday. "We weren't prepared."

"Is anyone ever prepared for death?" Russ gestured for her to turn right at the corner. "You had a good life with Matthew."

"He was a kind man."

"I'm surprised you didn't have more kids."

She was a minute in answering. "Me, too. I was so quick to get pregnant with Diane. I guess I wasn't meant to have more."

"Did you want more?"

"Uh-huh." But even as the word came out, she felt hesitant. Though she had never used birth control with Matthew, neither of them had been disturbed when she hadn't conceived. "With his being older, it was probably for the best."

"You could have more now."

Between strides, she shot him a doubtful look. "I'm forty-three."

"Easily done in this day and age."

She shot him another look, a chiding one this time. "Spoken like a man." Which he was. Quite definitely. She didn't have to shoot him another look to see the dark rumple of his hair, the lean strength of his shoulders, the muscular tone of his legs. "How about you? Didn't you want other children?"

"I've had hundreds over the years."

"Of your own."

He mulled over the question. "I wasn't sure I was worthy."

"Are you kidding?" She tried to make out his expression, but dusk shadowed his face.

His voice was sober, punctuated only by the rhythm of his pace. "I abandoned Diane. I wasn't sure I deserved another child. It's taken six years of building a relationship with her to give me back a little self-respect in that regard."

"So you want more kids now?"

He shrugged, shot a look behind him for traffic and gestured for her to make a left turn. "Got no wife."

"Which mystifies me. You should have married again."

"Didn't want to. No one would be good enough. You're a hard act to follow."

Her voice went breathless. "Don't say that."

"It's the truth."

"I have my faults."

"Like what?"

"Cowardice."

"When?"

"When you left." She didn't speak for several beats. "I should have stood up to my mother."

"You weren't in a position to do that. You said it yourself."

"I know. Still, I should have. Somehow."

As confessions went, it was filled with regret and, in that, was a world away from the anger he'd heard two nights before. Gone, too, was the bitterness he'd always felt when, in moments of self-pity, he allowed himself to think she could have done something to bring him back. They were moving on, past the pain, as they needed to do if they hoped to know each other in the here and now.

One shadow of the past, though, hadn't budged. "Cyn?"

"Hmm?"

"Does your mother know I'm here?"

"Not yet."

"But she knows I'm coming to the wedding."

"Yes."

"Does she know I'm walking Diane down the aisle?"

Cynthia ran on in silence.

"She doesn't," he said.

"See what a coward I am?"

He rallied to her defense. "You didn't know about it yourself until Monday."

"I should have called her then." The syncopated pat of their running shoes on the pavement was the only sound until she tacked on, "Then again, maybe it's best she not know. She can't make much of a fuss with everyone watching at the wedding." After another minute she darted Russ an uneasy look. "Can she?"

Russ didn't know, but the more he thought about it—which he did at some length after dropping Cynthia back home that night—the more he realized he didn't want to leave the matter to chance. Gertrude Hoffmann could be one unpleasant lady. Her narrow-mindedness had sabotaged his marriage. He wasn't letting it mar his daughter's wedding day.

To that end, he showed up at her house early the next morning. He remembered the way, having dropped Cynthia back there dozens of times. More often than not he had parked down the street and walked her to the house, so that Gertrude wouldn't hear the distinctly lower-class rumble of his car. Only once had he been inside.

He remembered being impressed by the size, the shine and the sophistication. But he'd been a boy then, and raw. Now he was a man with polish of his own, and while he could appreciate the stateliness of Gertrude Hoffmann's home, he wasn't terribly impressed. Cynthia's, which held an inherent warmth, was far more to his liking.

"My name is Russell Shaw," he told the uniformed maid who answered the door. "Mrs. Hoffmann isn't expecting me, but I'd like a word with her if she's home."

He was shown into the parlor, which amused him no end. The maid didn't know who he was, but making a judgment based on his clothing, his carriage and his confidence, had deemed him safe to let in. That was a switch from the judgment made twenty-six years before.

After no more than a minute, she returned. "If you'll come this way, Mr. Shaw." She led him across the hall and down a corridor into the dining room. There, at the far end of a huge table, at a place set with fine linen, bone china and sterling silver, sat Gertrude Hoffmann—and for a split second Russ understood what Diane had said about the woman being alone. There was no sadder image than that of a solitary figure amid opulence.

Then the second passed, and he saw a woman in her mid-sixties, well preserved and imperious-looking still. Her hair was pure white and perfectly coiffed, her face neatly made up, her blue blouse impeccably starched. She was in the middle of a breakfast of eggs and toast that had come from a scrolled chafing dish nearby. But her fork had been placed neatly across her plate and she was sitting back in her chair, elbows on its arms, fingers laced, staring at him.

"I was wondering whether you'd make it over here," she announced boldly. "If I were a gambling woman, I'd have lost money. I didn't think you'd have the courage to face me after all these years."

Russ wasn't put off by her bluntness. It dispensed with polite greetings and told him just where he stood. "I have the courage. I've always had it."

"Even when you deserted my daughter and granddaughter?" she asked archly.

With confidence, he said, "Mostly then. Leaving Cynthia and Diane was the hardest thing I've ever had to do. They were all I cared about in the world. More than anything I wanted to stay with them, but that would have been the selfish thing— the cowardly thing to do. I couldn't give them what they needed or deserved, or what I wanted them to have. Not without your help. So I sent them back to you. The way I see it, that took courage. The way I see it, you should be thanking me."

Her chin lifted a notch. "For embarrassing me? For causing upheaval in my home?"

"For returning your daughter to you, and for giving you a granddaughter who is better than either of us. She's the reason I'm here today. I love Diane. This is a special time for her. If there is to be unpleasantness, I want it to stay between you and me. She isn't to feel it."

Gertrude's gaze didn't waver, though her chin dropped slightly. "She was very angry with me for a while, all because of you."

"Justly so. You had no business telling her that I was dead. She had a right to know the truth."

"To what end? So she could chase after a man who had given every sign of not wanting her? You didn't contact my daughter after you ran out of here. Not once."

"Would you have wanted me to?"

"Heavens, no!"

"What would you have done if I had?"

"Gotten a court order to keep you away."

In a voice quiet with a common sense that chided, Russ said, "Do you have any idea what that would have done to Cynthia? Or to Diane?" When Gertrude didn't answer, he went on. "I left because I thought it was the best thing for both of them. I stayed away for the same reason. When I contacted Diane six years ago, it was because I felt she was old enough and because I couldn't stay away any longer. She's my daughter. There's no denying that fact."

Gertrude looked as if she did want to deny it but couldn't. Her frustration escaped in subtle ways—the faint compression of her lips, the shift of her fingers, her refusal to blink.

Russ refused to be intimidated by that unremitting stare. "I'm not sure how much she's told you about our relationship. We meet for lunch every few months. We've developed a mutual appreciation. I love hearing about what's going on in her life, she loves hearing about what's happening in mine. Do you know where I live?"

A muscle in her cheek moved. It could have been either a twitch or a gesture of dismissal. "She told me you lived at a school in Connecticut."

"Did she tell you that I'm the headmaster of that

school? I was chosen last year from a pool of three hundred candidates. It's a position of responsibility and prestige.''

Gertrude arched a pale brow. ''Is there a point to this self-promotion, Mr. Shaw?''

He smiled with the sudden understanding that she was rather harmless—arched brow, starched blouse, thinned lips and all. In a softer voice he said, ''It's Dr. Shaw, and indeed there is. I was up for a good part of last night thinking about this visit. I was prepared to spit in your eye—'' he held up a hand ''—not a terribly learned expression from a learned man, but apt. When I left here twenty-five years ago, I hated you. Since then I've come a long way in terms of who I am, what I do and how much money I make. I may not hate you now, but I'm not backing down. I'm here this week because Diane asked me to come. If she hadn't invited me to the wedding, I'd probably have come anyway and stood at the back of the church—just as I stood at the back during her graduation from Radcliffe, though she doesn't know that, and I wish you wouldn't tell her. She'd be upset, which would be pointless, since it's water under the bridge. I want her to be happy. That's all I've ever wanted.''

He paused for the briefest of instants, then reached the point of his visit. ''She's asked me to give her away at the wedding, and I've accepted. Cynthia just found out. She had already arranged for Ray Bauer to do it, and she wasn't thrilled at first, but she agrees that on Diane's day her wish should be respected. I'd like you to do the same.''

The silence in the dining room was abrupt. Russ made no move to break it. He was waiting for Gertrude's consent, and the fact that she didn't instantly offer it neither surprised nor bothered him. Cynthia had mentioned the woman's pride. She would answer him in her own sweet time—which was fine, as long as she gave him the answer he wanted.

He didn't expect the subtle shift of her features, this time not in frustration but in what looked surprisingly like remorse.

"There are people," she began more quietly than before, "who take me to be arrogant and bossy and bigoted, and rightly they should. I can be all of those things when I'm crossed, and some of those things even when I'm not. But whatever I do, I do because I believe it's the best thing." She looked off to the side, keeping her jaw firm to show she wasn't apologizing for anything. "I'll admit that I was a bit cruel cutting Cynthia off without a cent when you two eloped, but I was angry and hurt that she hadn't taken my advice, and I truly believed that only drastic measures would bring her back to me."

"She had a *baby*. You didn't come to see Diane once in those three months."

"Four months," Gertrude corrected, looking him in the eye now. "Cynthia stayed in that apartment for a whole month after you left, waiting for you to return, and she mourned you in earnest for months after. I'd be less than honest if I said that didn't bother me."

"You hated me that much?"

"I loved Cynthia that much. She was my only child, and she was heartbroken."

"But you weren't ready to go out and bring me back."

"No. I didn't think that would be in her best interest. Matthew was a far better match for her. He gave her the stability you couldn't have provided. But that's not my point. My point is that I love my daughter and don't want to see her unhappy. The same applies to my granddaughter. So. If your giving Diane away at the wedding will make her happy, I won't fight it."

Russ couldn't quite bring himself to thank her, though he did feel immensely relieved. He also felt a glimmer of understanding for the woman. Lips pursed, he reflected on that for a minute before nodding and turning to leave. Beneath the archway, he turned back and in a tentative voice asked, "Just for the record, if Cynthia hadn't called you, would you have gone looking for her?"

Gertrude's chin tipped up again. "I already had, and I'd already seen the baby. I used to sit in a rented car on the edge of the park on weekends and watch while you two handed her back and forth."

Russ's throat tightened. He stared at her, thinking about stubbornness and pride and loss. Then, with another nod, he turned, only to stop again. He didn't look back this time. "One last question. If Cynthia and I were to start seeing each other again, if she were to visit me in Connecticut, would you give her trouble?"

After what seemed an eternity to Russ, Gertrude

said, "Cynthia is a grown woman. A widow. I no longer have any control over her."

"She loves you and wants to please you. Would you give her trouble?"

The older woman's voice grew quiet. "Now, that wouldn't be in my best interest, would it?"

He did look back at her then. "What do you mean?"

"I have nothing to hold over Cynthia anymore. She is financially independent and socially secure. She doesn't need me the way she did twenty-five years ago. If she chooses to see you and I object, she's very well apt to defy me again, only this time she wouldn't have any reason to come back. Frankly, I don't care for the thought of being estranged from my only daughter at this point in my life."

The implication of what she was saying boggled Russ's mind. He wanted to make sure he'd heard right. "You wouldn't make life miserable for her?"

"Not on that score." One corner of her mouth moved in what Russ could have sworn was the germ of a smile. "On others, of course, I would. I'm Gertrude Hoffmann. It's in my nature to be demanding and iron-willed, even overbearing at times. The day I can't cause a stir on one matter or another will be the day they put me in the ground. Have you any more questions?"

Russ thought about it, then shook his head. With a final nod and a small wave of farewell, he showed himself to the front door and went out to the car. The day seemed suddenly much brighter.

Chapter Six

THE WEDDING REHEARSAL went off without a hitch on Thursday evening, and Cynthia couldn't have been more delighted. She was pleased to begin with, having gotten word shortly beforehand that Jimmy Schuler had regained consciousness. Added to that, the bridesmaids and groomsmen—bar one Jared Flynn—had all arrived in St. Louis intact, neither of the flower girls had misbehaved, and her mother hadn't said boo when Russ went through the motions of walking Diane down the central aisle of the church, so Cynthia was feeling good all over.

The feeling got even better as they moved from the church to Granatelli's, Nick's family's restaurant on the Hill, where the rehearsal dinner was to be held. The restaurant was small, but upscale and classy in its way, with white tablecloths, white linen napkins and fresh flowers. Candles on each of the tables, as well as paintings and photographs on the walls, gave it the homey atmosphere that suited Nick's family so well.

Cynthia liked the Granatellis, many of whom she'd met before. She liked Teresa, who, plump but stately, had a natural dignity to rival Gertrude's. She liked Dom, with his white moustache and commanding nose, and Uncle Vito, with the ever-present cigar that smelled up the place but looked so much a part of the man that no one dreamed of complaining. She liked Nick's sisters, Paula, Frankie and Sophia, and his brothers, Carlo and Vinnie—all blond, as was Nick, whom she adored. Mostly she liked the fact that Nick and Diane were in love, and that their love surmounted the differences in background that a generation before had caused such heartache. If Gertrude had any objections to the match, she hadn't dared say so to Cynthia. She must have known Cynthia would fight tooth and nail for her daughter's right to happiness.

So Cynthia was feeling good about that, too. And then there was Russ, who had hardly left her side since they'd arrived at the restaurant. She enjoyed having him there. She enjoyed introducing him to Nick's family, enjoyed the way he fitted into the group, enjoyed the way he held his own in conversation. She enjoyed the way he stood with an arm or a shoulder brushing hers, the way he brought her a drink from the bar, put a hand at her waist to guide her to a table, pulled out her chair. He was a gentleman, and though she had never found him lacking in that respect years before, this was different. He was socially suave and urbane, more so than she ever could have wished. Twenty-six years before she'd been bowled over by the boy in the soda shop; now she was bowled over by the man that boy had become.

She was sorry when the evening ended. Too soon, Russ drove her home and walked her to her door. Though her senses were keyed up for something warm and exciting—and though the longing look he gave her suggested he wanted it, too—he didn't kiss her. Instead, he offered to come by the next day and give her a hand doing whatever last-minute things had to be done. If for no other reason than to keep him close, she accepted the offer.

The result was heaven and hell at the very same time. Russ was with her while she opened newly arrived gifts with Diane, oversaw the tent and table raising in the yard and made a final run-through of the wedding events with Tammy. He sat patiently while she made calls to various out-of-town guests who were starting to arrive. He drove her to the jeweler's to pick up the bridesmaids' gifts, to the dry cleaner's to pick up things Diane would be taking on her honeymoon, to the hospital to visit Jimmy. He even drove her to the manicurist's, then wandered around outside until she was done.

Though he was a joy to be with—calm, accommodating and patient—his presence was a torment. He touched her, but never for long enough. He looked at her with desire, but never acted it out. He spoke in the low, intimate tone lovers used, the kind that stroked her inside and out, then took a step back while she reeled. By late afternoon she wasn't sure whether the shakiness she felt inside was mother-of-the-bride jitters or pure lust.

Russ had barely brought her back to the house when the phone started ringing again. Whispering asides to him about who each of the calls was from, she talked with a cousin who had arrived with her family from Cleveland, a former business associate of

Matthew's who was in with his wife from Denver, a friend of Gertrude's whom Cynthia had known forever. Then Diane called from Nick's, reporting that people were gathering at the Granatellis' and asking if they would be along soon. It was a perfect solution to Cynthia's problem. She could be with Russ, yet safe. The more people around, the more diffused her awareness of him would be.

That didn't turn out to be the case. The party at the Granatellis' was wonderful, but not once did Cynthia forget the man by her side. They talked together, moved together, laughed together every bit as naturally as when they'd been kids. Likewise, there were times when the party receded and they were alone, sharing a thought or a story or a reaction to something another person said as though they were the only ones in the room.

That happened increasingly as the evening went on. By eleven, Russ was feeling a distinct need to be alone with Cynthia, if only for a short time. Leaning close, he said, "Are you tired?"

She knew she should be. She knew she should go home to bed, given the eventful day that was ahead. But her senses were humming. She was more awake than she'd been in years. "I don't think I could sleep if I tried."

"Want to go for a ride?"

"I'd love to."

"Think anyone will miss us?"

She glanced around. The party was still in full swing. "Are you kidding?" Slipping a hand in his, she led him through the crowd to where Diane was laughing with a group of friends. "We're taking off, sweetheart. Shall I see you back home?"

"Sooner or later—probably later. Better still, don't wait up, Mom, okay? I'll be more relaxed that way. And I'll have everyone be quiet when we get back so we don't wake you up."

Cynthia touched her hair. She couldn't quite believe her baby was getting married in the morning. Then again, given the work she'd done planning the wedding, she could believe it quite well. "Don't forget, Franco and his crew are coming to do hair at ten. Pass the word."

Diane smiled. "I already have." She kissed Cynthia, then Russ. "See you tomorrow."

The air outside was hot and still. Russ didn't have to be told that a storm was coming on. Anyone could tell, what with the humidity and the dark, starless sky—even a person whose own senses had been storming for hours. His blood was hotter than the air, his arousal heavier than the humidity, and as for the darkness of the sky, that was the way he felt when he thought of leaving on Sunday. There was so much yet to be said, so much to be done. *So much.*

After tucking Cynthia into the car, he went to the driver's side and slid in behind the wheel, but he didn't turn on the ignition. Instead, he caught up her hand and brought it to his mouth.

"I don't want to go for a ride," he breathed against it. "Not really."

She was looking at him, sure that if she didn't kiss him soon she would die. "Me, neither. Russ?"

He rubbed her knuckles against his mouth. "I love you so much."

"Oh, God," she whispered, and opened her hand. She traced his lips for a minute, parted them and leaned over the gearshift to meet him halfway. Their mouths touched and fused, and it was as though twenty-five years of separation had never been. The fire, the balm, the bliss were so intense that by the time they parted for a breath, there were tears in her eyes.

"Can we go somewhere?" he whispered hoarsely.

"Please," she whispered back. "Quickly."

He drove one-handed. The other hand was wrapped in both of hers, anchored against her throat. Her eyes were on his face. He caught her gaze as often as he dared take his from the road. It was brilliant with excitement and need, both of which shone through the thick, dark night. Once, then a second time, he hastily pulled to the side of the road to kiss her again, and if his kisses held more raw need than finesse, he knew she understood. He could taste the hunger in her mouth, could feel the desire that set her slender body to shaking.

By the time they arrived at the inn, large drops of rain had begun to splatter the windshield. Leaving the doorman with a ten-dollar bill to park the car, Russ grabbed Cynthia's hand and ran inside. They took the stairs, moving as quickly as Cynthia's heels would allow, and when that wasn't fast enough, she slipped the shoes off and ran faster.

He fumbled with the door, finally unlocked it and pushed it open. The bed had been neatly turned back in his absence and a low light left on, but he barely noticed. As the door clicked shut behind them, he slid his fingers into her hair, covered her mouth with his and gave her a frantic kiss that spread to her cheeks, then her eyes.

"I can't believe you're here," he whispered.

"I'm here." She was unbuttoning his shirt, desperate to touch him. In a fluid motion that pushed the cotton fabric aside, she slid her palms over his chest and ribs to his waist. In the next breath, she put her mouth where her hands had touched.

Russ was in heaven. He braced shaky arms against the door on either side of her and bent his head over hers. "Sweetheart...sweetheart...what you do to me."

"I love you, Russ," she said, raising her face. Her mouth met his again, and this time, while their lips continued to nip and suck, they went at their clothes. Cynthia's halter dress fell to the floor not far from Russ's shirt and slacks. He released her bra and filled his hands with her breasts, while she pushed his shorts over his hips.

"Hurry," she cried, straining closer, frantic with need.

No less frantic himself, Russ kicked off his shorts, scooped her up and carried her to the bed. He set her down on her knees in the middle of it and, with time-out to touch all he bared, freed her of her silk panties. While they knelt facing each other, breathing harder than if they'd just come off a long run, he reached for the pins in her hair.

"I want this all over me. I've dreamed of it. It's so beautiful."

She helped him with the pins, helped him comb through her hair with his fingers until it flowed softly over her shoulders. Then, draping her elbows over his shoulders, she gave him her mouth. At the same time, he brought her body tightly against his, drew her thighs over his and entered her.

Her cry was muffled in his mouth. Seconds later, her back hit the bed and he began to love her inside with long, hot strokes. She wanted to savor them and everything else about his body, but the intensity was too great. Within minutes she erupted into a climax so powerful and prolonged that she was never to know where one orgasm ended and the next began.

For Russ, too, the pleasure went on and on. The memory of their lovemaking, which had kept him hard night after night for years, was nothing compared to the heat of the present. His body was slick with sweat by the time he finally let his weight go on her. He rolled to the side and drew her to him, tightening his arms when, still shaken by inner spasms, she began to cry.

"What, sweetheart? What is it?" But he knew even before she told him. He was feeling the same overwhelming emotion.

"I've missed you so much," she gulped through huge tears that wet his throat. "Part of me has been gone—"

"—gone all this time." His arms tightened until he feared he would crush her. His head was bent over hers, his breath was urgent against her temple. "There was always that empty spot. I kept thinking it would fill in—"

"—but it never did. I tried to put other things there, like Matthew and my friends and my causes—"

"—and my students and my courses, but it didn't work. There was always that void, and it hurt—"

"—*so much.*"

"Ahhh, sweetheart," he whispered, moving his head as he kissed her until he could reach her mouth again. "I love you, Cyn...love you, sweetheart." He rolled her over, then over again, kissing her all the while. Ending on top, he began to make love to her again, moving down her body, touching and tasting all the places he had missed for so long.

She writhed beneath him until she could take no more. "Now, Russ, *now.*"

Hard and heavy with need, he surged into her, then proceeded to make up for the time they had lost by loving her until she came again—only to realize that wasn't enough. He climaxed, but still he wanted her. The sounds she made, the touch of her hands and the motions of her body told him she felt the same.

They made love long into the night. Hours had passed before either of them was ready to settle onto the damp and rumpled sheets for long, and then it wasn't with exhaustion but with gales of breathless laughter that only two people who are pleased with themselves and in love with each other can produce.

"You haven't changed, Russell Shaw," she hummed against his shoulder. "You're as insatiable as ever."

He spread a hand over her backside to mold her

closer. "Look who's talking. I haven't had a workout like this in years."

"How many years?"

"Twenty-five."

"Mmm. That's good."

"And you? Did you drive Matthew wild like you do me?"

"It was different with Matthew. Pleasant, but sedate. There were never grounds for comparison."

"Mmm. That's good."

"But he was a fine man, Russ. He was kind. He loved me, and he loved Diane. I tried to be a good wife to him."

"From everything I've read and heard, you were."

She sighed. "But did I love him? Ahhh, there's the question. I tried to, but it never came close to the kind of all-consuming love I had with you." She tipped her head back and looked over the plane of his lean cheek to his eyes. "I prayed I'd never see you. I went out of my way over the years not to know what you were doing with your life. I never quite trusted that I wouldn't want to run off to be with you—or that you wouldn't turn and walk away from me again." Her eyes misted and her voice fell to a plaintive whimper. "You won't do that, Russ, will you?"

He brought her over on top of him. "No, love." He kissed her eyes. "I couldn't."

"It would kill me."

"It would kill me, too."

"So what are we going to do? You're leaving Sunday."

"Only if you can't find room for me in your house."

Her heart soared. "You'll stay?"

"Why not?"

"What about school?"

"I'm on summer vacation."

"You have the whole summer off?" Her mind leaped at the possibilities.

"Yes and no."

"What does that mean?" She held her breath.

"I'm due in England on the fifth of July. I'm committed to spending the summer in Oxford collaborating with a don there on a book on education."

She continued to hold her breath.

"Want to come with me?" he asked, and started to smile just as she did because he knew very well what her answer would be.

"I'd love to."

"I'll be busy. Writing a book takes time and concentration."

"That's okay. I'll catch up on all the reading I haven't been able to do this spring, and write letters and take walks."

"I was planning to rent a house in the Cotswolds. Does that sound okay?"

She grinned. "I think I could live with it."

"Then, when I'm done, I thought I'd spend a few days in London, and maybe drive north to Scotland for a few more. Would that be a problem?"

"Are you kidding?"

"I have to be back before Labor Day," he cautioned. "School doesn't begin until a week later, but there'll be plenty to do before then."

She rested her chin on his chest. "What's it like, your place at Hollings?"

"It's a Tudor, wood and brick, with a grape arbor and an old-fashioned well and lots of trees." He ran his fingers through her hair, spreading it around her. "You'll like it, Cyn. It's on campus but set apart so that there's plenty of privacy. It's the kind of house we used to talk about having one day. I mean, it's not as grand as yours—"

She put her hand over his mouth. "I don't care about grand. I care about *you.* You could live in a shack on the tundra and I'd follow you there. That's what I was trying to tell you Monday night. It's one of the reasons I was so crushed when you left me. I've had wealth, and, yes, it makes life easier. But it isn't worth diddly if I can't have you. Don't put me through that misery again, Russ. Don't ever, ever, *ever* do it."

Grasping her waist, he raised her just enough for a kiss. He was about to tell her that he wouldn't ever, ever, *ever* leave her again, when the kiss heated and spread, and before he could contain the flame, she was beneath him and he was inside her again.

It was a while later before he said the words, and by that time they were both so drowsy that the words were slurred. But Cynthia heard them, and held them to her heart as she fell asleep in his arms. Just to make sure she knew he meant them, he repeated them several hours later, when, with dawn sending shards of pale color over the Frontenac treetops, he drove her home.

IT WAS A GEM OF A DAY, sunny and dry after the rain the night before. The rich alto of the organ filled the air. With rosebuds in soft shades of cream, pink and peach on the pews and on arbors framing the altar, the church looked beautiful, as did the guests, who filled row after row, waiting expectantly for the processional to begin.

Cynthia, too, waited, her heart beating fast beneath the corsage that had been carefully pinned to her dusty pink gown. She had just been escorted down the aisle and now stood beside Gertrude, who looked surprisingly soft in dove gray. At a change in the music, she turned to watch the groomsmen enter. They were a handsome group. She smiled at each one whose eye she caught, but her attention inevitably returned to the rear of the church. The bridesmaids appeared one by one, looking as exquisite as she had intended in shades of peach, dusty rose and gray. The maid of honor passed as planned, then the flower girls, leaving soft pink petals in their wake.

The music changed again, and this time when Cynthia looked back, her breath caught in her throat. The two people she loved most in the world were there— Diane, looking more stunning than any bride had ever been in her gown of satin and beaded lace, with her cascading bouquet and the headpiece of flowers and veiling, that barely hid the glittering tear-shaped diamond earrings her father had given her that morning; and Russ, looking more handsome than any father of the bride had ever been with his white standing collar, his pale gray cutaway coat and trousers, his cream-colored boutonniere.

Tears came to her eyes as she watched them slowly approach. When she brushed them away, new ones simply took their place. She smiled through them as she caught Diane's eye, and when she found Russ looking at her, her smile grew even softer. He was a beautiful man inside and out, with a beautiful daughter who had been the focus of her passion for the twenty-five years he'd been gone from her life. Now he was back, and the passion would broaden and shift. She felt she was the luckiest woman in the world.

Russ must have read that in her eyes, because his own spoke of sheer adoration in the brief minute before he passed. As she faced front, Nick was approaching the foot of the altar. Gently, Russ lifted Diane's veil and kissed her cheek, then placed her hand in Nick's. By the time he had come to stand by Cynthia's side, the bride and groom were in the priest's care.

Cynthia felt Russ's fingers twine with hers. Looking up through her tears, she saw the sparkle of his own, and in that instant understood the precious second chance they'd been given. His fingers tightened possessively, and while Diane and Nick exchanged their vows, silently they did, too.

Their hearts heard every word.

Handsome as Sin

Kelsey Roberts

Chapter One

"Just play along with me," Ellie whispered to the bartender as she leaned against the bar. Her task was hindered by the rather imposing figure of a man who had occupied the same stool ever since the snow began sticking to the street two hours ago.

Josh gave her a conspiratorial smile and a flirtatious wink. "Anything for a beautiful woman."

"So I hear," she mumbled under her breath. She was turning away from the bar when she caught the other man's gaze.

The tall stranger had eyes the color of rare emeralds. A brilliant, sparkling green that reflected the white light overhead.

Normally friendly and outgoing, Ellie Tanner suddenly found herself without a voice. Actually, she amended, it wasn't that she'd lost her voice, it was more like a total loss for words. What do you say to a man who is as handsome as sin? A man with a perfect smile and even more perfect dimples?

She didn't have time to contemplate an answer because Mike Avery, his jacket dusted with a damp layer of fresh snow, burst through the door.

"Show time," she said, sighing.

After taking a second to brush the flakes off his coat, he shrugged it off and deposited it on one of the hooks on the wall. In keeping with one of his many personality flaws, he didn't seem to care that a small puddle of water was forming on the polished wood floor.

"Why are you here?" she asked without preamble, crossing her arms in front of her chest. In her peripheral vision, she saw the tall, blond stranger remove his Stetson and place it on the bar next to the penny he'd been playing with for the better part of an hour.

Great! she silently fumed. Nothing like an audience.

Mike stepped forward and attempted to place a kiss on her tightly clamped lips. Ellie turned her head at the last second. Mike had to settle for a brief brush against her cheek.

"Merry Christmas to you, too," he said.

"It isn't Christmas yet."

Mike's eyes narrowed, but her blatant rebuke didn't seem to be penetrating his thick skull any better than it had back in New York.

Just then, Josh came out from behind the bar and draped his arm across her shoulder. Ellie derived some small amount of satisfaction as she watched her former boyfriend try not to react.

"Josh Richardson, Mike Avery."

"Nice to meet you," Josh greeted, extending his

hand. "I didn't know Ellie had any friends here in Charleston."

Ellie drew her bottom lip between her teeth to keep from laughing aloud. Aside from being a great bartender and an even more legendary leech, Josh was also a very good actor. No, she corrected when she felt him brush his mouth against her hair, he was an *excellent* actor.

"What's going on here?" Beth asked as she came over, an empty tray balanced against her slender hip.

Ellie felt a momentary panic. What if Beth gave them away? The last thing she needed was for this well-meaning waitress to tell Mike the truth.

"Miss?"

Ellie was saved by the handsome man at the bar. His Texas accent and deep, sexy voice could not be ignored, especially by the obviously curious Beth. Somewhat reluctantly, Beth walked over to serve the lone customer waiting out the storm.

"What gives here?" Mike asked, his eyes fixed on Ellie.

"I don't know what you're talking about," she responded, slipping her arm around Josh's waist.

If it were physically possible, steam would have poured from Mike's ears. Instead, his face flushed an angry shade of red.

"You've been down here less than a week and you've already taken up with this guy?" He hooked his thumb in Josh's direction as if he were insignificant.

"I'm a quick study," Josh volunteered, baiting the

larger man. "And Ellie sure is a beautiful topic to study."

He was playing it all wrong, she thought to herself as she gently extracted herself from his arm. "Josh, honey," she purred. "Why don't you let me explain things to Mike. Besides…" She turned her eyes toward the bar. What she saw there made her heart skip a beat. Mr. Handsome as Sin was watching her with blatant interest. If that sexy half smile was any indication, he was enjoying the show, too. "You promised Rose you'd keep Chad out of the cherries."

When her pseudoadmirer spotted the two-year-old reaching into the tray of fruits, Josh abandoned her and raced to the end of the bar. Hesitantly, she turned to face the music.

THE PENNY WAS SMOOTH as he rubbed it between his fingers. Smooth and satisfying. Jake only wished he had had the time to send it to Greenfield before arriving in Charleston. He'd only been in town a couple hours and already his opinion of the city fell well short of positive. Or at least it had until he'd caught his first glimpse of the tall, willowy woman now seated at one of the round tables arranged near the glow of the fireplace.

This was the South, the place where people came to escape the snow-ladened winters up north. Raising his eyes to the large picture window, he felt himself frown as he watched the steady stream of fluttering white flakes floating down from an ominous gray sky.

"I hate the cold," he grumbled to the bartender as

he turned to rest his elbows on the bar, giving him a front-row view of the couple.

"Where're ya from?"

"Texas," Jake answered absently, his attention drawn to the woman's stunning profile. She was certainly something when she was mad. And she was nothing, if not mad. Whatever that muscle-bound jerk was saying to her had the lady seeing red. He could tell by the way her dainty hands were balled into furious little fists. He could also see it in the way her foot nervously tapped against the floor. But mostly he saw it in the flushed expression on her face.

Then he could hear it. Whoever she was, she wasn't shy about her feelings. Leaning back, he listened.

"...told you that months ago," she was saying, or rather shouting.

"Ellie, honey, we both know that you overreacted. You know how emotional you can be."

"Emotional?" she scoffed. "I'm not being emotional. I'm simply telling you I don't feel any emotions for you."

"Muscles" made a grab for her hand. She countered the move as easily as she'd deflected his earlier attempt to kiss her. Jake's admiration for the woman increased with every passing moment.

She wasn't a classic beauty, he decided. Her features didn't have the severe angles or the even distribution of perfection. No, this lady's mouth was slightly off center, her eyes too far apart. But there was an alluring quality to those blue-gray eyes, rimmed in inky lashes. A certain subtle sensuality that he doubted she was even aware of. No, this woman's charm was understated and natural. It was apparent in the almost regal way she held her head, totally unconcerned with the few strands of raven black hair that had fallen free from the gold barrette. It was apparent in her choice of cosmetics, or lack thereof, he noted when his eyes fixed on her slightly overfull lips. The rosy hue was a gift from nature, just like the long, shapely legs she crossed and uncrossed as she continued her heated conversation.

"...told you not to come."

Muscles frowned and loosened the knot of his tie where it met his thick neck. "I know you didn't mean it, Ellie."

"I always mean what I say, Mike. Your problem is that you don't listen."

He liked her accent. It told him she was from someplace up north. Instead of sounding harsh, it held a certain self-assuredness that he saw mirrored in the determined set of her delicate jaw.

"Ellie, I've come all this way," Muscles argued.

"For nothing," she told him. "I'm here to spend a nice quiet holiday with my family. And you aren't family."

"You didn't feel that way three months ago."

She blew an exasperated breath toward the bangs that feathered softly above those incredible eyes. Jake found himself enjoying the part of the voyeur. In fact, this was definitely an interesting way to wait out the unexpected snowstorm that had paralyzed the city.

"It's over, Mike," she was telling him. "It's been over and it will continue to be over."

"Because of him?" Muscles asked, tilting his large head in the direction of the bar.

Something flashed in the woman's eyes, but it was gone before Jake could put a proper name to it. He was further distracted from the couple when the waitress stomped up to the bar and scooted between two of the stools. She didn't give Jake a second look, her eyes were biting into the guy behind the bar.

"Need something?" he heard Josh inquire.

"Rose said to cut everyone off. She doesn't want us serving alcohol when the roads are this bad."

"Roads...cars," said the little boy who had been in and out of the restaurant. He struggled to pull himself up onto the seat next to Jake. "I Chad," he said, offering a toothy grin.

Jake smiled at the little boy, who looked so much like the woman he'd been admiring. "Jake," he said, extending his hand to the kid.

"Hat," Chad returned, pointing to the Stetson Jake had placed on the bar.

Seeing the child's curiosity, he put the penny down and retrieved his hat, balancing it on the little boy's dark head.

"Hat," he said again.

"Expensive hat," Jake told him.

But before he'd gotten the last word out, the child had bounded from the stool and scurried off behind the metal doors that led to the kitchen.

"Don't worry," the bartender said. "He'll bring it back as soon as he shows it to Rose."

Reluctantly Jake turned away from the couple and looked at the bartender. "Rose?"

"One of the owners. Chad's folks own the other half."

"Her?" he asked, indicating Ellie.

The bartender's grin bordered on wolfish. "Nope, luckily for me, she's a free agent."

Jake had to agree. Especially when he turned back and saw that she had gotten to her feet. He placed her body in the delectable category. Curves, but not overdone. The floral-print dress clung to her in all the right places, yet left enough to the imagination to inspire a few fantasies.

"You're a lucky man," he said as he turned back to the bar. "She's a pretty lady."

After draping the towel over his shoulder, Josh leaned forward, his eyes fixed on the couple. "I can't believe that loser followed her all the way here from New York."

"I can," Jake said under his breath. If she was his lady, he'd definitely keep her within arm's reach. In fact, he thought, continuing to fantasize as he turned back around, he could think of a whole list of things he'd do if he had a woman like that.

He would not, however, have his hand in a viselike grip on her upper arm. Jake waited, thinking Josh should intercede. Even though the lady was tall, Muscles outweighed her by at least a hundred pounds. He could tell by the wince on her face that he was hurting her.

Sensing the bartender wasn't going to spring into action, he stepped from the stool, his boots scraping the floor as he calmly sauntered over.

"Afternoon," he drawled, fixing his eyes on Muscles.

"Yes?" the man returned, clearly irritated by the intrusion. "Do you mind? This is a private conversation."

Jake hoisted one foot onto the seat of the chair and sighed pensively. "That's not how I see it. The way you've been yelling and carrying on, most everybody here knows the lady doesn't want you around."

"I can handle this," she interrupted, placing her hand against Jake's forearm.

He made a point of looking at her then. Her eyes were even more blue up close.

"I'm sure you can, ma'am," he answered easily. "But my mama wouldn't hold too kindly if I was to let this guy get away with roughing you up that way."

As if just aware of it, she looked to where Muscles' thick fingers circled her upper arm. "Let go," she said in a soft command.

"We need to talk," Muscles argued. "Alone," he added with a dismissive glare at Jake.

"Seems to me," he began slowly, "the lady pretty much said all she needed to say. I believe she gave you your walking papers."

"Back off," Muscles warned as an angry red stain seeped up over his collar. "This is between me and my fiancée."

"Ex-fiancée," she corrected. "I'm involved with Josh now. Right Josh?" she called across the room.

"Anything you say, sugar," he answered with a wink.

The other waitress, the one they called Beth,

groaned. Jake had to admit he shared the sentiment. The bartender didn't seem like much of an improvement over this clown.

"You haven't been here long enough to get involved with anyone," Muscles argued.

"What can I say?" She sighed heavily as her lashes fluttered over her eyes. "Love at first sight."

"Which brings me back to my original point, friend," Jake interjected. "I think the lady has made it pretty clear that you aren't welcome here." Jake lowered his leg and took a step so that he was right up in the other man's face. "I believe she asked you to leave. Now."

"Josh!" Ellie called, her voice slightly panicked. "I think you'd better get over here."

The bartender came over and got between the two men. "Rose doesn't allow fighting. You two have a problem, take it outside."

"I don't have a problem," Jake said. "I was only doing your job."

Ellie rubbed her hands over her face and said, "Mike, you have to leave. You should never have come here in the first place."

She watched the indecision on his face and silently prayed he would comply. The last thing she wanted or needed was for this collection of men to start brawling in the middle of her sister-in-law's restaurant. Dylan would kill her.

"Please, Mike?" she asked in a softer tone.

"For now," he grunted before turning on his heel and heading for the door. Angrily, he yanked his coat from the hook on the wall, nearly pulling the hook out along with the jacket.

"Be careful," she called out. "The roads are really slippery."

Mike's only response was to slam the door. The action shook the ornaments on the Christmas tree perched in the far corner of the room.

"Thanks," she said to Josh, then turned her attention to the tall, handsome man.

Having him in such close proximity made her breath catch in her throat. His hair was blond and stylishly long, falling well below the collar of his chambray shirt. She could just make out the impression of the hat she'd seen her nephew Chad race off with a few minutes earlier. But it was his eyes that had stolen the starch from her knees. They were so clear and green that she had the uncomfortable feeling that he could see right into her thoughts.

In order to talk to him, Ellie had to lift her chin. It was an unusual occurrence; at nearly six feet tall, she rarely had to look up to a man. "There wasn't any need for you to intercede," she told him firmly but politely.

"I didn't see it that way," he drawled in a sexy Southern accent that told her he wasn't a native of the area. "My mama was real clear on protecting the fairer sex."

Ellie felt her blood begin to boil and it had nothing to do with his display of even white teeth or those boyishly charming dimples on either side of his mouth. "Josh and I had things under control. Didn't we, Josh?"

The bartender shrugged. "I could have taken him. No problem."

The tall man said nothing. He didn't have to. He had a full vocabulary of eloquent looks that easily communicated his doubts.

Chad came bouncing back into the room then, followed by Rose. The hat was still clutched in the little boy's chubby fingers. He raced over to the tall man and thrust the hat forward. "Jake's hat," he announced.

Rose wasn't as quick as the small child, possibly because of her stiletto heels, or then again, it might have had something to do with her skintight Lycra pants. Though her choice of clothing was showy, her smile was genuine.

"Are you the one dumb enough to let him get his hands on an expensive thing like this?" Rose asked as she wrestled the hat away from Chad.

"Guilty as charged," he answered easily. "He's a cute kid. Really bright."

Ellie was gaping at the tall man, wondering where on earth the uneducated, good-ol'-boy drawl had gone. He was speaking to Rose in the polished voice of a professional.

"Rose Porter," she introduced.

"Jake Devereaux," he said as he shook the woman's hand.

Then, turning slightly amused eyes on Ellie, he asked, "And you are?"

"Ellie Tanner."

"And the guy with the neck the same size as his thigh?"

She tried not to smile. "Mike Avery. We work together back in Albany."

"More than work," Jake speculated. "I got the impression he wanted you home for the holidays."

Jake was about six feet four inches of trouble. Ellie sensed it in the same way a small animal senses a predator. He was a lankier, smarter version of Mike, so she decided immediately to nip her own curiosity in the bud. It was fairly easy to accomplish, especially when she looked up and saw the smug look in his emerald eyes.

"Sorry to do this to you, Jake, but I'm closing the Tattoo, so you'll have to be on your way," Rose announced. "The roads are only supposed to get worse and I doubt we'll be inundated with business."

"We're closing?" Beth asked. When Rose nodded, the waitress's lower lip protruded in a definite pout. "But I need the tips. I've got a new coat on layaway that I—"

"You shouldn't buy things you can't afford," Rose interrupted. "Besides, take a look outside. I don't think the good people of Charleston will want to risk life and limb for a plate of grilled sea bass."

"Hey, Ellie," Josh began as he placed a hand at her waist. "How about giving me a lift home? I'm no good at driving in the snow."

"I can take you," Beth suggested. "You live on my way."

Josh laughed. "You're no better at driving in this stuff than I am. I think I'd rather put my life in the hands of a pro."

"Organize yourselves quickly," Rose insisted. "I want to get out of here as soon as possible."

"What about Chad?" Ellie asked. "You want me to take him with me?"

Rose shook her head. Thanks to an abundance of hair spray, not a single teased curl came free. "The house is less than a mile away and I promised him we'd stop at the toy store to see if they have any sleds. This may be his one and only chance to go sledding."

"Tell Shelby I'll be home soon, then. Let's get our coats," she suggested. Ellie was careful not to make eye contact with Jake as she led the others toward the kitchen.

The coats were all piled in a small closet near the rear exit. Everyone bundled up, wrapping layer upon layer of mismatched winter gear on their bodies. Ellie smiled but said nothing. She guessed these Southerners would freeze to death inside a week back in Albany. This was a simple snow shower. They were dressing as if Charleston was about to experience a blizzard instead of the predicted inch and a half.

"The front door," Rose said with a groan as soon as she'd hoisted Chad and his ten pounds of coat, hat, mittens and scarf into her arms. "I forgot to lock it after that Jake fellow."

"I'll lock it," Ellie offered.

"Don't be long," Josh purred.

Rose gave him an admonishing look and Beth simply grunted at the lecherous suggestion behind the words.

Thanks to years as a criminologist for the New

York State Police, Ellie was quite comfortable walking through a strange place in dim lighting.

There was, however, just enough light spilling through the windows for her to see him well. Too well. Jake Devereaux was behind the bar, with both hands inside the cash register.

Chapter Two

Ellie let out a yell that brought Josh and Beth racing from the kitchen. The next few minutes went by in a flurry of arms, legs, punches and grunts.

Upon seeing the melee, Rose shielded Chad's face from the violence as the two men tumbled out from behind the bar. The struggle continued as chairs were toppled and tables were upended.

"Watch the tree!" Rose called as the men skittered across the floor, dangerously close.

"Watch his right!" Beth called too late.

They grimaced in unison when Jake's fist landed solidly against the other man's cheek.

"Stop it," Ellie heard Jake exclaim as he dodged blows as effortlessly as a professional. "I can explain."

"Thief," Josh growled as he butted Jake with his head.

The two men went sailing backward. Ellie heard Rose exclaim, "Oh my God," a fraction of a second before the Christmas tree came crashing down.

Glass shattered and several of the lights exploded in a series of multicolored pops.

"Do something," Beth whined.

Ellie, thinking this was not an appropriate thing for her nephew to see, went into the fray and grabbed Josh by the back of his coat. "Stop this right now," she insisted as she gave a hard jerk. It wasn't her strength but probably the fact that her action caused his shirt to act like a noose. Whatever the reason, it earned her Josh's cooperation. Instinctively she knew Jake wouldn't continue the fight. With the exception of a few punches meant to deter the aggressor, Jake had gone out of his way to keep from hurting the bartender. Still, seeing his readied stance and balled fists, Ellie had no doubt that this man could pound Josh into a bloody pulp with little or no effort.

"What is going on here?" she demanded as she watched Josh struggle for breath.

Jake tested his jaw by opening and closing his mouth in an exaggerated action. "I was looking for something."

"Money?" Rose accused, one brow arched toward the mass of lacquered hair.

"My money," Jake corrected. "I had a special coin with me that he must have—"

"Yeah, right," Josh grumbled. "And to think I didn't even charge you for the cup of coffee."

"Thanks," Jake answered wryly. "But the point remains that I had this item with me when I came in—"

"And you think that gives you the right to break into my register?" Rose said with a sneer.

"I was out the door before I realized I didn't have it," Jake explained. "I thought you all had left so I simply went looking for it on my own."

"Call the police," Beth insisted. "He's probably wanted."

Jake didn't even flinch at the suggestion. Instead, he took a moment to pull several strands of tinsel from the front of his jeans. "I can assure you, I am not a thief and I was only looking for something that belonged to me. If you don't believe me, I suggest you check the amount of cash in the drawer. You'll probably find that your cash drawer is exactly one cent over."

"You mean to tell me you were trying to steal a penny?" Ellie asked, astonished.

Rose handed the wide-eyed little boy to Ellie as she went over to the register. After a few minutes she said, "He's right. Nothing's missing."

Again Jake didn't react in any visible way. His casual, relaxed features piqued her curiosity. Of course, the fact that he was drop-dead gorgeous didn't help, either.

Remember Mike, she silently admonished. Though New Year's Day was still two weeks away, Ellie had already made a resolution—no more alpha males. And Jake was nothing if not an alpha. It was apparent from the hard set of his jaw. This man fairly screamed arrogance bred of too much testosterone, and she wasn't about to let history repeat itself.

"So," Beth began as she dabbed at Josh's bloodied lip with a napkin. "Are we going to have him arrested?"

Josh shrugged away from Beth. Ellie guessed the action was the result of having so many people witness his thrashing.

"I should," Rose huffed as she went over to survey the damage that was once her Christmas tree. She sank down to her knees. "Look at this!" she whined. "Do either of you two barbarians have any idea how long it's taken me to collect these?"

Ellie offered a conciliatory smile. "Maybe we can glue them together."

Rose grunted in response. "This one," she said, holding up a fragment depicting part of a nostril, "was painted by a woman Elvis kissed in Germany. I have the certificate of authenticity at home."

"I'll be happy to share the cost of replacing what was broken," Jake offered.

Rose glared at him. The hostility in her eyes reminded Ellie never to get on this woman's bad side.

"They aren't replaceable," Rose said.

"Neither is my penny," Jake said.

Rose got up slowly, still clutching the small piece of the King's nose in her hand. "Do you really think an Elvis Presley collectible and a penny are in the same category, Devereaux? We're talking Elvis here. Much more important than a dead president cast in copper."

Jake moved then, drawing Ellie's eyes to the definition of muscles where his well-worn jeans hugged powerful thighs. She shouldn't be watching his legs, she admonished. Nor should she care that his sheepskin jacket hung from broad, even shoulders. It was as ridiculous as fixating on the fact that he didn't just walk, no, this man swaggered with a pure male confidence that reminded her of an old movie hero. The kind that breezed into town, saved the day, then disappeared without a backward glance.

"Hot," Chad said as he wiggled in her arms.

"Yes he is," Ellie mumbled. "Rose, maybe your daughter-in-law can do something with the pieces. Isn't she some sort of preservationist?"

"Yes," Rose answered. "But I don't think Tory can fix all these in time for the holidays."

"So buy some new ones," Josh suggested, a touch of annoyance in his voice.

"You have no appreciation for the King," Rose said. "If you did, you wouldn't make such a stupid suggestion."

"Forgive me," Josh said on a sigh. "I guess listening to his music hour after hour, night after night, has kinda turned me off the guy."

Rose glared harder. "You can always find another job. Hey!" she called out, turning in the direction of the bar. "What the hell do you think you're doing?"

Ellie followed Rose's angry gaze and found Jake on his hands and knees, crawling between the bar stools.

Jake looked over and Ellie was amazed at the mild annoyance she saw in his eyes. "I'm looking for my penny."

"To hell with your penny," Rose said as she stomped over to the man. "Is it worth a fortune? Is that it?"

Jake shrugged and said, "Not really."

"Then get up off my floor and get out of my place."

"As soon as I find my penny."

Without taking her eyes off the man, Rose said, "I'll give you exactly two seconds to get out of here, or I'm calling the cops and having you arrested for attempted robbery."

"You don't seem to understand," Jake said in a calm but firm voice. "I *need* that penny."

"And I needed my Christmas tree. Out."

"It will just take—"

"Josh," Rose called, "see this jerk out." Rose stepped back to allow an eager Josh access to Jake. "Consider your penny—if there ever was one—partial payment for the damage you did."

The two men squared off, and for a brief second Ellie was afraid another fight might break out. "Here," Ellie said as she handed her nephew to Josh. "You hold Chad and I'll see Mr. Devereaux out."

There was a faintly amused light in his eyes as she took hold of his sleeve. "What about my penny?" he asked.

Guiding him toward the door, Ellie grabbed his hat off the table and thrust it against his stomach. It was a mistake. Brushing her fingers against the solid muscle at his waist caused a tiny tingle of awareness to spread from her hand to her arm, before shooting down her spine. "I'll look for your penny tomorrow. The weather is getting worse and I have to get Josh home. I hardly think now is the appropriate time to argue over a penny. Besides, you just destroyed several of Rose's most prized possessions. If you don't get out of here, she'll have you in jail so fast you won't know what hit you."

When they reached the door, Jake turned, and his eyes met and held hers. "Are you always the peacemaker?"

Ellie schooled herself not to react to the low, seductive quality of his voice. "I'm the middle child. I learned the fine art of mediation before I learned my alphabet."

Shaking his head, he sighed. The action caused a wave of warm, mint-scented breath to wash across her uplifted face. "And here I was hoping you were trying to tell me you liked me."

Ellie blinked. "I'd like you gone."

"Here," he said as he pulled a book of matches from the pocket of his jacket. "I'm staying at the Manor House. Call me tomorrow when you find my penny."

Ellie accepted the matchbook, knowing full well she wasn't going to call him. Every instinct in her body told her Jake Devereaux wasn't the kind of man a sane woman called.

She locked the door and slipped the matchbook into her pocket. Rose still looked despondent, Josh was apparently still fuming and, for some unknown reason, Beth's bottom lip was thrust out in a pout.

"Shall we?" Ellie suggested.

"Sled!" Chad yelled excitedly, throwing himself toward Rose. "Sled!"

"I know," Rose said as she took the little boy from Josh. "We'll go now."

"Now," Chad parroted.

Rose looked out the window and Ellie read the frown on her face. The reason for the deep lines became apparent as soon as she turned. Jake Devereaux was standing on the porch, just staring.

"I'm calling the cops," Rose decided.

"Sled!" Chad argued, kicking his feet. "Go now!"

"I'll be happy to take him home," Ellie suggested.

"You're taking me home," Josh reminded her.

Beth stepped up and tried to loop her arm through his. "I can drop you off."

"Forget it," Rose said, sighing. "The alarm's on. He can stand out there in the snow until his nose freezes off. Let's just get out of here before we get snowed in for the night."

The group shuffled out of the bar, leaving Jake with his nose pressed against the frosted glass. Ellie half expected him to appear at the back door and found herself oddly disappointed when he failed to appear.

After a quick round of good-byes, Ellie settled behind the wheel of her rented car. Josh slid in beside her, blowing air into his cupped hands.

"Gloves help," she suggested with a wry smile.

"I usually manage to find someplace warm to stick my hands."

"One more crack like that and I'll be happy to tell you where to stick them."

Josh raised his hands, palms out. "You can't fault a guy for trying."

"Yes," she promised him. "I can."

Ellie had just pulled onto the main street when Josh asked, "Is that what your little vacation is all about? You having difficulty with your love life?"

She shrugged. "Not trouble, exactly."

"That's not the impression I got when that gorilla showed up."

"Mike is having a hard time dealing with rejection."

"Not used to being the dumpee?"

She glanced over at him, smiling. "He's probably no better at it than you are."

"I've never been dumped." Josh blew on his fingernails and buffed them theatrically.

"There's a first time for everything," she warned.

"Not for this kid," he answered. "I let them know right up front that I'm not into 'happily ever after.'"

"You know something," Ellie said as she carefully slowed for a traffic light. "Susan was right, you are slime."

Josh laughed. "I see our psychic waitress has already given you the word on me."

"Susan, Rose, Beth, Shelby..."

"I get the picture," he said.

"But at least you're honest slime."

"A regular Boy Scout. Not like that shady Devereaux character."

Ellie felt her smile slip. "I wonder whether that bit about the penny was real."

"You think he was really after a penny? Or just there to rip us off?"

"Who knows. But if I had a valuable coin, I sure wouldn't be stupid enough to lose it in a bar."

"He didn't seem like the stupid type," Josh stated after he told her to make a left turn at the next corner. "That's why I think all that crap about the coin was a put-on."

"You're probably right. I just feel terrible for Rose. Those ornaments looked like they were completely destroyed."

"Good."

"Josh!" she admonished. "They meant a lot to her. You should feel terrible since it was partially your fault."

"My fault? I was only trying to stop that guy from ripping her off."

"You could have been more careful."

"I'll remember that the next time I'm tossing some ugly drunk out of the bar."

"He wasn't an ugly drunk." *Where did that come from?* she wondered. "Anyway, I think you should try to replace some of the things that were broken."

"Let *him* replace them," Josh grumbled. "Or better still, maybe now we can have a normal Christmas tree."

"I thought it was kind of unique," Ellie admitted.

"Right. What about that one that played 'Blue Christmas' over and over again?"

"That one was a little hard to take."

"It didn't have an Off button," Josh continued to rant. "What kind of manufacturer makes a musical ornament with no Off button."

"An Elvis fan."

"This is it," Josh said, pointing to a modest apartment building on the left. "Want to come in and see my etchings?"

Ellie groaned. "Keep your etchings to yourself, thank you very much. But I will use your ladies' room before I head back to Shelby's."

"Fine by me. But you enter at your own risk."

"Lovely," she mumbled as she cut the engine and got out of the car.

The snow had tapered to little more than flurries. Chad's dream of sledding didn't look too good as she followed Josh up the short walkway. She estimated there was less than an inch of total accumulation.

Josh unlocked the door to his ground-level apartment. Ellie immediately noticed two things. First, it was surprisingly neat, except for the clutter of holiday decorations waiting to be hung. Second, the whole place smelled of a rather sweet, almost feminine, floral air freshener.

"First door on the left," he said as he tossed his coat over one of the boxes.

"I can't believe you had the audacity to criticize Rose's tree."

Josh looked at her with surprise in his eyes. "What?"

"I assume these are for your tree?" She lifted the carefully wrapped strand of lights and allowed them to dangle in the air between them. "Chili-pepper lights?"

"I'll have you know they are quite in vogue these days."

"On a silver foil tree?" she asked, glancing at the partially assembled tree near a large window.

"I guess you'd rather have ode to Elvis?"

Ellie shook her head. "I'm a glass-ornament, colored-lights, strings-of-popcorn kind of girl."

"How boring."

"It's better than silver foil," she taunted as she headed toward the bathroom.

Foil was obviously a passion of Josh's. The wallpaper in the small powder room was some sort of Grecian motif, a silver background with silhouettes of naked couples in black contrast. Ellie laughed softly. When she heard the thudding sound in the other room she instantly felt guilty. Obviously Josh had heard her snickering at his wallpaper and was letting her know it by banging around in the living room.

Ellie spent a few extra minutes fixing her hair, trying to think of something kind to say. After all, who was she to criticize this man's decor. Even if it was a bit odd.

"Thanks," she called as she walked down the hall. She was immediately struck by how cold it was in the apartment. Almost as cold as it was outside.

She walked toward Josh, who was seated on the sofa with his back to her, obviously pouting.

"I'm sorry I snickered at your tree and at your wallpaper," she began as she continued to approach. She spoke louder to overcome the sound of an approaching emergency vehicle. "It really is a pretty tree and the chili peppers will—"

Ellie stopped in midsentence as she rounded the

couch. Josh's eyes were open wide, bulging. His face was a grotesque contortion, pasty white with blue, swollen lips. The strand of chili-pepper lights was wound tightly around his throat.

Chapter Three

"That siren is the cops."

Ellie let out a small, frightened noise and her eyes flew to the sound of the newly familiar male voice.

Jake Devereaux dangled in the window frame, one leg in and one leg out. "Unless you want to get caught here with the late Josh, I suggest you come with me."

The sirens grew louder. "You killed him?" she breathed as her hand clamped over her mouth to stifle a scream.

"Of course I didn't kill him," Jake said calmly. "I was under the impression that you did."

Dropping her hand, she yelled, "Me?" above the siren.

"I was just letting myself in when I heard you come down the hall." His green eyes scanned the room. "I assume you're the culprit. I don't see any other suspects. Do you?"

"I didn't kill anyone," she told him.

"If you didn't, and I didn't, I suggest we get out

of here before the cops arrive.'' He held one gloved hand out to her.

''Leave with you?''

''That's the idea. If you get moving now.''

''But shouldn't we stay here and tell them—''

''What?'' he interrupted impatiently. ''That I was breaking in and found him dead? Or that you were the only one here when he died?''

The sirens came to a halt along with her heartbeat. ''If we run, we look guilty.''

''Suit yourself.'' He shrugged as he hoisted his leg up onto the windowsill. ''But while you're waiting to bare your soul, think about who might have called the cops.''

''What?''

''Someone called the cops. My guess is that whoever it was wanted them to find you alone with the stiff.''

''Oh, God,'' she groaned.

''Last chance,'' Jake said as he jumped onto the ground below.

Acting on fear, Ellie went to the window. His large hands circled her waist and he lifted her out and down, placing her softly on the slushy ground. She was only vaguely aware of a faint tearing sound above the loud thunder of footsteps echoing from inside the apartment building.

Soundlessly, Jake closed the window and grabbed her hand. He tugged her in the direction of the woods that lined the south edge of the building. ''Where are you taking me?''

''Hush.''

Wet, heavy branches slapped at her cheeks as they trudged over the uneven terrain. The snow had turned to sleet, which pelted the leaves and stung the backs of her exposed hands.

Ellie focused on his shoulders, too stunned and too shocked to do much more than follow. The image of Josh's face chased her through the woods. It didn't seem real. There had been no ominous sounds, nothing to alert her that a murder was being committed while she was in the bathroom. It didn't make any sense. Unless *he* was the killer.

Ellie stopped suddenly, digging the heels of her half boots into the soaked ground.

Jake turned to her, annoyance shining in his eyes, which were little more than harsh, angry slits. "Why are you stopping? We can't let them find us out here."

Ellie made a futile attempt to tug her hand free from his. "I don't think running is the right thing to do," she argued. "Especially with you."

Jake shoved back the brim of his hat. Small pellets of ice showered down on his broad shoulders. "I'm your best hope right now. Unless you have a better plan in mind."

"And you do?"

He let out an exasperated sigh. "We'll go through the woods, then double back to my car. Hopefully the cops will think we're nothing more than a couple of idiots out for a romantic stroll in the snow."

"That's your plan?" she scoffed, swatting a strand of limp, wet hair from her face. "We're soaking wet.

We'll attract their attention in a heartbeat. Cops aren't stupid, you know.''

"I'm betting they'll be so engrossed in preserving the crime scene that they won't even notice us."

"They will when I get into my car."

Jake stroked his chin. At least he seemed to be considering her argument. Ellie watched him intently, trying to discern if the man holding her hand could be the killer. Secretly, she wished all murderers had warts and fangs, then they'd be easy to spot. Looking up into his handsome face, she tried to find a clue, something tangible that would tell her whether or not to trust this guy.

All she saw were perfect, chiseled features and the promise of dimples on either side of his mouth. *Great,* she thought. *I'm supposed to be trying to pick up some sixth sense, and all I can do is admire his dimples. Do killers have dimples?* she wondered.

"You'll have to leave your car right where it is," he said.

"It's a rental."

Jake rolled his eyes. "Which they'll be able to trace, but probably not right away."

Ellie's suspicions were growing in leaps and bounds. This man knew as much, if not more, about police procedure than she did. "Are you a cop?" she asked, forcing her voice to remain steady.

He offered a lazy smile. "Hardly."

"You sound like one. Phrases like 'preserving the crime scene' and—"

"I watch a lot of TV," he said with a shrug. "So,"

he began as he eased his hold on her hand. "Are you coming or not?"

Not, the intelligent sphere of her brain answered. Her lips, however, ushered forth the words, "Lead on."

"Smart girl," he drawled, taking her hand and pulling her farther into the mossy woods.

Ellie glanced back over her shoulder. She guessed they were about two hundred yards from the building, but she could easily make out the flashes of red and blue lights from the police vehicles. Apparently they had swarmed to the building like ants to a picnic.

"There's too many of them," she said.

"Too many what?"

"Officers," she said as she quickened her pace so that she was at his side.

"The more the merrier," Jake responded glibly. "Isn't that what they say?"

"Not if they want to preserve the integrity of the evidence."

This time it was Jake who stopped suddenly. He looked down at her as the sleet continued to bounce off his Stetson. Some of the tiny ice pellets ricocheted and struck Ellie.

"What do you know about evidence? Don't tell me you're a cop?" The last question came out as something of a groan.

"I'm not an officer."

"But?"

"I'm not," she told him emphatically before she lowered her eyes.

He caught her chin between his thumb and forefinger, applying just enough pressure to force her to meet his gaze.

"Then what are you?"

"A tourist?" she suggested. If he was a killer, the last thing she wanted to do was give him a reason to kill her, too. "I'm a scientist."

His head fell to one side and he regarded her suspiciously for a long second. A definite frown curved the corners of his mouth downward. "You don't look like a scientist."

"I left my lab coat at home," she said. He didn't look like a killer, either, but then again, neither did Ted Bundy. "I'm freezing," she told him. "Can we keep going, please?"

Something flashed in those eyes, something so fleeting that Ellie didn't have the chance to put a name to it. She relaxed a little when he marched on. He probably couldn't murder her and walk at the same time. Especially not on this icy ground.

Ellie slipped several times, each time clutching Jake's arm to keep from falling. He seemed to sense whenever she was about to lose her footing, and his reactions were quick and efficient.

They emerged from the woods several blocks north of the apartment building. As soon as they stepped onto the sidewalk, Jake surprised her by draping his arm across her shoulder. His pace slowed as her panic rose.

"Why are we going this way?" she asked. Her eyes fixed on the distant sight of emergency vehicles and police cars blocking the road ahead.

"My car is this way."

"How will we get past all the cops?" Ellie persisted, trying in vain to shrug off his arm.

"Cooperate, Ellie," he said, squeezing her shoulder to punctuate the remark. "We're simply going to wander over to my car. If the cops stop us, I'll do the talking."

"Going to confess?" she mumbled under her breath.

The deep, throaty sound of his laughter did strange things to her stomach. Here she was antagonizing a potential killer and all she could do was sit back while her hormones obliterated her common sense.

"Not me," he said. "How about you? You can always stop and let them know you were alone with Josh when he met his untimely demise."

"Obviously I wasn't alone with him," Ellie snapped. "I didn't kill him, so someone else had to be in the apartment."

"And they simply evaporated after the dirty deed?"

Ellie pursed her lips and concentrated. Nothing came to mind. Nothing except the obvious. "You were in the apartment."

"Half in," he corrected. "I was just entering when you came down the hall."

"Then the killer must have used the front door, since you had the window all tied up."

She saw him shake his head. "I was watching the front door."

Ellie stopped walking and gaped up at him. "How long were you there?"

"Same as you and the bartender. I followed you from The Rose Tattoo."

She tried not to let the sudden infusion of fear show on her face. "Why did you follow me?"

"Actually, I was following the penny."

Ellie blinked.

"The 1955 Ben Franklin," he prompted. "The bartender had to have it. No one else was anywhere near me when I was in the restaurant."

She was barely aware of the sound of approaching footsteps as she tried furiously to sort through the bits and pieces fragmented in her mind. There was the fight. There was Jake's obvious fixation with the stupid penny. There was the fact that he had followed them. There was the fact that she had seen no one else. There was—

"I'm Officer Sonnenmark," a young, thin blond man in uniform said.

Ellie, startled by the sudden appearance of the policeman, instinctively pressed herself against Jake. She swallowed hard, trying, on the one hand, to keep from blurting out her suspicions. On the other hand, she was trying not to react to the solid, warm outline of his body where it touched her own. Shock, she decided. She had to be in shock; it was the only explanation for her juvenile and erratic, not to mention illegal, behavior for the past several minutes.

"Unusual weather," Jake drawled, tipping his hat like the perfect Texas gentleman. "Something happen?" he continued with an innocent tone that could have earned him an Academy Award.

Officer Sonnenmark nodded, his boyish face com-

pletely devoid of emotion. "Y'all live around here?"
Thankfully, the question was delivered to Jake.

"Nope," Jake drawled. "We wanted to get a little
inland, you know. Take a walk in the snow without
having to fight the breeze off the harbor. It sure was
pretty, but I'm afraid my blood just isn't thick enough
to stand the cold."

Sonnenmark nodded and smiled down at Ellie.
"Your husband may be romantic, but you look about
frozen to death."

"You'd think he was trying to kill me," Ellie said
through a fake smile. "I'm soaked through to the
skin. I've been telling him for the past hour that I've
had enough of this wilderness hike."

"Now, dear," Jake began as his gloved fingertips
bit into the flesh of her upper arm. "You know I
would never do anything to hurt you. I just thought
a little walk would be invigorating. And a nice break
from the kids."

"Y'all got kids?" Sonnenmark asked.

"Six," Jake replied without missing a beat. "All
boys."

"Hell," the officer said, giving Jake an admiration-
filled punch on the arm. "Since you got six kids at
home, I guess any excuse to get out of the house
works."

"Any excuse," Ellie repeated as she glared up at
Jake's relaxed jawline.

"What kind of trouble did you have?"

The officer bent forward, lowering his voice to an
almost conspiratorial tone. "Murder. Guy in that

apartment building there. Richardson was his name. You folks didn't happen to see—''

"Naw," Jake drawled. "We didn't see anything. Didn't even hear a gunshot."

The officer leaned even closer. "No gunshot to hear. The poor guy was strangled with his own damned Christmas decorations." Then, as if suddenly remembering Ellie was present, his face colored slightly. "Sorry, ma'am. Excuse my language." He touched his fingers to the edge of the plastic covering the brim of his police hat.

"I'd appreciate it if you would be so kind as to excuse us. I'm freezing," Ellie said to the officer.

Jake wrapped his other arm around her, pulling her against him and placing an unanticipated kiss against her cheek. The frozen skin tingled and warmed almost immediately, and it was everything Ellie could do to keep from shoving him away.

"I'd best get her home and warm her up," Jake told the officer, none-too-subtly hinting at just how he expected to accomplish the task.

"Sure thing," the officer said. "Your kids are probably ready for supper, anyway."

"Exactly," Ellie said with a nod. Then, glaring up at Jake, she added, "We wouldn't want the little darlings to go hungry, would we?"

His green eyes darkened slightly. "No one should go hungry," he fairly purred against her ear.

"What was that for?" she demanded in a harsh whisper as soon as the officer was out of earshot.

"I was ad-libbing," he answered as he allowed his hand to fall away from her shoulder.

Ellie told herself that the sudden chill was the result of the dropping temperature. It couldn't possibly have anything to do with the fact that he was no longer touching her. After all, she didn't want him to touch her, not with the same hands that in all likelihood had killed poor Josh.

Jake led her to a sleek Mercedes and held open the door. The interior smelled of leather and it had the feel of newness. It also had the feel of money. As her eyes scanned the elaborate collection of controls on the dashboard, she decided the car must have cost as much as her annual salary.

"Lead on." He mimicked her earlier words as he slid behind the wheel and started the engine.

Drawing her bottom lip between her teeth, Ellie's brain worked at warp speed. "Uh…you need to head back in the direction of The Rose Tattoo."

Misty rain accompanied the dusk as he drove back toward town. Ellie cautiously watched him out of the corner of her eye. How could someone so gorgeous be a killer? she wondered. Just her luck. The first really attractive man she meets turns out to be a thief at the very best, a killer at the very worst.

"Still trying to figure out how I did it?"

Ellie's mouth opened but nothing came out.

He smiled then, an action that she felt all the way down to her toes. The effect was from more than just the attractive combination of dimples and even, white teeth. There was something almost hypnotic in the simple action, something that seemed to draw her to this man like the proverbial moth. Only with this man,

Ellie knew with relative certainty that she'd be consumed by the flames.

"I was thinking about the murder," she hedged.

He nodded, apparently unfazed by the whole situation. "Whoever it was obviously wanted to make sure you were caught at the scene."

"That's ridiculous. I don't have any enemies."

"Really?" One pale brow arched high on his forehead. "What about that guy at the bar? The one with no neck."

"Mike has a neck," she insisted.

"The size of a tree trunk."

"He works out."

"With a bottle of steroids?"

"No," she told him on an exasperated breath. "He has a very stressful job. He works out to release some of the stress."

"What does he do?"

"He's a detective."

Jake let out a low whistle. "So that's how you know so much about police work."

"Pretty much," she said, lowering her eyes to study her hands. "Mike investigates murders, he doesn't commit them."

"Unless maybe he bought that little scene you staged with the bartender?"

Ellie shifted in the bucket seat, angling herself so that she could glare at his profile. "That's crazy. Mike is not the violent type."

"Really?" Jake asked, almost taunting her as he abruptly swerved over to the curb and threw the car in park. "Then what are these?"

Taking one of her arms, Jake pulled it free of her coat and rolled up her sleeve. Even in the dim light of early evening, she could easily make out the small, roundish bruises where Mike had gripped her arm.

"He doesn't always realize his own strength," she said.

Tossing her arm down in obvious disgust, Jake said, "Right. Have you always made excuses for him? Is that why your relationship with that Neanderthal ended?"

Ellie didn't bother to fix her sleeve, but simply stuffed her balled fist through the armhole of her coat and stiffened in the seat. "My relationship with Mike is hardly any of your business."

"Excuse me," Jake grumbled as he pulled back onto the road.

For several minutes the only conversation consisted of Ellie's minimal directions to take a left or a right. The tension inside the passenger compartment was as thick as the fog slowly settling over the city.

"Turn here," Ellie instructed. "Stop at the third house."

"Nice neighborhood."

"I'll be sure to tell my brother and his wife that you approve."

Jake eased the car to a halt in front of the empty driveway. Ellie swallowed her trepidation as she reached for the door handle.

"Aren't you going to invite me in for a cup of coffee?"

She met his slightly amused eyes. "No. If you can

afford to buy a Mercedes, I'd say you can afford to buy your own coffee.''

''Tea?''

''No.''

''Brandy?''

''No.''

''Maybe I could use—''

''No.'' Ellie got out of the car and slammed the door before he could think of any other idiotic pretexts under which she would let him inside. It wasn't that she was inhospitable, she was simply protecting her family.

Calmly she strolled up the flagstone walkway, silently praying the whole way.

She reached the front door and pressed the bell. Her heart was racing as she waited, knowing full well that Jake was still parked at the curb.

The porch light came on and the door opened a small crack. Ellie tilted her head and spoke to the portion of the face visible through the small opening.

''Mrs. Baxter, it's me, Ellie Tanner, from over on Chestnut Street. Dylan's sister.''

Chapter Four

The white-haired woman's face registered surprised recognition as the door was unlatched and pulled completely open.

"What are you doing out in this weather?" she chided. "And you're soaked through to the bone."

"I had some trouble with my car," Ellie explained as she slipped inside the house. It smelled of buttery baked goods and freshly ground cinnamon. "Rentals," she added with a shrug.

"Do you need to call for a tow?"

Ellie glanced over her shoulder and saw Jake still parked at the curb. She could hear the hum of the idling engine. Knowing she couldn't very well let him discover where she really lived, Ellie smiled as she reached for the door. "I'm letting in a terrible draft."

Mrs. Baxter looked at her with kind, gentle eyes. "I'm so sorry," she began. "How rude of me. Come into the kitchen. I've had the oven going since early morning. We'll have you toasty in no time."

With one last, satisfied glance back, Ellie closed the door and followed the gracious older woman down a hallway filled with mementos of a full and happy life. There were photos of her children from birth through college, and of the newest generation of Baxters. It reminded Ellie of her own mother's house.

"I don't want to impose," she told the other woman. "I was hoping you wouldn't mind if I cut through your house, just to get out of the cold for a while."

Mrs. Baxter ushered her into a large kitchen. The round table was covered with a variety of tins, partially filled with delicious-smelling goodies.

"Gifts," she explained as she wiped her hands on the front of her well-worn apron. "With Mr. Baxter's surgery this year, I'm a little behind on my baking."

"I'm sure your family will understand."

"These aren't for family," she said. "I send a little something to the ladies I used to work with."

Ellie took in a deep breath. Listening to Mrs. Baxter, being in this kitchen, was almost enough to make her forget the horrible image of Josh on the sofa.

"Have you been retired long?"

Mrs. Baxter placed her hands on her ample hips and nodded. "It was way back during the war. We all worked at the base, assembling military equipment for the boys in Europe."

"You were like Rosie the Riveter?" Ellie asked.

"You bet," Mrs. Baxter answered. There was a definite pride in her wistful expression. "Worked eight-, sometimes ten-hour shifts. By the time Mr. Baxter came home, I had enough saved to buy this house."

"What a great story," Ellie said.

In response to a chime from the stove, Mrs. Baxter donned padded mitts and turned her attention to the oven. "It was different back then," she said. "We women didn't have as many choices as you gals do today, but at least we had security. We knew that when we got married, it would be till the death. My one son is on his third wife. Doesn't have a clue what the word commitment means."

"I know the type," Ellie lamented as she carefully sat on the edge of one of the chairs, trying not to get the cushion wet.

"I take it you aren't married?"

"No."

"Do you want to be?"

Ellie smiled at the woman's candor. "Yes. I'm just afraid I'll choose the wrong guy. So far, I have a track record of nothing but losers. Sometimes I think I'm wearing some sort of invisible sign that only jerks can see—Date Her, She's Desperate."

Mrs. Baxter's laugh was soft and very reassuring. It reminded Ellie so much of her own mother's laugh that she felt a small pang of homesickness.

"The right man will come along eventually. Patience, my dear."

"Will he be wearing a sign?" Ellie asked.

"Most definitely." Mrs. Baxter waved her spatula dramatically as she spoke. "I believe in fate," she said, her expression distant and contented. "I knew the first time I laid eyes on Mr. Baxter that he was the man for me."

"Love at first sight?"

"Hardly," Mrs. Baxter snorted. "He was coming

out of a club—one of those dance clubs we had in the old days—falling down drunk.''

"And you fell in love?"

"Actually, he fell on me."

Ellie smiled.

"Even though he reeked of whiskey, one feel of those strong shoulders and I was gone."

The memory of Jake's strong, muscled body flashed in her mind. Ellie shook her head, hoping to rid herself of such outrageous thoughts.

"Well," Ellie began as she rose slowly. "I had better be on my way. Shelby is probably frantic by now."

Mrs. Baxter went to the window, shoving back the dainty lace curtains before she said, "I think you're a little late, my dear."

Ellie hurried to the window. Even in the shadows of early evening she had no trouble making out the insignia on the car parked in front of her brother and sister-in-law's home.

"Looks like she's already called the police."

Closing her eyes for a brief second, Ellie sucked in a breath. *Now what?* she wondered. *How am I going to talk my way out of this?*

"You'd best hurry along," Mrs. Baxter was saying. "Shelby must be worried sick if she's already alerted the authorities. I suppose it has something to do with what happened to poor little Chad a while back. Kidnapping is the sort of thing that stays with a mother always, you know. I guess it's only natural for Shelby to react quickly when a family member is missing."

"I hadn't thought of that," Ellie admitted. Great, she silently castigated as she let herself out the back door. "I've left the scene of a murder," she grumbled as she worked her way toward the house. "I've probably assisted a murderer in making his escape. And now I've probably scared Shelby half out of her mind. If the cops don't kill me, Dylan absolutely will."

Every light in the house was on, which pretty much eliminated the possibility of sneaking in the back way. No, Ellie acknowledged as she shifted her handbag to the opposite shoulder, there was nothing to do but walk in the front door and hope she could explain her behavior in a calm, rational way.

Sucking in a deep breath, she lifted the drenched hem of her skirt and gingerly maneuvered up the icy steps. She was frantically running various excuses through her mind when the door suddenly flew open.

She was greeted by a pair of glaring green eyes. "Well it's about damn time," Rose yelled. "Shelby's been frantic, especially since the cops arrived."

Ellie lowered her eyes. "I'm sorry she called the police," she tried again.

"Get in out of the cold," Rose grumbled, reaching out and grabbing a handful of Ellie's damp sweater. "And she didn't call the cops. They showed up because of the murder."

Ellie, paralyzed by fear, looked into the hallway, fully expecting a whole battalion of officers to be waiting there, handcuffs dangling from their eager fingers.

"Why are they here?" she asked.

"Josh," Rose answered, her voice softer and with just a trace of sadness.

Ellie's eyes darted into the living room. Spotting the two uniformed men with Shelby, she felt her heart pound urgently.

As nonchalantly as possible, she positioned herself so that Rose stood between her and the officers. Placing her arm around the shorter woman, who was reciting the facts of the case, Ellie managed to get to the foot of the stairs without attracting the attention of the police.

Leaving Rose with a saddened, slightly perturbed look on her face, Ellie dashed up the stairs. She raced past her nephew, who was sitting in the middle of his room, apparently playing with one of his small toys. Cushioning the sound of her footsteps, Ellie moved past her sleeping niece, into the guest room. Wasting no time, she peeled away the layers of wet clothing, balled them up and tossed them in the back of the closet. As a forensic scientist, she knew better then to leave the clothes in plain view. There was no way for her to know how many fibers or other trace elements she had picked up during her short stay in Josh's apartment. She could dispose of them later, when the house wasn't crawling with police.

"Blast," she cursed as she hopped and danced her way into her jeans. She cursed again when she heard the soft rapping at her door. "Just a second," she called as she yanked a sweatshirt over her head.

"The police want to talk to you," Shelby said in that soft, feminine drawl.

Ellie noted that there was some redness around her

sister-in-law's eyes. "Me?" she asked, struggling to add surprise to her voice.

Shelby nodded. "Rose said she told you that something terrible has happened."

Lowering her eyes, Ellie said, "Josh."

"It must have happened just after you left him off. That's why the police need to talk to you."

"Of course," she managed to say past the lump of trepidation clogging her throat. "I guess they won't mind my damp hair."

"How did you get so wet?" Shelby asked as the two women moved back toward the stairs.

"I couldn't get the car started."

"You're joking? Why didn't you call me. No wonder it's taken you this long. Josh's place is nearly five miles from here."

"It was a hike," Ellie commented, conveniently leaving out the fact that she hadn't hiked alone.

"You should have called me, Ellie. Rose or I could have come. Dylan won't like it when he finds out his baby sister was roaming the streets of Charleston at night in the snow."

"I'm not a baby," Ellie remarked as she began a slow descent of the stairs. "I won't tell him if you don't?" she suggested.

Shelby's expression was sympathetic, but it also indicated that there were no secrets between husband and wife. Ellie envied that, given their past.

She was ushered into the living room, where two rather imposing men she judged to be somewhere in their mid-forties sat sipping coffee. They half rose as she entered.

Ellie folded her slightly trembling hands and quickly tucked herself into the lone chair opposite the formal sofa.

"Would you like something warm to drink?" Shelby asked.

"Great," Ellie told her as she nervously brushed at her damp hair.

One of the detectives produced a small notepad and pen from his pocket and leaned forward, his dark eyes fixed on Ellie.

"I'm Detective Greavy. This is Detective Simmons."

"Hello."

"You left The Rose Tattoo with Mr. Richardson approximately two hours ago?"

She nodded.

"How is it you came to drive him home?"

"He asked." Ellie kept her eyes fixed on the dried floral arrangement at the center of the coffee table. "He was leery of driving in this weather."

The lead detective's brows arched as he scribbled. "Approximately what time did you arrive at Mr. Richardson's apartment?"

"Four-thirty, maybe a few minutes later."

"And you went inside?" Greavy asked, his brown eyes as piercing as his question.

Ellie shook her head. "I just dropped him off."

"So you were never inside his apartment?"

"No."

"Then—" Greavy reached inside his jacket and produced a small, clear evidence bag "—how do you explain this?" He passed her the sealed bag.

Regarding the item, Ellie winced, knowing full well she would now have to backpedal out of her falsehoods. Her eyes met Greavy's, but sensing no ally there, she turned to his partner. His soft blue eyes seemed a bit less intimidating than Greavy's cold brown ones. "Doesn't this match the dress you were wearing when you dashed up the stairs?"

Placing a guilty smile on her face, she said, "I think I'd like to take back what I said about not going in."

"Then this is a piece of the dress you were wearing earlier?" Simmons asked.

"Probably," she admitted. "I ran out of there so fast, I must have caught it on something."

"Why did you run out?" Greavy queried.

"I wanted to get home," Ellie said.

"Do you always tear your clothing on your way out of a room?" Greavy pressed.

"No. I'm sure it was just a fluke."

Shelby appeared then, balancing on a tightrope of tension as she moved over to stand next to Ellie, handing her a mug of coffee. "What's that?" she asked.

"I tore my dress at Josh's place."

She watched as her sister-in-law, obviously shocked, looked from Ellie to the swatch of fabric, to the policemen, then back again. "They can't possibly believe that you had anything to do with Josh's murder?"

Ellie shrugged nervously. "Ask them."

Shelby turned angry blue eyes on the two men. "My husband is a federal agent. Ellie is a forensic specialist with the New York State Police. You can't possibly believe that she had anything to do with a murder.''

Greavy and Simmons exchanged benign expressions. Greavy then said, ''Why did you lie about being inside?''

''I was afraid you would jump to exactly the conclusion you've jumped to right now. I didn't lay a hand on Josh. I had nothing to do with his murder.''

''Really?'' Greavy said, sounding skeptical. ''Then can you explain why we found the material from your dress on the windowsill?''

''I...um...sorta left by the window.''

''You did what?'' Rose bellowed from the hallway.

Ellie got up and moved stiffly to the window. She gently fingered the sheer curtain, parting it slightly. Looking out into the darkness, she told them her story. ''It wasn't until I walked around the front of the sofa that I realized he was dead.''

''And you didn't hear anything?'' Greavy asked just as Shelby came to Ellie's side.

''A few knocking sounds. They weren't even loud enough to cause concern. I told you, I thought Josh had heard me laughing at his wallpaper.''

''Then what happened?'' Simmons asked. ''Why'd you use the window?''

''I heard the sirens and I panicked,'' she answered, then, sucking in a fortifying breath, she turned and faced the two detectives. ''There was a man coming in the window. He helped me down.''

''Wait a second,'' Greavy thundered. ''Are you telling me you saw the killer?''

Shaking her head, Ellie said, "No. I'm just telling you someone else was there."

Greavy cursed. "Can you describe him?"

"His name is Jake Devereaux."

"The thief from the Tattoo?" Rose cut in.

"The same."

"Guy sure gets around," Rose grumbled. "I guess I should have had him arrested, after all."

"I don't think he did it," Ellie said in a small voice. She wondered why she was defending him. It was incredibly stupid, not to mention baseless. "He said he was just coming in the window when he saw me come down the hall."

"Where can we find this Devereaux?" Greavy asked.

Ellie gave him the name of the hotel Jake had mentioned at The Rose Tattoo. "He said he'd been watching Josh's apartment."

"Watching for what?"

"For Josh, I guess," Ellie speculated. "He thought Josh had his penny and he—"

"Penny?" Shelby asked.

"He ruined my Elvis tree over that penny," Rose lamented. "He and Josh got into a fight and destroyed the whole thing."

"This Devereaux guy and the deceased had a fight?" Greavy asked. "When?"

"Right around four, just before we closed," Rose said.

The two detectives got to their feet. "Is there anything else you'd like to tell us, Miss Tanner?"

Ellie shrugged. "Not that I can think of. I'm sorry I lied about being inside. I know better."

Greavy's expression seemed to soften. "Since you've given us Devereaux, I guess we can call it even."

Somehow, knowing that they would probably arrest Jake for the murder didn't exactly make Ellie feel relieved. Much later, when she was alone in the quiet of the den, watching fire lick at the logs in the glass-enclosed fireplace, she envisioned the tall, blond Texan with those attractive dimples being finger-printed, photographed and finally jailed for the murder of Josh Richardson. Oddly, the images saddened her.

"You're being silly," she grumbled softly. "The guy is probably guilty and I should be thanking my lucky stars that I got out of there with my life."

Ellie shivered just as a sharp series of knocks split the midnight quiet.

"I see my brother hasn't broken his habit of losing his key," she told Foolish, Dylan's mixed-breed canine, as he followed her to the door.

Crouching slightly, Ellie checked the peephole. Her heart stopped when she saw the shadowy figure on the opposite side of the door.

"What are you doing here?" she demanded just after she yanked open the door.

Jake tipped his hat and gave her a patient smile. It didn't reach his eyes. No, his eyes were sparkling with anger.

"You didn't waste much time telling the cops about me," he said as he slipped inside.

"What did you think I'd do?"

"Oh," he said as he appeared to be taking in the comfortable surroundings, "I was pretty sure you'd tell. I just thought you'd wait more than an hour."

"How did you find me?"

Jake turned then and reached out both arms. His palms flattened on the wall, effectively capturing her head. Ellie met the challenge in his expression as she soaked in the scent of him. It was a purely masculine scent that actually caused goose bumps to form on her arms. His hat was pushed back on his forehead, allowing a few strands of light hair to tickle the thick lashes rimming those intense eyes.

"You owe me," Jake said in a low, almost threatening voice.

"What?" Ellie stammered.

"I did quite a tap dance trying to keep us both from being arrested. I came by so you could thank me."

"How did you know where to find me?"

Jake smiled. "Was I supposed to buy that little scene back there with the old woman one street over?"

Ellie's eyes grew wide but she didn't say anything in her own defense. What could she say?

"You shouldn't have picked the only house on the street without a swing set in the backyard."

"You knew I wasn't telling you the truth because there was no swing set?"

"I met Chad, remember? And it took you too long to get in the door."

"I guess I'm not very good at clandestine activity," she admitted, trying not to react to the fact that he had moved fractionally closer. So close that she could actually feel the heat emanating from his large frame.

His mouth hovered just above hers. "No, you're not. Are you any good at kissing?"

She groaned and ducked away from him. "In your dreams, Devereaux." She went to the door and held it open for him. Foolish, the dog, took instant advantage of the situation and darted out into the night. Ellie cursed under her breath. "Great, now I have to chase the dog."

"That's probably a good idea."

"Why?"

"Because then you won't be home when the cops come to arrest you."

Chapter Five

"That's crazy!"

Jake shrugged, feeling a twinge of guilt for the fear he saw shadowing her eyes. "Crazy, no. An exaggeration, yes. Now that I'm in the clear, they're pretty much focusing on you."

She gaped up at him, her expression a mixture of shock and anger. "How did you get in the clear?"

"I believe they checked my alibi."

"What alibi?"

"The very nice gentleman who assured them I was in his coffee shop at the time they received the call telling them that a murder had been committed by a woman at 407 East Bay."

"What call?" she echoed loudly.

"Apparently, the cops got an anonymous 911 call claiming a woman had murdered Josh. I checked the time on the call—it came in right about the time I saw you coming down the hall at Josh's."

He watched as she shook her head, apparently trying to make sense of his statement. "Is there someplace where we can sit?" he asked softly.

Obviously stunned, Ellie led him into the den and took a seat on the sofa. He leaned against the fireplace mantel, taking in the room. It reminded him a bit of his place back in Tyler. It was a small, cozy room filled with rich wood accents and an eclectic collection of American antiques. Some of the pieces were fairly pricey and he found himself habitually drawn to the nicer items.

"Why did you come here?" she asked in a voice barely audible above the crackle of the fire.

"I thought you ought to know that you're in a hell of a lot of trouble."

"And you're not?"

Removing his hat, Jake allowed it to dangle between his thumb and fingertip. "Not anymore. Remember, I've got an alibi."

"But you told me—"

"I didn't say it was an honest alibi, just a verifiable one."

He watched her eyes grow larger. "Are you telling me you fabricated an alibi and the police bought it?"

Jake shrugged but decided it would probably be a better idea to steer her away from this topic for the time being. "We need to concentrate on you right now. Do you still have the dress you were wearing this afternoon?"

"What?"

"The dress," he repeated. "The one the cops have a piece of. I suggest you burn it in the—"

"That's illegal. It's tampering with evidence. I could go to jail for that alone. Besides, they confiscated the dress immediately following the interrogation."

"If your prints are on those lights, the dress will be more circumstantial evidence for them to pile on top of you."

"The Christmas-tree lights?"

"The murder weapon," he elaborated. Then he watched the color drain from her face. "Don't tell me," he said with a groan. "You didn't touch them?"

"I teased Josh about the lights and I'm afraid I did. I only picked them up for a second."

Tossing his hat on one of the chairs, Jake moved over and took a seat next to her on the sofa. She smelled faintly of some sort of herbal soap that he found distracting. It was almost as distracting as the way her dark hair reflected the flames from the fire.

"Then you must be glad to see me."

She looked at him with trepidation in her wide eyes. "Why would I be glad? For all I know you're a murderer."

Tilting his head, he regarded her for a silent moment, watching the gentle rise and fall of her slender body with each intake of breath. "You know I didn't do it."

"How do I know that?"

"You're too smart to be sitting here calmly chatting with me if you truly thought I was the killer."

His statement had exactly the effect he'd expected. Apparently, Ellie liked the fact that he respected her intelligence. Now all he needed was a way to use it to his advantage.

"So I'm not completely convinced you're the

killer," she admitted grudgingly. "You still fabricated an alibi and lied to the police."

"So did you," he told her. He liked the slight stain of embarrassment on her high cheekbones. "Greavy told me you were...evasive," he added.

As she raked her hands through her hair, Jake noted the look of frustration and felt the first stirrings of protectiveness. It was idiotic, he told himself. He wasn't in any position to help Ellie out of whatever lay in front of her. His only concern had to be the penny. He had to get it back before the opening of the Asian art exhibit at the Charleston Gallery, so he could leave town immediately afterward. As soon as the job was finished.

"If my boss hears that I gave a false statement to the police down here, I'll be fired in a heartbeat."

Absently, he crossed one booted leg over the other. "What exactly do you do for the police back in New York?"

"I'm a forensic-evidence technician. Currently assigned to the trace unit."

He nodded. "Hairs and fibers?"

"Microscopic analysis of hairs, fibers, almost any material that can host biological evidence for recovery and analysis."

"Sounds dull."

"I guess it is, compared to your brawling and climbing in and out of windows. Tell me," she began as she shifted to tuck her leg beneath her, "do you have a job? Or do you just roam from place to place getting into trouble?"

He offered her his most charming smile. "I'm a professor at East Texas University."

She was especially attractive with her mouth hanging open in disbelief.

"I teach history."

Her eyes went from his face to his rather rumpled shirt, to his well-worn jeans, then finally to his custom-made boots.

"You don't look much like the academic type. I didn't think teachers could afford expensive cars and boots."

Stroking the stubble on his chin, Jake said, "Most can't."

"I also don't understand what you're doing here."

"I came to make you a deal."

He watched as her mouth clamped shut. Several seconds passed before she asked, "What do you mean, *deal?*"

"Bargain, agreement," he explained. "I help you, you help me."

"Help you what?" she asked, her voice going up an octave or two. "Not to mention why. Why would I help you?"

"Because I can prove you aren't the killer."

Her head tilted slightly to one side, allowing some of the raven strands to spill over her slender shoulder. "I know I'm not the killer. I don't need you to prove it to me."

"Not to you," he said. "To the police."

Her expression brightened. "Really?"

Jake nodded. "On one condition."

It was like watching curtains being drawn against

a brilliant sun. Ellie's face was masked in uncertainty and there was a hesitancy in her eyes. "Condition?"

"Right." Jake rose and collected his hat. "You scratch my back..."

"I don't scratch."

He cast her a sidelong glance. "Okay, poor choice of words. I need your help and you need mine. If we work together, we both benefit."

"What could you possibly need from me?" she asked.

"My penny."

He watched as she rolled her eyes. "You mean my future is dependent upon that penny you claim you lost?"

"Did lose. And—" he tugged the Stetson on his head before finishing his thought "—you have access to all the people and places where the penny might be. If you help me search the homes of all The Rose Tattoo employees, I'll help you find your killer."

"Let me get this straight," she said, clearing her throat. "A history professor from some Texas university I've never heard of is going to solve a crime just to retrieve a penny—one that you've already said wasn't worth a whole lot of money?"

"Right." He shifted his position on the sofa. "It's a collectible. The owners don't normally sell them on the market. I went to a great deal of trouble to get that penny."

The smile she offered was an interesting mixture of wariness and amusement.

"Trust me, Ellie. I'll make sure the real killer is caught."

"Why?"

"Why what?"

"Why do you want to help me?"

Jake shifted his weight and lowered his eyes, debating just how much he wanted to tell her. The penny was only a portion of what he needed from her, but he doubted now was the time to clue her in on that.

"Would you believe I'm just a nice guy who wants to come to the aid of a beautiful woman?"

"No," she answered instantly.

"Okay," he said. "Then how about I'm doing this because I need someone who knows all the employees and the management at The Rose Tattoo so that I can find my penny. With you at my side, I can search without appearing too conspicuous. I don't think Peg Bundy will let me in the front door at this point."

"Peg Bundy?"

"The Porter woman, the one with the outlandish clothes, big hair and even bigger mouth."

He watched as her spine stiffened slightly. That was good, he decided. It told him that if he could gain her trust, she'd be a loyal ally.

"You aren't exactly in Rose's good graces at the moment. But Beth and Susan would probably welcome you with open arms."

"See, that's how you can help me. I don't want a welcome mat, I want a private opportunity to check out their apartments."

"I don't know, Jake."

He took a step closer, so that mere inches separated them. Gently, he captured her chin between his thumb and forefinger and tilted her face up toward his. It was all part of the game, all of it except the way his heart had skipped a beat as he looked deep into those fathomless blue eyes. "Please help me, Ellie. Please?"

"I'll think about it."

"Then I'll be back tomorrow for your answer." Without ever consciously meaning to do so, Jake tipped his head and brushed a feathery kiss across her warm lips. He left quickly while surprise held Ellie silent.

"HERE? LAST NIGHT?" Shelby yelped, clutching her throat. "And you let him in?"

"He said he came by to warn me that the police were focusing on me," Ellie said as she raised the cup of coffee to her lips.

"Why didn't you say something before Dylan left?" Shelby shifted the baby to the opposite shoulder.

Chad had slurped down some cereal and dashed back up to his room, babbling something about having to check his secret treasure. Ellie wished she had a secret treasure, one that included an alibi for last night.

"Dylan was in a rush to catch his plane," she told Shelby. "Given the fact that he's off on a dangerous assignment, I didn't think it was such a hot idea to casually mention that I was under suspicion for murder while he was kissing you all good-bye."

"He won't like this."

"I'm not exactly thrilled, either," Ellie admitted.

"If what Jake said was true, the police don't have any suspects but me."

"That's insane," Shelby said with conviction. "You have to think, Ellie. There must have been something, a noise, voices, something that will help the police find the real killer."

Shelby placed Cassidy in an elaborate swing with lots of toys and gadgets attached to it. She then sank down in a chair across from Ellie. "I thought Devereaux was the killer."

Ellie ran her fingertip around the rim of her mug, unable to meet her sister-in-law's piercing eyes. "I don't think so."

"Oh, no," Shelby breathed. "Have you lost your mind?"

"You didn't see him at that windowsill. He was too calm to have just brutally murdered Josh. Besides, he just doesn't act like a killer."

"That isn't what Rose thinks."

"Rose is just miffed because of the Christmas tree," Ellie offered. "And because she caught Jake with his hand in the till."

"Sounds like two very good reasons to think he might be the killer."

Ellie stood and let out a long breath. "I know," she admitted. "I'm not being rational." She went to the counter and poured herself some more coffee. Purposefully, she kept her back to Shelby. "I know it sounds nuts, but I just have a feeling about Jake. My instincts tell me he isn't the one who killed Josh."

"Instincts?" Shelby repeated cautiously. "Are

these the same instincts that told you to accept Mike's marriage proposal?''

"Ouch," Ellie said as she turned around. "Is everyone in this family going to ram that down my throat at every turn? Come on, Shelby. I came here for the holidays because I thought you and Dylan would cut me some slack. It was a mistake and I gave the guy his ring back. It's over.''

"Is that why he showed up at The Rose Tattoo yesterday?''

Ellie shrugged. "Who knows with Mike. He hasn't exactly taken this well.''

"What are you going to do?" Shelby asked.

"Ignore him and hope he goes back to New York before I do.''

"What if he doesn't?''

Closing her eyes, Ellie sat dejectedly. Then an evil smile curved the corner of her lips. "Maybe he'll trip and fall into the icy waters of the Ashley River. Then I could stop looking over my shoulder.''

"It seems to me that now you'll be looking over them both. One for Mike and now one for Devereaux.''

Ellie gave a dispirited laugh. "Mike's temper still scares me.''

Shelby reached over and patted the back of her hand. "And Devereaux?''

"He makes me weak in the knees.''

Chapter Six

All that remained of the previous evening's snow was a layer of frozen precipitation, leaving the town blanketed in a sheen of picturesque ice. Every tree Ellie passed on her way down Bay Street was decorated with a shimmering display of icicles. That, coupled with the elaborate Christmas decorations on every door and lamppost made her think that Norman Rockwell was alive and well in Charleston, South Carolina.

As she maneuvered Shelby's car up the alleyway next to the Tattoo, she noticed two men on the sidewalk about a half block south of the restaurant. The Stetson was a dead giveaway and her pulse reacted instantly. Jake's face was shielded by the low brim of his hat, but there was no mistaking those broad shoulders, trim waist and long legs. She was so busy gaping at Jake and his companion, Ellie nearly rammed into the row of trash cans.

Is he a cop? Ellie wondered as she glanced quickly at the dark-haired man standing with Jake. All morning she'd been waiting for some uniformed man to come and drag her down to jail. That fear had made it impossible for her to do her Christmas shopping, thus the entire morning had turned into a waste of time and energy.

Parking the car, Ellie grabbed her shoulder bag and entered the Tattoo through the kitchen. Instantly the scent of grilled food and rich desserts filled her nostrils. The mood of those working in the kitchen was somber, which was only natural given the fact that Josh had been dead less than twenty-four hours.

The image of Josh's lifeless body flashed through her mind, chasing her up the back staircase to Shelby's office.

She found Rose seated at her desk with the telephone held slightly away from her perfectly coiffed hair. Ellie smiled as she took one of the seats between the two desks. She wondered briefly where Shelby was, and then decided that her sister-in-law probably left the room so she wouldn't have to listen to the rather colorful string of adjectives Rose was using. Ellie was amazed at the way Rose pointed her finger as she ranted. The tip of her saberlike red nail pounded against the desk top as each demand was communicated to the party on the other end.

Hoping to appear polite, Ellie began looking around the office, reading the various things framed along the wall. There were several pictures, as well as awards and articles. She was impressed to discover that The Rose Tattoo had been selected as one of Charleston's ten best restaurants. Ellie began reading one of the newspaper reviews as she heard Rose suggest, in a rather loud voice, that the supplier do to himself something that sounded rather impossible, before slamming the receiver onto the cradle.

"Jackass," Rose grumbled.

Ellie offered a sympathetic smile. "Maybe it isn't such a good idea for you to be conducting business so soon after—"

"It is if we want to pay the bills," Rose cut in. "Don't get me wrong, I'll miss Josh." Rose's green eyes sparkled mischievously. "As will most of the single women within a twenty-mile radius."

"Was he really that much of a ladies' man?"

"Lech is a better description."

"Rose!"

"Well," she defended as she patted her hair. "He was a nice pig, but a pig nonetheless."

"A nice pig?"

"Sure." Rose straightened a small pile of papers on her desk. "He went out with anyone and everyone."

"Then he was a pig," Ellie readily agreed.

"But he never led any of them on. Josh was always up front. Right after saying hello, he usually announced he wasn't marriage material."

Ellie smiled. "He said as much to me last night when we were on the way to his place."

Rose's expression suddenly grew serious. Steepling her fingers, she leaned forward and rested her elbows on top of her desk. "You want to tell me what actually happened last night?"

Shelby came in then, saving Ellie from having to relive the horrible experience of finding Josh dead.

However, things did not appear to be looking up when Jake Devereaux came in right behind Shelby.

"What the hell are you doing here?" Rose bellowed.

Jake removed his hat. It was only then that Ellie noticed he carried a rather large white box, complete with a huge, bordering-on-gaudy, rose ribbon.

Jake's eyes met and held hers. Ellie immediately felt her pulse quicken. "Hello, Ellie."

"Jake," she managed in the coolest tone she could muster.

"I'd like a few minutes of your time, Rose."

"I'd like a few feet of your hide," Rose countered.

Those darned dimples, Ellie groaned inwardly as she watched Jake smile at the older woman.

"Come on, Ellie," Shelby said as she yanked Ellie's purse strap. "Mr. Devereaux and Rose need some time alone."

"Humph!" Rose grunted. "The way I see it, Devereaux needs some time all right. Behind bars."

Ellie was still snickering as she followed Shelby down the stairs, through the kitchen and into the restaurant. Beth and Susan were seated at a large table in front of the fireplace. Sheets of paper were scattered around mugs of rich-smelling coffee.

Susan looked up first, her dark eyes rimmed with the telltale circles of a woman deprived of sleep. Beth was somber and appeared to be struggling to keep her tears in check. Ellie didn't know either of the waitresses well enough to offer many words, so she quietly took the seat next to Shelby.

"I'll get them," Beth said as a couple entered the restaurant.

"It seems weird without Josh here," Susan offered, staring over at the bar. "I can still sense his aura."

Ellie's brows wrinkled questioningly, but Shelby signaled her not to ask.

Susan sighed, then continued, "Rose says we're supposed to mix our own drinks until she hires someone else. She's got an interview set up for this afternoon."

"That quickly?" Ellie asked. "How would anyone know you all have an opening?"

"She's probably just gone back into our personnel files and called a former applicant. Luckily for us, it isn't too hard to find an out-of-work bartender," Shelby explained.

"But he won't be like Josh," Susan said with a sniff.

Beth came back just as Susan was finishing her comment. Her blue eyes blazed as she said, "I suppose you think you're an expert on Josh, too?"

Visibly taken aback by the accusation in Beth's tone, Susan lurched back in her seat. "Hold on. Why are you so mad at me?"

"Because everyone around here this morning has had something negative to say about Josh. To hear you all talk, you make him sound like a slimeball. You," she continued, pointing her finger at Shelby, "even had the audacity to suggest we plan a memorial service for all his friends."

"What's wrong with that?" Ellie queried cautiously.

"Because!" Beth wailed. "She didn't mean friends—she was talking about his former girl-friends."

"You have to admit, he did have more than his fair share of lady friends," Susan said.

"I meant no harm," Shelby explained in the soft, cultured voice Ellie suspected was just one of the reasons her brother had married her.

Beth crossed her arms tightly over her bosom. "Well, I think it should be private. Just for us."

"Your aura is screaming red," Susan observed. "I think some tea and a few hours of meditation might help you get some calm back into your life."

"Can't do that," Beth said. "I have to work. Remember, we shut the place down when Rose's son gets married. But when an employee is brutally murdered—" she paused and gave Ellie a long, pointed stare "—it's business as usual."

"You don't think I had anything to do with it?" Ellie gasped.

Beth turned and faced her, venom spewing from her eyes. "You were the last one to see him. I heard the cops went to see you last night."

"Stop this," Shelby insisted. "Ellie's only involvement with the murder was being unlucky enough to have found poor Josh."

Beth didn't appear to be the least bit appeased. "I heard she was the only one in the apartment when he was killed. Isn't that true?"

"Beth," Rose's voice thundered through the room, reaching them just a scant second before the woman herself. "I could hear you clear into the kitchen. Our patrons didn't come here to listen to your ranting and raving.''

Ellie was having a hard time listening to Rose's comments. She was trying to figure out why Jake was right behind Rose, wearing a Cheshire-cat grin on his face. Ellie was put off-balance by the fact that Jake's green eyes were fixed on hers. It was disarming, to say the least.

''...serve the customers, and Shelby and I will put together something tasteful and respectful. Understand?''

''What about her?'' Beth asked, hooking her thumb in Ellie's direction. ''Will the prime suspect be invited to the memorial service?''

''Keep it up,'' Rose warned, ''and you won't be. Ellie is not a killer. She is a member of your boss's family. You'd do well to remember that fact.''

''She's not taking this very well,'' Susan said as soon as Beth had slammed her way into the kitchen.

Rose snorted. ''You'd think she and Josh were a thing.''

''Josh tried,'' Susan said on an expelled breath. ''But then, I think he hit on everyone but me.''

''Maybe your aura wasn't right,'' Rose suggested with a barely contained grin, then turned, all smiles and batting eyelashes, to Jake. ''Would you be a dear and help me put these on the tree?''

''My pleasure, ma'am.''

Ellie and Shelby exchanged shocked looks as Jake and Rose went over to the sparsely decorated tree and began adding items from the box Jake had been carrying earlier. Rose could be heard tittering during the lull in the music coming from the jukebox.

"I've never heard her make that sound," Shelby whispered. "Look at those!"

"They look a lot like the ones that broke," Ellie acknowledged.

"He's cute and thoughtful," Shelby observed. "Dangerous combination."

"Tell me about it." Ellie groaned, then spent the better part of an hour watching Jake and Rose restore the tree to its original glory. Blissfully, Jake had either forgotten or decided not to replace the ornament that played "Blue Christmas" relentlessly. That thought reminded her of her drive with Josh and immediately her spirits fell.

"The King is honored. All's right with the world," Jake said as he came up to the table, turned the chair backward and tossed one well-muscled leg over the back before settling down. "Why the long face?"

"It was very nice of you to replace Rose's ornaments," Ellie said, keeping her eyes fixed on the square tips of his fingers. "That stuff must have cost a fortune. Where'd you find it so fast?"

"There are several collectible shops near the Omni. You can get darned near anything with a Gold Card these days."

"And where'd you get the money?" she asked. "That stuff couldn't have come cheap."

Jake shrugged. "I'm blessed with a few family dollars to supplement my teaching salary."

The scent of his cologne reached her, enveloping her almost like a hug. Shaking her head, she tried to rid herself of such crazy thoughts. "I guess you can be on your way now that you've made restitution."

"We've got a deal."

Ellie's head came up. "Not anymore. Rose loves you."

"We agreed last night," he said before casually reaching for her mug. With their eyes locked, Jake lifted the mug to his lips and took a long swallow, never once breaking the magnetic contact locking their eyes.

Ellie found herself holding her breath. She should have told him how crass his behavior was. She should have told him to get out of her sight. Instead, she sat mesmerized, virtually hypnotized by those emerald eyes with their thick, honey-colored lashes.

"Ready?" he asked.

"For what?" she managed in a helium-high voice that brought a deep, warm stain to her cheeks.

"I thought we'd take a look around his apartment."

"Go back to the scene of the murder?" she said, nearly choking.

"Unless you can levitate."

"I STILL THINK this is a bad idea," she said for the fifth time in as many blocks. I don't want any part of returning to Josh's place. Susan swears my bad karma will permeate the place."

Jake's soft laughter did interesting things to her insides.

"We can't search Beth and Susan's apartments this early, so I thought we could kill some time checking things out. And who knows what else might crop up.''

"Meaning?'' Ellie asked, shifting on the smooth leather seat so that she could take in his handsome profile.

"I need to find that penny.''

"What is so blasted important about that penny?''

"It is *very* important that I retrieve the penny soon,'' he said.

Ellie blinked twice. "So that's why we're going back inside?''

"Yep.''

"You're crazy! What if someone sees us and calls the police?''

He turned slowly, his face split by a sly grin. "We have an airtight alibi.''

"You're nuts if you think I'm going to break the law. As you so eloquently pointed out last night, I'm their prime suspect. The last thing I need is to get caught nosing around the scene.''

"According to Grayson Pryce, curator of the Charleston Gallery, you and I have been in a private viewing room from noon until the party.''

"Whoa! Back up,'' Ellie said, shaking her head in disbelief. "Who is Grayson whatever his name is, and what gallery? And what party?''

"You're my date for a small, private function at the gallery this evening. I've known Grayson for years, so he didn't even flinch when I called and told him I needed him to cover for me this afternoon.''

"You told him you were spending the day breaking and entering?''

Jake stopped the Mercedes for a light, turned and tapped her chin with the tip of his finger. His voice was low and sultry as he said, "No, I told him I was spending the afternoon in bed with a lady who has a very possessive boyfriend."

"Wonderful," Ellie said, slapping his hand away. "The police think I'm a killer and now some man I don't even know thinks I'm a hooker."

"Hooker?" Jake repeated, laughing aloud. "Grayson doesn't think you're a hooker. He thinks you're a ravishing woman with a body to die for."

Ellie groaned and covered her face with her hands. "Why does he think that?"

"Because that's how I described you."

"I don't know whether to thank you or slap you," she said as Jake pulled into the lot next to her abandoned rental.

"I'd take a kiss," he suggested.

"Good," she answered with a huge smile. "Then kiss off."

Ellie was out of the car in a flash, then, coming to an abrupt halt, she stood staring at the yellow tape flapping in the chilly breeze. It was a somber reminder of what had happened the night before. Wrapping herself in her own arms, she was only vaguely aware of Jake coming up behind her.

"They've obviously finished here."

"I know. The tape's been pulled."

"Sorry," he said against her ear. "You're the evidence expert here."

The feel of Jake's large hand splayed against her

back was alternately soothing and thrilling. Never in her life had she ever felt such conflicting emotions about a man. Considering the recent disaster with Mike, she would be out of her mind to allow herself to get involved, even short-term, with a man like Jake.

"Shall we?"

"Shall we what?" she asked as he nudged her forward.

"Check to see if the police overlooked anything."

"Police aren't stupid."

"They also aren't usually well versed on rare coins, either."

"This is totally illegal, you know," she warned as she moved with him into the hallway. Odd, she thought, only her footsteps seemed to be echoing through the building's interior—his were silent.

"Hang on," Jake said as he stepped up to a door and knocked. Obviously satisfied that the occupants weren't home, he reached up and unscrewed the light bulb from the fixture above their door.

"What are you doing?" Ellie asked, moving from foot to foot in order to keep an eye on the parking lot. Somehow she'd taken on the role of lookout, and she didn't particularly care for the job.

"Just watch," he told her.

Pulling a handkerchief from his back pocket, Jake carefully wrapped the bulb in the cloth, placed it beneath his boot and gently shattered the glass.

As he kneeled down, Ellie stopped watching for cars and started paying attention to the flattering way the worn denim outlined his well-muscled thighs. As he moved, her eyes seemed drawn to the breadth of his shoulders, then the deep lines of concentration around his eyes and mouth. She realized her mouth had gone dry.

"Success!" he called as he got to his feet, displaying the metal end of the bulb with its filaments exposed.

"You consider it a success to dissect a harmless light bulb?"

Jake gave her a half smile and a wink before he moved to the door still blocked with evidence tape. Intrigued, Ellie stepped forward, got up on tiptoes and watched, fascinated, as he picked the lock with the filaments.

"Geez" was all she could manage.

Jake's expression was purely predatory as he said, "I'm incredible with my hands."

Soundlessly he pushed open the door, using his coat sleeve to prevent leaving prints.

"Your precautions won't matter if Josh's neighbors come home and find that little pile of glass you dumped in the corner."

"Keep your voice down and start looking. You're trained to examine crime scenes. Help me," he instructed.

"Not me," she countered. "I'm not touching a thing. I have too much to lose."

"Fine," he said, a trace of annoyance marring his drawl. "Just stand there and look pretty. I like my women that way."

"I'll bet you do," she said between clenched teeth. "It must be heartbreaking for you when they pop and deflate."

Jake stopped dead in his tracks and spun around. "I sure wouldn't have pegged you as the kinda girl who'd know anything about inflatable sex dolls."

"I'm an evidence tech, Jake. I see lots of strange things."

He appeared to be considering her statement, at least she thought so, because his expression became unreadable. Then, almost instantly, he was in front of her, his handsome face looming over hers. He moved quickly, silently. Ellie didn't know what to do. She only knew that her curiosity about this man was nearly overwhelming. Especially when he was this close. She wondered what it would feel like to lay her head against his solid chest; how it would feel to be cradled in those strong arms. Her eyes found his mouth and her fantasies came in rapid succession.

Her eyes widened when he lowered his head. Would it be like the previous evening? When he'd simply teased her with that feathery touch of his mouth? Or would it be more substantial, more satisfying?

"Ellie?"

"Yes?"

"I'm desperate here. I really don't know what the police would have done last night. You would know. Now, come on, I need you."

So much for fantasies, she thought when he abruptly turned on his heel and went into the kitchen. As she heard the sounds of drawers and cabinets being opened and closed, she remained fixed in her spot. She wasn't going to help him. She didn't give a flying hoot about his blasted penny. Nope. Jake, she knew, was wasting his time. Ellie learned early in her career that a team would have gone over this place with the proverbial fine-tooth comb. He probably wasn't going to find anything even remotely helpful. Unless the techs were sloppy, since the crime scene was so obvious and they had the 911 call. In which case, she may well find something to clear her own name. No, she thought, they wouldn't have been that sloppy.

"Your testosterone is showing," she commented when he moved his search into the living room.

"Meaning?" he asked as he got down and began feeling around under the sofa on which Josh had met his demise.

"You're acting like a typical male."

"I am a typical male."

Not with those dimples, she thought. "You can't admit that this is a stupid idea."

"It isn't stupid."

"Right," she scoffed. "And I'll bet you stop to ask directions when you're lost."

Jake cast her a withering look. "Sometimes I do."

"And sometimes I weld pipes. Look," she began with an exasperated sigh, "I'll start searching because I want out of here as soon as possible. I can't afford to get caught here."

"Ellie," he began slowly. "Either help me or stop lecturing me. I know this is risky, but it could lead us to the real killer."

Not likely, Ellie thought. "If I check the bedroom for your precious penny, can we get out of here?"

"Yes."

"Thank heavens," she muttered as she hurried down the hall.

Josh's bed didn't look as if it had been made in the past decade. Ellie tripped on the edge of the rumpled bedspread as she moved toward the nightstand. Using a pencil from the notepad next to the bed, she carefully opened the drawer. Inside she found a variety of items to protect Josh from the litany of diseases out there: a breath-freshening spray, a small bottle of massage oil and a photograph.

Pulling the picture from beneath the other items, she smiled at the familiar faces. It was a group shot in what appeared to be a recent photo. Rose, Shelby, Dylan, Beth, Susan, Josh and the chef, whose name she could never remember, were all huddled together. Judging from their attire, this had probably been taken at the wedding of Rose's son J.D.

Using the picture, she shuffled the items around until she was satisfied no 1955 Ben Franklin penny was hiding in the drawer. She moved over to the dresser and performed much the same ritual. No penny, just a colorful array of the skimpiest men's underwear she'd ever encountered. Ellie was still smiling when she went to the closet.

Jake came in as she opened one of the double doors.

"Find anything?"

"All of it X-rated," she joked.

"I found some pictures in that desk in the living room that made *me* blush."

Ellie laughed. "Shucks, the only one I saw was that one in the nightstand."

While she checked the pockets of the clothing, Jake checked out the picture.

"This is really pointless," she began. "Josh never even came into this room before he was killed."

"You don't know that. You were in the little girls' room, right?"

"Little girls'?" she called over her shoulder just as her hand felt something deep in the pocket of a well-worn letter jacket she guessed was from Josh's high school days.

After scanning the note she'd extracted, she said, "Apparently our friend Josh was a two-timer way back in high school. Look at this."

Dropping the edge of the bedspread, Jake came over and took the envelope and note from her.

Ellie sighed dramatically, placed the back of her hand to her forehead and said, "Can't you just see some poor seventeen-year-old writing that to Josh after seeing him at the mall with another girl? I'll bet she cried for months."

"How old was Josh?" he asked.

"Late twenties."

Jake's expression hardened. "Congratulations, Ellie. I think you've given us our first lead on finding the killer."

"What?" she said, snatching the note back. "A typed note from a lovesick teenybopper is a clue?"

"Read it."

"You said there would only be me," she recited, then looked up to meet his gaze. "I don't get it."

"Look at the character in the upper left," he instructed.

"It's that duckling from the comic strip. I've seen it."

"So have I," he said slowly. "That strip replaced one of my favorites. It's only been in syndication for a year."

Chapter Seven

"I still don't understand why you think this might be important," she said to him as they pulled away from Ellie's house.

Out of the corner of one eye, Jake saw her holding the typed note in one hand and the photo in the other, but that wasn't the reason for his distraction. Ellie had changed for their trip to the gallery. Though he'd explained that the attire for this sort of affair ran the full range—from tuxedos to turbans—she had insisted on changing. Secretly he was thrilled with her choice. It was a simple black velvet dress with some sort of beaded design sewn all over the snug-fitting bodice. The sleeves tapered down to her dainty wrists, which she had accented with simple gold bracelets. A small, black silk bag lay in her lap just above where her long legs, clad in sheer black hosiery, peeked out to tease him. He took in a deep breath, holding it in order to taste the subtle perfume he was certain she had dabbed at the base of her throat. The scoop neckline revealed just a hint of the swell of her breasts, leaving his imagination running rampant. He could easily see himself reaching over to nibble the creamy white skin just below her ear, while his hands snaked up to free the pins holding her hair.

"Earth to Jake?"

"Sorry," he said, coughing. "I was thinking."

"About the killer?"

"No." Though she certainly was killer looking in that dress, he thought.

"I thought that was part of your deal. I keep searching the employees' homes for your penny and you find the killer."

"I'm working on it."

"Jake?" she began as she uncrossed, then recrossed those incredible legs. "What's so important about that penny, anyway? I mean, can't you just go to some coin shop and replace it?"

"It isn't like that, Ellie. A replacement is never as good as the original."

"Is that why you replaced all of Rose's Elvis stuff? Which, incidentally, won't get you completely back in her good graces. There's still the matter of your having your hand in her cash register." One perfectly shaped brow arched above her eye.

"Elvis memorabilia isn't exactly in the same category as my penny."

"Then why'd you do it? And what did you mean by *family money*?"

Luckily Jake didn't have to answer. Pressing a button on the driver's-side door, he unlocked the car. Stepping out into the brisk evening air, he saw him, standing by the front door, his face illuminated by the red glow of a cigarette. He let out a low curse.

"I got the door, thanks," Ellie said as she walked around to meet him. "I'll bet when you buy a Mercedes there's an etiquette section in the manual."

"I was going to get the door for you," he said as he looked at her upturned face. "I just got distracted for a second." He allowed his eyes to take in the full length of her body. She was thin, but not skinny. The dress, what little there was of it, hugged the curvy outline of her body. But it was her legs that again caused him to take in a sharp, quick breath. Those shiny, black spiked heels made them the same height. They also made him wonder what it would be like to run his palms over that sheer nylon.

"Is my slip showing?" she asked impatiently.

"You have a slip on under that thing?"

HER CHEEKS were still warm as she allowed Jake to lead her into the gallery. She caught their reflection in the glass double doors and, she had to admit, they were a sight. Jake in his jeans, crisp white shirt, funky tie and raw-silk jacket; Ellie dressed all in shimmering black. They were a study in contrasts. His hair was very light, almost wheat colored. Hers was very dark. Yet they were virtually the same height. She had no doubt that a handsome man like Jake with a tall woman on his arm would surely attract attention.

"People are staring," she whispered as they entered a plushly carpeted foyer lined with glass display cases.

"You're a beautiful woman," he returned as he took her hand and wrapped it around his arm.

She could feel the definition of muscle beneath the

soft fabric and struggled with the urge to give it a squeeze, just to see if it was really that hard.

There were dozens of people, most holding champagne glasses, scattered through the maze of rooms. Ellie's favorite was a tiny woman with a huge hat and a long, jeweled cigarette holder. It didn't take her long to decide that she was way out of her element. There were people with their ears pierced at least a dozen times. Gender was often hard to discern. One woman had her nose pierced, still another had a ring hooked through her navel.

"Ouch," she whispered as they stood across from that woman at the elaborate buffet table.

Discreetly, she directed Jake's attention to the woman's belly button.

"That's nothing," he said.

"I bet it hurt."

"It's very popular among the artsy set these days. They love to have various parts of their anatomy permanently decorated. I'll bet her belly button isn't the most outrageous thing she has pierced."

"You're kidding?" Ellie asked excitedly. "Like what else?" she prompted as she lifted a delicate pastry filled with an asparagus tip.

"You don't want to know."

"Yes I do," she insisted as she gave his arm a gentle squeeze. The muscle was real, all right, definitely real.

It became apparent that Jake wasn't going to elaborate. She would just have to content herself with idle speculation as she watched the woman flit through the crowd.

When a waitress came by, Jake got them both glasses of champagne. It was only then that she noticed Jake staring at a small article in the glass case next to where they were standing. Ellie moved closer in order to read the small card beneath the antique box. She was staring at a hand-painted ceramic box from the Ming Dynasty, on loan from a Mr. and Mrs. Heller of Hamburg, Germany.

"It's beautiful," she said in awe as she marveled at the tiny paintings depicting the Pacific Basin. The detail was incredible, especially since the object couldn't have been more than a two-by-two-inch square.

"There are only three known in existence," he explained.

"What is it?"

"The real name is impossible for me to pronounce," he said with a rather sheepish grin. "It was used by members of the upper class to hold small amounts of opium."

"Drug smuggling?"

Jake laughed, as did the couple standing to their left. Ellie was so embarrassed that she dragged Jake away from the box to an area of the gallery where cloisonné eggs were on display.

"I feel like a real jerk. Art was never my strong suit."

Jake took her hand and directed her into a small, private enclave. His hands rested at her waist, his fingers just brushing the curve of her hips.

Ellie felt his warm breath wash over her face. She felt a heat where his palms pressed against her body.

Without any warning, every cell in her body seemed to electrify with a strong, uncontrollable current. She was aware of everything. The flecks of gold mixed into the green of his eyes. The tiny lines at the corners of his eyes. The way the sun had turned his skin a rich, golden color that seemed the perfect complement to his light hair. She noticed the way his hair curled over the collar of his shirt, the way his Adam's apple moved above the knot of his tie.

She swallowed, trying to quell the desire she felt churning up from the pit of her stomach. This was crazy. This was insanity. "We can't do this," she said in a husky voice that belied her words.

Spreading his legs, Jake moved forward, trapping her between him and the wall. A small sound slipped past her slightly parted lips as she lifted her hands to his shoulders. Their eyes locked as his palms slowly moved up her sides, just barely grazing the swell of her breasts before he cupped her face in his hands.

It seemed as if Jake searched her eyes for an eternity, quietly seeking something. But what?

"You think this is crazy, huh?"

She should say yes. She should nod. Instead, she laced her fingers up through his hair and pulled him to her.

The initial contact should have been hesitant and awkward. But it wasn't. Not with Jake. This was something entirely different. It was all heat and contradictions. His lips were soft but their magic was rough and demanding. When his tongue reached out to taste the seam of her lips, Ellie heard the rumbling sound deep down in his throat. That only served to heighten the sensations bombarding her. She was aware of nothing but him. The way he kissed her with practiced expertise. The gentle feel of his thumbs toying with the outline of her cheekbones. The natural feel of opening her mouth, inviting—no, needing more. The strength she felt emanating from him, from all the places he had pressed against her. She could feel a soft mat of hair through the thin fabric of his shirt, the definition of his physique through the craggy roughness of his jeans and the smooth softness of his jacket.

Ellie slid her hands inside his jacket, molding the firm muscles as she explored his torso. Jake's reaction was swift and determined. He pressed harder, trapping her hands and allowing her to feel the undeniable evidence of his arousal. Her mind began to swim in the flood of what she was feeling. Too much was happening. All of her senses were on fire, burning nearly out of control. It was the most incredible thing she'd ever experienced. Her knees were actually becoming weak from it all. Her heartbeat was pounding in her ears.

As if somehow sensing this, Jake abandoned her mouth and kissed a warm path across her cheek to her throat. He nibbled and kissed, teased and taunted his way along her jawline until he reached her earlobe. The sensation of his breath against her ear both tickled and thrilled her. She made a small sound and half opened her heavy-lidded eyes.

Using what little strength she had, she shoved him with all her strength. Jake teetered back, his face contorted in confusion.

Plastering a smile on her face, Ellie spoke through clenched teeth. "We seem to have an audience."

Jake turned so that he stood between her and the silver-haired man and his attractive redheaded companion who had been watching them for God knew how long.

Mortified didn't seem like a strong enough word to describe what Ellie was feeling at that moment. Toying with her hair, she lowered her eyes and silently prayed that the floor would open and swallow her whole. She hadn't been caught necking for the better part of fifteen years. Somehow it was acceptable behavior for a teenager. Two adults should have known better than to get caught groping each other in a public building in the middle of a fancy party.

"Ellie?" Jake was saying as he reached around, took her hand and tugged her out from behind him. "I'd like you to meet Grayson, the curator here."

"Nice to meet you," Ellie squeaked as she reluctantly placed her hand in his. The look in his eyes suggested that maybe this wasn't the first time this man had caught Jake in a compromising position.

"My pleasure, Miss Tanner. I trust you're *enjoying* yourself?"

Ellie nodded, hoping her face wasn't completely crimson. It probably was, if the heat she felt was an accurate barometer.

"Jake, I believe you may know Melissa Kelly."

Jake nodded and offered the rather stiff woman his hand. She smiled and accepted it, though the smile didn't reach her eyes.

Then she turned her icy brown eyes on Ellie. "And you are Jake's...companion for the evening?"

He gave her hand a gentle squeeze. At least Ellie hadn't imagined the ugly inference behind the woman's words.

"Ellie was kind enough to accompany me," Jake answered for her. He then craned his neck and peered around. "Where's your date, Melissa? Don't tell me you couldn't get one...again?"

The redhead handled the dig with aplomb, which told Ellie the two probably had a history. Somehow she couldn't imagine the two of them together. Melissa could have been the ice-queen poster model. She just couldn't see this woman climbing out of windows, running through the woods or lying to the police. Any one of those activities might ruin her manicure. Ellie didn't think Melissa could handle a smudged nail. She seemed too unyielding, too anal retentive. She was also incredibly beautiful.

"Gee, Jake. It didn't occur to me to bring a date to an official function. But then again—" she paused and gave Ellie a very unflattering once-over "—most of what you do wouldn't occur to me. She does know what kind of man you are, doesn't she?"

"She's getting to know me pretty well, Melissa. Thanks for asking."

"Oh." Melissa adjusted the large, gold metallic purse beneath her arm and looked directly at Ellie. "I wasn't asking. I was warning."

"Game, set and match," Ellie said in a stage whisper as Melissa sauntered away.

Grayson laughed. "Well put, my dear. Melissa certainly isn't timid. I assumed you and Melissa traveled in some of the same circles, but I had no idea there was some...er...tension between the two of you or I wouldn't have brought her by."

"No problem, Gray," Jake said as he patted the older man on the shoulder. "I'm just sorry for your sake," he added as he turned to Ellie.

"I guess this makes us even," she said.

"Even?" Jake asked, his brow arched high on his forehead.

"It was only yesterday when you got to referee Michael and me," Ellie reminded him.

"Michael?" Grayson piped up. "Is he a somewhat large gentleman with a rather pronounced accent?"

"Define accent," Jake said.

"Up north. New York, New Jersey—one of those."

"No neck?" Jake continued.

Grayson smiled in spite of himself. "Well, yes. He is an overdeveloped sort." Grayson frowned and added, "I believe he's here this evening."

Ellie made a sound of disbelief. "That isn't possible. Michael probably hasn't been to an art gallery since a grade school field trip."

Grayson's smile returned. "Then I believe we are definitely speaking about the same gentleman. He actually *touched* one of the sculptures. Stepped up over the cording and felt the biceps."

"That's Michael," Ellie said, sighing. "I wonder what he's doing here?"

"He showed the host at the door a badge. Apparently he indicated that he was here on official business.''

Ellie's entire body stiffened, a reaction obviously noticed by Jake. He dropped her hand and slipped his arm around her shoulder, pulling her close against him. ''We can leave,'' Jake said against her ear.

''But you've only shown me about half the exhibits.''

He smiled down at her and said, ''We can come back another time. Right, Grayson?''

''Always,'' he said before inclining his head slightly and excusing himself.

''We can go back to my place,'' Jake suggested.

The mere thought of that brought about a resurgence of her hormones. ''I don't think that's a good idea,'' Ellie told him. ''I seem to forget my proper upbringing whenever you touch me.''

Jake's expression was playful as he offered a wink. ''Glad to hear it. Then we definitely need to go.''

Knowing Michael was somewhere in the gallery, Ellie decided she would leave with Jake, then clue him in that he was to take her back to Shelby's. He had the ability to make her swoon but not the power to completely overcome her reason. Besides, she didn't relish the thought of another run-in with Melissa. Leaving was a good idea.

As they weaved their way back toward the front entrance, Ellie caught a glimpse of a man in her peripheral vision. He looked familiar, but she couldn't place him. When Jake stopped once more in front of the display case guarding the small Ming box, Ellie casually glanced around.

"Did you happen to see a dark-haired man in a black suit?" she asked.

"Only about fifty of them," Jake said with a small chuckle. "Could you be a little more specific?"

"Not really." She frowned. "He looked sort of familiar but I can't place him."

"It's probably all the tuxedos. Most men look alike in tuxes."

"Why don't you wear one? From the way Grayson and that lovely Melissa woman talked, you must go to a lot of these things."

Jake grinned as he took her hand. "I teach art history. They excuse me from the dress code because I'm an academic and not a collector."

"Then what about that expensive car you drive?"

He leaned down and whispered, "That's my little secret. Don't tell or they'll make me dress up in a monkey suit from here on out."

"You'd look very handsome in a tuxedo," Ellie told him as they exited the building.

"There you are!"

Ellie recognized the voice at the same instant she felt the viselike hand clamp around her upper arm. She let out a small cry of pain just as Jake swung into action.

The pointed toe of his boot caught Michael right in the midsection, folding the large man like a rag doll.

"Stop it!" Ellie yelled as Jake made another move. "Just call the police. I have a restraining order."

Jake kneed the recovering Michael, this time sending him to the pavement, writhing and holding his stomach. "That should keep him quiet until we can call—"

The sound of a siren split the night air. Ellie remained hunched in the doorway, where others from the party were beginning to congregate.

Grayson pushed through the crowd and went over to where Jake stood over Michael's rolling and moaning form. The two men conversed quietly, but Ellie couldn't hear over the sound of the sirens. It was an eerie replay of the previous evening, only this time she couldn't wait for the police to come. This time they were the good guys.

The first squad car came to a screeching halt outside the gallery so that Michael was illuminated in the headlights. Two uniformed men got out just as a second car arrived. Ellie couldn't see the officers' faces because of the bright headlamps. Carefully, she moved over next to Jake, slipping her hand into her purse.

"Hold it!" one of the officers yelled.

Suddenly Ellie found herself staring down the barrels of four service revolvers. Several of the patrons yelped and scurried inside.

Ellie froze. "I'm just getting the copy of my restraining order."

"Put the bag on the ground and step back!"

"Wait a minute," Jake began.

"On the ground!"

"Detective Greavy?" Ellie stammered. "Is that you? It's Ellie Tanner," she began in a rush of breath.

"Put the bag on the ground and step back," he said

again, though this time his command wasn't quite as menacing.

Ellie did as instructed just as Michael was regaining his faculties. "Please," she pleaded with the officers still barricaded behind the open doors of their squad cars. "I have a restraining order against that man. He isn't supposed to be within a hundred yards of me."

Michael scrambled to get to his feet, but a well-placed boot in the small of his back sent him sprawling back down. He cursed long and loud.

"Hold him," Greavy said to the uniformed men as he walked over and picked up Ellie's bag. He came a few steps closer, then turned as if he had some sort of radar attached to his back. "You!" he barked at Jake. "Stand still."

Turning back to Ellie, he said, "Ms. Tanner, you are under arrest for the murder of Josh Richardson."

Chapter Eight

It was, without question, the worst night of Ellie's life. After being booked and stripped of her clothing and her dignity, she'd shared a large cell with a dozen assorted women, most of them repeat felons. As the rotund female deputy extracted her from the cell, she silently wondered if she would one day be able to laugh about her discussions with Gertie, who was in for assaulting her mother-in-law. Or June, who preferred to be called Boogie and who had been picked up on an outstanding bench warrant. Or any of the other variations on life-forms she had endured for the past eleven and a half hours.

"The van will be here in a few minutes," the deputy said as she handed Ellie a bag containing her shoes. They'd taken her shoes, claiming the heels could be used as a weapon.

"Sit there on that bench," she was further instructed. "And don't talk. No talking allowed here or on the bus."

Ellie joined a row of sullen women on a metal bench adjacent to the area where she'd been booked the night before. The room smelled of stale coffee and cigarette smoke. Mindful of the plastic bands handcuffing her wrists, she managed to slip her shoes on after discarding the paper booties provided by her jailers.

She was able to catch a glimpse of her image in a large glass window opposite the bench. It wasn't a pretty sight. Much of her hair had come free and hung limply around her face. Dark smudges of mascara marred her cheeks, remnants of the many tears she had shed during the night.

As she sat there, quiet and still suffering from the shock of being arrested for murder, she closed her eyes and thought of Jake. He had shown such concern as the police were loading her into the car. She only hoped he had fulfilled his promise and that Shelby would be waiting at the courthouse when her bail was set.

Bail. She stifled a moan. Where on earth was she going to get money for bail? Worse yet, what if they wouldn't grant her bail?

"ARE YOU OKAY?" Shelby whispered across the smooth wooden rail that separated prisoners from the gallery in the large courtroom.

"I'm fine," she lied. "Just a bit wrinkled and in desperate need of a long bath."

Her eyes scanned the room and she saw Beth, Rose and Susan, but no sign of Jake. Her heart fell with the realization that he hadn't come to court. Then again, she could hardly blame him, under the circumstances.

"I've retained Max Jennings to represent you," Shelby said.

A middle-aged man who looked rather bored stepped forward and shook her hand. "Mrs. Tanner tells me you'll be pleading not guilty."

"Of course I am," Ellie answered without hesitation.

A woman with crisp black hair that matched her judicial robe entered the room, beginning the formal session.

Ellie was directed to a seat to await her turn. Her attorney shared the row with her friends as the waiting began.

Ellie wasn't called until nearly noon. The bailiff led her to the counsel table, where she was joined by Mr. Jennings. His cologne was strong. That, mixed with her incredible nervousness, brought on a sudden wave of nausea. It didn't help when she heard the clerk bellow, "State of South Carolina versus Eleanor Tanner. Charge is murder in the first degree."

The judge looked at her over the lenses of her half glasses. Ellie clutched her churning stomach as the judge scrutinized her.

"Can I get counsels' names for the record, please?" the judge asked.

"Linda Patterson for the people."

"Maxwell Jennings for the defendant." Jennings opened his briefcase and said, "The defendant waives formal reading of the charges and would like to enter a plea of not guilty."

"So noted," the judge said as she wrote something

down on a pad in front of her. "Do the people have a recommendation?"

The prosecutor, whom Ellie guessed to be about her own age, shuffled some papers before saying, "Miss Tanner has no real ties to the community. She presents a substantial risk for flight. Therefore, the people request no bail be granted."

"What?" Ellie squealed.

The judge gave her a stern look and Jennings squeezed her wrist.

"Forgive my client's outburst, Your Honor."

"See that it doesn't happen again."

"Yes, ma'am." Jennings leaned over and whispered. "This judge is a stickler for propriety. Keep quiet, no matter what."

Taking in a deep breath, Ellie closed her mouth and her eyes, struggling with tears of frustration and fear. One night in jail was bad enough. To think she might remain incarcerated indefinitely was too awful to even imagine.

She took another deep breath and her tortured mind played a cruel trick. For just an instant, she actually thought she smelled Jake's cologne. That masculine, woodsy scent she found so appealing.

"Mr. Jennings, I'll hear argument on bail," the judge instructed.

"Miss Tanner is a resident of the state of New York, where she is employed by the state crime lab as a forensic technician. Contrary to the representations made by the state, Ms. Tanner does have ties to Charleston. Her brother, who is an ATF agent, lives here in the city. Her sister-in-law owns and runs a business here in Charleston. Being as my client has no prior record, not even a traffic citation, denying bail would be completely unreasonable under the circumstances.''

The judge glared at Ellie, giving her the distinct impression that she was about to hear the worst.

''With all due respect to the district attorney, we do still operate under the presumption of 'innocent until proven guilty.' Bail is set at one million dollars. Cash or bond.''

The sound of the gavel rang in her ears. ''One million dollars?'' she echoed numbly. ''I don't have that kind of money.''

''We can get a bond for ten percent. We only need one hundred thousand dollars cash.''

''I don't have that kind of money, either,'' Ellie stated as if in a trance.

''I do.''

Whipping around, Ellie came face-to-face with a wary-looking Jake. He offered a tired smile.

''See if you can get them to keep her in the holding cell while I go pay the clerk?'' Jake told Jennings.

Just like that, she thought several minutes later while she was alone in a small room reserved for attorney-client visits. ''Where does a college professor from some small school in Texas get his hands on one hundred thousand dollars?''

A series of light raps on the door was her only answer. Shelby and Rose slipped inside under the watchful eye of the guard standing in the hallway.

''You look terrible,'' Shelby crooned as she gave

Ellie a warm hug. "I can't wait to get you home. Gina and I will pamper you."

"Gina is good at pampering," Rose added. "She thinks she's royalty, so pampering is an art form to that one. She used to be a professional model, so she knows all about massages, pedicures and the like."

As soon as Shelby stepped aside, Rose offered a brief hug. "She's right, you do look like hell."

"Rose," Shelby warned, then turned her concerned eyes on Ellie. "I have a call in to Dylan, but so far I haven't heard back."

Ellie grasped Shelby's wrist and asked, "You didn't call my folks, did you?"

Shelby shook her head. "I thought it would be best if they heard it from you."

"Hopefully," she began, "they won't have to hear at all."

"How are you going to keep this from them?"

"I'm going to find the killer myself," Ellie stated emphatically.

"That's crazy!" Shelby argued.

"Really?" Rose asked, bracing her hands against the patent-leather belt cinching her waist. "Seems to me that you went off investigating on your own when Chad was missing."

"That was different. Chad is my son."

"And this is my life," Ellie argued. "After last night, I'll do anything to stay out of jail." She shivered at the memory. "And Jake said he'd help me."

One of Rose's penciled brows arched distrustingly. "The brawler with the bucks and the penny?"

"He replaced your ornaments," Ellie defended,

wondering why she was defending Jake when even she had lingering doubts about him. "And he's paying my bail."

"And you thought he was the killer," Rose pointed out with her usual candor. "I'm still not convinced he isn't involved."

"He didn't kill Josh any more than I did."

"How do you *know* that?" Shelby asked in a soft voice.

"I can't really know. But I feel sure he isn't a murderer."

"Because he's a great kisser?" Rose said with obvious disgust. "So was my ex, but that doesn't make a man worth a damn."

"It isn't about kissing. I just know that Jake is not a killer. If he was guilty, why would he be bailing me out? Why would he offer to help me find the real killer?"

"Because he wants something from you," Rose answered. "That's how men work."

"Rose," Shelby admonished. "Okay, Ellie. If you believe Jake is innocent, how can you explain his presence at the scene? You didn't kill Josh, and Jake was the only other person there."

"Not true," Ellie insisted. "The killer was there. That's the only explanation."

"So, WHERE do you want to go?" Jake asked as he held open the door of his Mercedes.

"Home," she assured him. "I need to wash the hours of incarceration off me and then I'm burning this dress."

"Now that would be a crime," he said as he fastened his seat belt.

His eyes roamed over her, his expression one of definite approval. It did wonders for her battered self-esteem.

"Home it is."

"Shelby and Gina are going to pamper me."

"Gina?"

"She's Shelby's friend and nanny. Gina helps with the kids but she also does a ton of other stuff around the house. Rose doesn't like her much, but the kids are crazy about her and Dylan says she's really taken a lot of the pressure off Shelby."

"Does Rose like anyone?"

Ellie smiled. "She likes Shelby and the kids. So far I haven't seen her exactly go out of her way to cultivate friendships."

"But your sister-in-law is so gregarious."

The use of that word set alarms off in her brain. She recalled their first meeting, when he spoke in that good-old-boy drawl. Then last night, as he was showing her the various items on display at the gallery, he'd sounded like a trained curator. Now he sounded like the college professor he purported to be. About a zillion unanswered questions zipped through her mind.

"Thank you for posting my bail."

"You're welcome."

"How'd you do it?"

"I went to the clerk's office and—"

"I didn't mean specifically. I meant where did you get that kind of money on such short notice? After all, you're the guy hanging around looking for a flaming penny."

"You're yelling," he said calmly.

"I'm not yelling, I'm just very curious."

"Because I had the money? Or because I paid your bond?"

"Both."

"Didn't your mother ever tell you about not looking gift horses in the mouth?" he drawled.

"Of course she did. She also told me never to take gifts from strangers."

"I believe that's candy, not gifts."

"You're dodging my question."

"I got the money out of one of my accounts. I had it wired to me after you were arrested last night."

"That much money?"

"Actually," he said as he raked his fingers through his hair, "I had more than that sent. I figured you'd cost me between three and four hundred."

Ellie simply gaped at him.

After taking a quick look at her, he asked, "What?"

"You're rich."

He chuckled. "I'm comfortable."

"You're *really* rich," she repeated. "Only rich people say they're comfortable."

"My grandparents were rich, my father was frugal, so I got the bulk of the money. Is that a problem for you?"

Ellie thought for several seconds before she answered. "I think so. If I had money, I sure wouldn't get up and go to work every morning at eight-thirty."

"I rarely teach before ten."

"If you don't have to work, why do you?"

"Why wouldn't I?"

"I don't know," she admitted. "I suppose I just thought all rich people did was attend charity functions and donate money to have buildings named after them and stuff. I never thought of rich people as having real jobs with W-2's and everything."

"Sorry to disappoint you."

Ellie could have argued that statement for hours. Disappointing? Impossible. The man was gorgeous, funny, generous, intelligent—everything but disappointing.

"So, now that I've told you my secret, why don't you tell me about Michael?"

"Ancient history."

"Not when I saw that restraining order in your purse."

"You went through my purse?"

"You told me to call Shelby," he said. "I was only looking for her phone number. And why are you carting around that note and the photo we found when we searched Josh's apartment?"

"I don't know," she answered. "I took the picture to give to Shelby since she seemed so fond of Josh. I don't even remember sticking that note in there since it could have come from anyone in the past year. The way I hear it, Josh has had more trysts in a year than ten men have in a lifetime."

"Well, it's a good thing you handed me your bag. Can you imagine what the cops would have thought if they'd found that note and that picture on you when you were arrested?''

Ellie closed her eyes and rested her head against the seat back. There was no doubt in her mind that the police would have jumped all over that stuff.

''So,'' he prompted, ''are you gonna tell me about Michael?''

''Are you going to tell me why you bailed me out of jail?''

''We made a deal. I need my penny, and now, more than ever, you need to find out who killed Josh.''

''Hold on there,'' Ellie said, her hands waving for emphasis. ''This whole thing is too bizarre. We hardly know each other, and yet, you post enormous bail. You claim to be a teacher, yet you insist you can solve a murder. You tell me you have money out the wazoo, yet you're hell-bent on retrieving a penny.''

''Makes me an interesting guy, huh?'' he said with a wink.

''It makes you unbelievable,'' she admitted. ''For all I know, you killed Josh.''

''Think, Ellie,'' he said with a certain edge to his tone. ''If I killed Josh, would it make any sense for me to bail you out of jail? Wouldn't I want you behind bars, branded as the murderer?''

With a loud sigh, Ellie sat back, trying to make some sense of this. ''Okay, if your motives are pure, and you've got money to toss around, why don't you just go out and buy another penny to replace the one you lost? Aren't there coin shops in Charleston? You said it wasn't all that rare.''

"Collectibles are just that. The owners don't sell, they hoard. The penny isn't all that rare in the monetary sense. But the penny I lost at The Rose Tattoo has a particular mark on it. The owner would never accept a duplicate."

"The owner? You mean it isn't yours?"

Tight lines appeared around his mouth and eyes and his jaw muscles grew taught. "I was returning it to its rightful owner."

"So that's why it's so important?" Ellie felt slightly better. Her little voice of reason was appeased by his admission. It allowed her to put her lingering doubts about him back into the far recesses of her mind.

"That's why," he responded, apparently relaxing a little. "I'm going to help you because we made a deal."

"We may have made a deal..." Ellie said as she tentatively placed her hand on his arm. She was still a bit awed by the solid feel of his body. Her palm tingled as the nerve endings came to life, memorizing the feel of him. Almost immediately she recalled what it had felt like to be in his arms, to feel the soft caresses as he kissed her senseless. "I still don't understand what makes you think you can solve a crime."

Nodding, Jake gave her a quick look, then dropped one hand from the wheel, placing it on her knee. "When I'm not in front of a class, I'm scouring various shops and sources, tracking down objects for private collectors. I figure finding a murderer can't be much harder than finding a rare stamp or a long-missing painting.''

"So where'd he get the money?" Shelby asked the next morning as they sat at the table finishing their coffee.

"He's rich—family money—and apparently he gets commissions from fancy collectors for tracing down their lost or stolen stuff.''

"What kind of stuff?" Rose asked, her tone skeptical.

"Like the coin he lost at the Tattoo.''

Rose sighed theatrically and fussed with the plain black pantsuit she'd donned for the memorial service later that day. Ellie could tell by the way Rose kept adjusting the simple outfit that she wasn't comfortable sans leopard print and Lycra.

"We've been all over the bar area and the restaurant,'' Shelby said. "We even had the cleaning service check the vacuum-cleaner bag, just in case.''

"Which means there probably never was a penny,'' Rose snorted. "Jake is probably setting us up for some sort of fake claim. He'll probably find some sleazy lawyer to sue us for not guarding the darned thing.'' Rose's cheeks began to turn red as her anger festered. "He can ruin us. Remember that McDonald's thing. The coffee was too hot and it ended up costing them four hundred thousand when all was said and done.''

"Rose,'' Ellie interrupted in a calm tone. "The man replaced most of your Elvis ornaments. He paid my bail. That hardly sounds like the beginnings of an elaborate extortion scheme.''

A sudden hush fell over the room and Ellie saw that both Rose and Shelby had turned to stare at Gina, who had been sitting mutely by, bouncing Cassidy on her lap.

''What?'' Ellie asked, frustration forcing her voice up a notch.

''Nothing,'' Gina said softly, her large brown eyes downcast. ''It was something that happened a while back.''

''It's in the past,'' Rose added, her tone suddenly verging on the compassionate as she spoke to the tall, elegant woman who had lived with Dylan and Shelby since just after Cassidy's birth. ''And we never thought of it as blackmail.''

The woman was generally quiet and hadn't exactly warmed up to Ellie. Gina, with her flawless, chocolate-colored skin and near-perfect features, seemed awfully reserved for such a beautiful woman. It was Ellie's experience that most attractive women were basically outgoing. Gina was hard to figure out.

Chad came bounding into the room then, skidding on the tile floor and ricocheting, intentionally, against the side of the refrigerator. A wide grin dominated his chubby little face. He was a beautiful little boy, even if he did have just a touch of the devil in him.

''Me going, too,'' he announced.

Shelby knelt in front of her son, tucking the end of his shirt into his pants for the fifth time that morning. ''You can't go, sweetheart. This is only for grown-ups. You'll stay here with Gina and Cassidy.''

"No."

"Chad, honey," Shelby cooed. "You cannot come with Mommy."

The little boy's lower lip began to tremble. "Fine," he fairly shouted. "Then I just play with Chad's secret treasure."

"That's a good idea," Shelby said brightly.

"Yeah," Rose agreed. "Go play with your treasure." Rose rolled her eyes and said, "As spoiled as you are, you've got enough treasures to play with until the turn of the century."

"What kind of treasure is it?" Ellie asked.

Chad looked up at her, his big blue eyes wide and earnest. "It a secret," he insisted. "Chad's secret."

"Okay," Ellie said, swallowing a laugh. "It sounds really special."

"I coulda getted you outta jail," Chad announced, his small chest puffing out. "I rich now."

"We'd best be going," Rose said. "You go on up and play with your treasure, Chad. We'll be back soon."

ALL THE FURNISHINGS at The Rose Tattoo had been arranged so that the chairs faced the fireplace. The Christmas decorations had been temporarily removed from the mantel for the occasion.

Ellie had a new understanding of the word *pariah*. She could literally feel the eyes boring into her back, hear the faint whispers of accusation as she entered the room. She should have listened to her common sense and stayed home with Chad and his make-believe treasure. It was far superior to having a room

full of virtual strangers glaring at her. The worst of-
fender seemed to be Beth. She had actually let out a
horrified gasp upon seeing Ellie arrive. It wasn't long
before the words "Josh's murderer" filtered through
the crowd.

Ellie sat next to Shelby and Rose, feeling very uncomfortable until Jake sauntered in and took the seat
beside her.

"What the hell are you doing here?" she demanded in a whisper.

"Isn't it appropriate etiquette for murder suspects
to sit together at the memorial service?"

Chapter Nine

Several excruciatingly painful hours later, less than a dozen people remained at the Tattoo. Mickey, the chef, and most of the kitchen staff had transformed the dining room from a makeshift chapel back into a trendy eatery. Solemn hymns had been replaced by one of Elvis's Christmas albums.

It was truly amazing, Ellie thought as she joined Rose, Shelby, Beth and Susan at one of the tables. Susan had already shed her mourning garb and was tying a black apron over her slacks. Beth seemed to be lingering, sadly watching the steam rise off the mug of tea clutched in her hands.

As she took a seat, Ellie happened to look out at the side porch. There, through the frosted window, she could just make out Jake and a dark-haired man involved in a rather animated conversation.

"Who's that?" she asked as she placed her diet soda and her purse on the table.

"He's our new bartender," Rose answered after looking over her shoulder. "Your Jake is probably lecturing him about that damn penny."

Your Jake, Ellie's brain repeated.

"So," Beth began in a definitely hostile voice. "Don't you think it was a little strange of you to come to Josh's memorial service? Given the fact that you're the one who killed him."

"If I ever hear anything like that come out of your mouth again," Rose warned, "you'll be looking for a job *and* a few of your teeth."

"Really, Beth," Shelby admonished. "My sister-in-law had nothing to do with Josh's death. She came here this morning at my insistence."

"Wow, Beth," Susan chimed in. "You're really taking this hard. I went to my channeler last night and she's assured me Josh is on his way back. His energy should reappear any minute."

"Excuse me?" Ellie asked.

Susan patiently folded her hands in front of her and said, "All life is energy. Josh was a negative force when he was alive. His energy has to return in order to work off the negatives. My channeler made contact and they were preparing him for his return. Even if he didn't have all those negatives to atone for, there's always the stuff about being murdered. No one that's been murdered can go to the other place until the guilty party is brought to some sort of justice. That's why so many souls get caught between the two places. No closure."

Rose rolled her eyes. Shelby smiled politely and Beth jumped up and marched out of the room, muttering.

"Should I have held off hiring Manetti?" Rose

asked, gesturing toward the new bartender. "I mean if Josh is coming back..."

Susan pouted for a moment. "I know you don't believe the same things I do," she all but whined. "But we spent a long time channeling with Josh. He said a lot of very interesting things."

"Let me get this straight," Rose said. "You and one of your pyramid-worshiping friends got together and had a chat with Josh? Like in the movie *Ghost?*"

"Rose," Susan said, rolling her eyes. "Pyramids have their own soothing powers. They aren't even used in channeling."

"Pardon me," Rose said, chuckling.

Beth came back then, carrying her apron in her hand. As she laid it on the table, Ellie reached out automatically to move her purse. In the process, the photograph and the note slipped out.

"What's this?" Rose asked, grabbing the picture and looking at it.

Horrified by the prospect of having to explain that she and Jake had entered Josh's apartment, Ellie stuffed the note in her bag and said, "Oh that. I saw that at your house," she said to Shelby. "I just brought it along to the memorial service. I'm not really sure why."

Rose passed the picture to Shelby. After looking at it Shelby said, "I don't remember this."

"Sure you do," Rose said. "That was taken after J.D. and Tory's wedding."

"I know that," Shelby corrected. "I just don't remember this particular picture."

"Maybe it's Dylan's," Ellie suggested as she watched the photograph being passed to Susan.

"That's just how Josh looked in my vision," she announced. "He was smiling and content."

"What are you talking about?" Beth moaned. As soon as she was filled in, she asked, "And why should we believe all this channeling garbage?"

"Well, for one thing, Josh told me Ellie didn't kill him."

"Sure," Beth said with a sneer. "You're getting weirder by the minute, you know that? I could take the numerology, the psychic babble, the tarot readings. But this is going too far. Some of us really cared for Josh. Your using the tragedy of his murder to add to your list of otherworldly accomplishments makes me sick."

"Calm down, Beth," Rose ordered. "Susan doesn't mean any harm."

"It's the truth, though," Susan insisted. "Josh was emphatic that Ellie wasn't his killer."

"Well, then," Beth said, "I'm sure her attorney will want you to testify on her behalf."

"Stop being so nasty, Beth," Shelby said in the same tone she used on her son. "There's no need to be sarcastic."

"Me? You're ragging on me when she's the one having a meaningful dialogue with a dead person."

"It isn't a dialogue," Susan explained. "It isn't like hearing voices. It's a totally different kind of communication."

"Well," Beth began as she got to her feet, apparently completely disgusted. "Did he tell you the name of the murderer?"

Susan shook her head. "We lost contact before he could tell us the story."

"Too bad," Beth said. "I'm sure Ellie would have appreciated the information. Of course, I don't know whether they cover channeling in the rules of evidence. Who knows, though? Could be an exception to the hearsay rule."

"Don't let her bother you," Rose said as soon as Beth had gone back behind the bar. "She was his friend and I think it's natural for her to feel angry."

"She doesn't have to take it out on me." Susan frowned. "He was my friend, too. But you don't hear me saying mean things."

Just strange things, Ellie thought as she took a sip of her drink. Really strange.

"I LIKED your other black dress much better," Josh whispered against her ear as they stood together in the garden path behind the Tattoo. He liked the fresh scent of her hair and longed to take her into his arms. She looked so fragile, even with that brave smile plastered on her pale lips. In the fading light he could see she was teetering on the edge.

"Are you sure you want to be seen talking to me?"

"Why wouldn't I?"

Ellie looked up at him, her eyes wide, barely masking the caldron of emotions he saw boiling up toward the surface. "I'm a murderer. Half the people who came into the Tattoo tonight pointed at me and whispered. It was like the memorial service all over again.''

"You did make the morning papers," he reminded her. "A beautiful woman accused of murder is a pretty sensational thing. Especially given the murder weapon."

"They called me *Eleanor Tanner, the Suspected Christmas Killer,* in the headline."

"I saw it," he said as he reached up to pull the edges of her coat together.

The action allowed his knuckles to brush the soft underside of her upturned face. Her skin was chilled and he felt her shiver as he pulled her closer to him.

"What's that?" he asked, pointing to a building at the end of the path.

"The dependency. They have entertainment on the weekends during the winter. Nightly at all other times."

"Can we go in?"

She looked up at him with indecision in her eyes.

"Come on," he said, tugging her along with him through the shadows of the stately oaks that lined the walkway. When they got to the door, Jake reached into the back pocket of his jeans and pulled out his wallet. Then, after giving the dead bolt a quick inspection, he extracted one of his credit cards.

"Allow me," Ellie said, reaching around him and turning the knob. With a devilish grin, she added, "They were working on sets today and I heard Shelby say she'd lock it up on her way home after dinner."

"Is anyone in here?" he asked as he followed her through the doorway.

"I saw the van pull out about half an hour ago."

He heard her feeling around in the darkness, then there was a click and the back portion of the room filled with light.

It was a fairly narrow room, dominated by an arrangement of small, round tables and a large, long stage. On the stage he saw a huge artificial Christmas tree partially put together and some background flats angled against the wall.

"They're doing a production of the *Nutcracker* through New Year's," Ellie explained.

"Were you a dancer?" he asked as he slipped her coat off her shoulders.

"Me? No way. I have absolutely no rhythm. My little sister, Diana, is the dancer. She started twirling at about three months and hasn't stopped since."

He laughed as he pulled out a chair for her. "So there's three of you?"

"Six."

He whistled, thinking of his own happy years as an only child. "That must have been tough. Did you ever get time to yourself?"

"The third Wednesday of the month," she joked.

He found himself absolutely captivated by the humorous light in her eyes. Dragging his chair closer, he positioned himself so that her knees were between his as he reached out and took her hands in his. "You're very pretty when you laugh."

"I used to laugh all the time," she told him. A small hint of sadness returned as she spoke. "You just had the misfortune to meet me at the lowest point in my life."

"Everything will work out," Jake promised. Funny, he thought as he raised her hand to his lips. He meant it. He would do everything in his power to see that she got out of trouble. Problem was, he didn't have the first clue as to how to go about it.

Her hand was warm as he placed a kiss between each dainty knuckle. His eyes locked with hers as he did the same thing to her other hand. He noted her pupils swelling, making her eyes turn an exotic navy blue. He'd never seen anything like it.

In one easy move, he shifted Ellie from her chair into his lap. The slight stiffening he felt wasn't enough to discourage him, though it did serve as a warning.

"Don't worry, Ellie," he said in a soft, soothing voice. "I'm only going to hold you. Seems to me you could use a hug after the day you've had."

"That sounds good," she murmured, resting her head against his shoulder. "But something tells me you and I won't stop at comforting hugs and friendly kisses."

"I sure hope not, ma'am," he drawled as he began stroking her hair.

"Why is that?" she asked.

"Why is what?"

"Why do we have such chemistry?"

"I think it's supposed to be that way," he said as his fingers moved down to trace the outline of her throat. He could feel the rapid pulse and it instilled in him a certain masculine power—knowing he could have this effect on her was a heady thing.

So heady that a moan rumbled around in his throat.

"Your skin is so soft," he said. "And you always smell so good."

"Thank you."

"Especially your hair." He lifted a handful to his nose and inhaled deeply, closing his eyes as the herbal-floral mixture reached him.

Ellie then surprised him. He felt her hand slip inside his jacket and begin to explore his chest. He moaned again as his body began to react to the feel of her touching him.

"I like your hands, too," he said, lifting her arm to plant a kiss against her palm. He turned her wrist and was about to place another series of kisses along her knuckles when the time on her watch penetrated his fogged brain.

A quarter to seven? he thought as he jumped to his feet, very nearly tossing Ellie unceremoniously on her fanny. "I'm sorry," he said as he pulled her to her feet. Grabbing her coat off the back of the chair, Jake thrust it at her, saying, "I'm really sorry but I didn't realize the time. I have to get to a very important appointment."

Her expression didn't exactly make him feel exonerated.

He tried again. "Really, Ellie. I'll come by tonight."

"No, thanks."

She didn't bother to put on her coat as she moved to the door in long, purposeful strides, her back stiff, her expression unyielding.

"I really am sorry," he said again as they stepped into the chilly night air.

"Fine" was all she said before she headed for her brother's house, never once looking back in his direction.

ELLIE WAS HOME before seven o'clock. She'd showered and tugged on her robe before eight. She'd tried to read Chad a story, but even he had shunned her, claiming he needed to spend some time finding a special hiding place for his secret treasure. Cassidy was already asleep and Shelby was busy working in her den.

Feeling restless, Ellie went down to the kitchen to get a drink. She was in the process of pouring juice into a glass when she saw the shadowy figure lurking by the back door.

Placing the bottle on the counter, she unlatched the door and threw it open, calling out Jake's name in the process.

"I want it," The shadowy figure growled in a low voice.

"Excuse me?" Ellie said, searching vainly for the porch light switch in order to get a look at the man dressed all in black.

"I want the penny. It belongs to me." He moved forward, trying to force his way through the opening.

Using all her strength, Ellie shoved against the door and let out ear-piercing cry for help. It seemed like hours before Shelby's hurried footsteps overcame her frightened, raspy breathing.

"What on earth?" Shelby yelled as she joined Ellie in fending off the intruder.

Chapter Ten

"Who was that?" Shelby asked.

"At first I thought it was Jake," Ellie said as she pushed back the curtain with still-trembling fingers and peered out into the circle of illumination created by the light. The figure was long gone by the time she'd found the switch. "I don't know, but he was really scary."

"Did he say something about your arrest?"

Ellie shook her head. "He told me he wanted the penny. He said it was his. I think he would have attacked me if you hadn't come when you did. It wasn't about the murder, which is odd. He wanted that damned penny."

"Jake's penny?"

"I guess." Ellie shrugged as she reached down and scratched Foolish between the ears. "You aren't much of a watchdog, are you?" she asked as her heart rate returned to normal.

Shelby touched her arm. "Don't you think it's time you called your folks and told them what's happening? It would be horrible if they found out another way. Especially if we're going to have threatening, late-night callers.''

Alarmed by the fear she saw in Shelby's eyes, Ellie felt the guilt settle over her like a blanket. ''I'll call them,'' she relented. ''But I need to make another call first.''

''To whom?''

''I've got to call my office. I can't let them find out by accident, either.''

It took Ellie the better part of an hour to explain to her boss why she might need to use some of her annual leave to remain in Charleston. His initial shock turned to outrage and he offered the assistance of the entire SID unit. Ellie was in the process of thanking him politely when she had a thought. ''Dave, do you think you could get someone in the detective division to run a check on a guy from Tyler, Texas?''

''No problem,'' he said without hesitation. ''Let me get a pen and paper, then give me everything you've got.''

The second call wasn't quite as easy. Her parents were devastated and Ellie had to think fast to keep them in New York. The sound of her mother's soft sobs and promises to pray nearly sent Ellie into a renewed fit of tears.

''It may be over quickly,'' Ellie said with false brightness. ''There's a preliminary hearing in two days. The judge might just toss the whole thing out at that point.''

''What about Dylan?'' her father asked. ''Can he do anything?''

Ellie didn't have the heart to tell her father that

Dylan was on assignment and they hadn't been able to reach him yet. "He's doing everything he can," she hedged.

After promising to call the minute the hearing was over, Ellie hung up and let out a deep, exhausted sigh. She needed an aspirin and went into the living room in search of her purse. The hallway was dark—apparently everyone had gone to bed. Just as well, she thought. She really wasn't in the mood to recite her conversation with her parents and she knew Shelby would be curious.

She was just about to step over Foolish's prone form when she heard the light knocking on the front door. Wary from her earlier experience, Ellie flipped on the light and took advantage of the peephole.

"*This* time I'm cautious," she said after yanking open the door, "and it's you."

Jake tipped the brim of his Stetson and said, "Nice to see you, too."

He stepped past her, a tall, dark, shadowy figure, clad in black from head to toe.

"You weren't here earlier were you?" she asked, though she knew the mystery man on the porch wasn't much over five-seven, tops.

"No, why?"

Foolish lifted his head, sniffed once, then stretched out and went back to sleep. Ellie sidestepped the dog and went into the living room with Jake just behind her. She knew he was there because of the telltale scent that seemed to be doing wonders for her nerves, while wreaking havoc on her hormones.

"You look like you're in bad shape. Has something

else happened?'' he asked as he took the seat next to her on the sofa.

Ellie nodded as she began to rummage through her purse. Her eyebrows drew together as she continued to search. The feel of Jake's thigh against hers didn't do much for her concentration.

''They're gone,'' Ellie finally announced after emptying the contents of her purse onto the coffee table.

''What's gone?''

''The note and the picture.''

''From Josh's place?''

''Uh-huh.'' She groped through the items once more just to make certain.

''Were you expecting them to be missing?'' he asked.

''No, why?''

Pointing at her purse, he said, ''You were in such a hurry to go through your purse, I didn't even get a kiss hello.''

She offered him a warning glance. ''You weren't getting a kiss, Jake. I was looking for an aspirin. Who would have taken them out of my purse, and why?''

''Shelby?'' he suggested. Then, apparently in response to the narrowing of her eyes, he added, ''Well, she's probably had the most access to your purse.''

''This is too weird.'' She sighed, leaning back against the cushions. ''First, some guy sneaks into the backyard, tries to break the door down and demands the penny. Now I find someone has been in my purse.''

''Who was at your back door?'' Jake demanded, as

she felt the slight sting of his fingers digging into the flesh of her shoulders.

"I don't know," Ellie assured him. "Some little man dressed in dark clothes with a hat pulled halfway down his face. He had a gravelly voice and only said two lines."

"Do you know who he was? Have you heard the voice before?"

"If I had recognized the voice, I would know who he was. Then I wouldn't be calling him some funny little man. I'd be saying 'Fred' came by and threatened me."

"What *exactly* did he say?"

"He wanted the penny. He said it belonged to him."

She watched as Jake's features seemed to relax almost instantly. It was equally peculiar when he let his hands slip away.

"Your concern is touching," Ellie said.

"I think I know who it might have been."

"Who?"

"A guy named Frank Moore. He's in his early fifties, has a sandpaper voice and dresses like something out of a forties gangster flick."

"It could have been him. Who is he? Why does he claim the penny belongs to him?"

"He's a thief and a liar. He simply wants the penny for himself. He isn't the rightful owner," Jake told her. "He was probably just shooting blind by coming here. Did he offer you money?"

"No. But I got the feeling that if I said I had the penny, he would have beaten me to a pulp and then taken it. Why does he think the penny belongs to him?''

"Because he stole it."

Blinking, Ellie felt her mouth drop open. "How brazen can you get? The penny is yours and the thief who stole it is running around trying to do it again? Why don't you call the police and have him arrested. My personal experience has been that they really enjoy making arrests in this town."

Jake's soft laughter soothed her as he pulled her into the circle of his arms. "Don't worry, Ellie. I'll get this all sorted out. You leave Frank Moore to me."

"Why did he steal it from you in the first place?"

After a slight pause, Jake said, "He didn't steal it from me."

"That's right, I forgot," she said as her palm flattened against his chest just above his rapidly beating heart. "You don't own these things, you just retrieve them for people. What about the real owner? Won't he want to press charges?"

Kissing her hair, Jake said, "Hush up about the penny. I didn't come here to discuss having people arrested."

"What did you come here for?" she asked, lifting her head in order to meet his eyes. His pupils were dark and dilated.

"For you," he said as he brushed her slightly parted lips with his own.

The kiss was dizzying in its intensity. Jake tasted of mint and felt wonderfully warm and solid. Ellie drank in the scent of him, returning the passion in his kiss with equal measure.

When he reached for the top fold of her robe, Ellie clamped down on his hand. "I don't think so," she said against his mouth.

He lifted away from her, looking disappointed but not beaten. "Really?"

"Really," she told him as she placed a kiss on his mouth. "This isn't the right time. It definitely isn't the right place. My brother would kill me if he heard I was fooling around on his sofa with Chad and Cassidy just at the top of the stairs."

"Then would you consider accepting an invitation to my hotel room tomorrow morning?" he asked softly. "I really want to be with you, Ellie. Please?"

"I think so," she answered, feeling her cheeks redden with the intimate negotiations.

"How about ten tomorrow morning? I'll spoil you with breakfast and then, who knows... Deal?"

"Deal."

ELLIE TOOK EXTRA TIME with everything the next morning. Her hair was perfect, her makeup subtle but enhancing. And after trying on nearly everything she'd brought from New York, she settled on simply wearing jeans and a pale blue sweater that opened down the front with a row of tiny pearl buttons. Her stomach flipped as she envisioned Jake's large fingers slowly, seductively unhooking each tiny button in turn. She had settled for simply pinning her hair atop her head, leaving wispy tendrils to frame her face. After checking her reflection in the hallway mirror,

Ellie set off for the downtown hotel where Jake was staying.

The snowstorm that had helped to ensnare her in the murder was nothing more than a bad memory. On this day the temperature was a balmy fifty-seven. Why, she wondered as she searched the historic district for a parking spot, did it have to wait until now to warm up? If only it hadn't snowed that night.

"You wouldn't have met Jake," she said as she slipped the car into a spot a few blocks west of the hotel.

The walk allowed her to do some thinking. Most of it centered on Jake. She knew that once she entered his room, there would be no going back. Could she walk away easily when it was over? Would he hang around until after her trial?

It was hard to contemplate her future when she wasn't even sure she had one. By the time she entered the New Orleans-style building, she knew one thing. She wasn't doing this just because it was a diversion. She wasn't doing it out of some sense of obligation because he'd paid her bail. As her hand balled into a loose fist to knock, she knew beyond any doubt that she was doing this because what she felt for Jake was real. And strong. And very, very special. The fact that she hadn't known him long didn't seem to matter.

As she stood, growing impatient, she reasoned that if it was possible to hate a person on sight, it was also possible to fall in love in short order.

Love?

The mere word was enough to send shivers down her spine. She thought she had been in love with Michael, but three days with Jake made her more certain than ever that she had made the right decision canceling the wedding. Michael's subsequent behavior had gone further to strengthen her resolve.

She knocked again, making that transformation between being impatient and being annoyed. If the guy stood her up, she'd positively die. The only plus side of being stood up was knowing that the state couldn't prosecute her if she died.

"Stop it," she mumbled to herself. "I'm growing maudlin. Must be the murder charges hanging over my head."

She knocked, no, pounded this time and still nothing. On a whim, Ellie tried the knob. It turned. The smile came back to her lips as she entered and called out his name. He was probably in the bedroom waiting for her, champagne chilling next to the bed. Wasn't that how all rich people had affairs?

"Jake?" she called again, more as a warning than anything else. "I'm here."

Finding the bedroom door ajar, she fluffed her bangs, held her breath, then gave the door a little shove.

Jake was there on the bed, all right, bleeding and unconscious.

Chapter Eleven

"Jake!" she screamed as she dropped her purse and rushed to his side. His cheek was swollen and bruised. A small trail of dried blood had trickled from the corner of his mouth. "My God," she breathed as she smoothed back his hair and saw yet another injury. A large, reddish goose-egg-size bump dominated his forehead.

"Sorry I didn't get the door," he rasped, his eyes flickering open.

"What happened?" she asked as she carefully sat down next to him. It was only then that she became aware of the state of the room. The lamp was on the floor, the drawers were all open and various articles of clothing were strewn about. "Who did this?"

Jake tried to move and it resulted in a strangled, pain-filled noise seething out from between his tightly clenched teeth.

"Don't move," she instructed as her hands went to his ribs. Carefully, she felt along his torso and was relieved when she didn't detect an obvious fracture.

"You've got great hands," Jake managed to choke out.

Smiling down at him, she said, "That was going to be my line."

"I was all set to oblige you until my little session with Frank Moore."

"That little creep who came to my house last night did all this?" she asked, her arm moving in an arc around the room.

"He had a little help. That's how Moore works. He doesn't like to get his hands dirty."

"Speaking of hands," she began, lifting his for inspection. "Your knuckles are about twice their normal size."

"I did defend myself."

"Did you win?"

Tilting his head to one side, Jake attempted a smile. His slightly puffy lower lip didn't quite make it. "Does this mean you aren't horrified?"

"Three brothers prepared me well for this sort of stuff." Ellie got up and went into the bathroom. After dampening a washcloth, she returned to the bedroom, only to find him shrugging off his shirt. Her mouth went dry at seeing him naked to the waist. His shoulders were broad and well-defined. Unlike the light hair on his head, his massive chest was covered in a downy mat of brown hair that tapered invitingly lower.

A few red circles were visible in the area of his ribs, no doubt the beginnings of bruises. She sat down, trying hard not to let the display of bare, bronzed muscle distract her from the task at hand.

First she dabbed gently at his mouth, keeping her eyes fixed on his injury. Jake's rumbling moans didn't help much; in fact, she was having a hard time keeping her hand from shaking.

"Be still and be quiet," she snapped.

"I can't help it if I moan when you touch me."

"Jake!" she reprimanded. "Please don't make something sexual out of this. I'm just tending to your wounds."

"I have lots of wounds, you know. Moore's man was very thorough."

She gave him a warning look. "You're making this very difficult," she told him as she dabbed the cold cloth on the lump on his head. "You should probably go to the emergency room. Or see a doctor, at the very least."

"No time. Besides, I'm a quick healer and we have errands to run." Jake again started to rise, winced and allowed his head to fall back against the pillow.

"I don't think you'll be running anywhere for a while. Lie back," she instructed as she adjusted his pillows. "I'll call room service and get some ice and something for you to eat."

Ellie took the cloth back into the bath. "When did this happen?" she called out.

"Moore came by right after I got home last night. He must have been watching your place. I suppose that he decided after threatening you, his best bet was to come after me for the penny."

"Oh, Jake!" Ellie began, alarm quickening her voice. "What about Shelby and the kids? You don't think this Moore person would—"

"No way," Jake cut in. "He said you were too shocked to be the one holding the penny. You must have put on quite an act. Do you have any other hidden talents?"

"I'll never tell," she teased as she lifted the receiver. Ellie ordered him a huge breakfast and a large amount of ice. As soon as it was delivered, she made ice packs, chatted about her family while he ate, then sat with him until he dozed off.

Ellie stood and watched him sleeping, feeling her heart fill with love with each passing second. Falling in love so quickly wasn't smart or rational, but she knew as she watched the even rhythm of his breathing that she was definitely in love.

"I'M A NEW MAN," Jake announced as he entered the sitting area wearing only his jeans and a smile.

"The new you limps," she observed dryly.

Jake came over and planted a rather loud but tentative kiss on her lips. It was a quick one, which led her to believe he wasn't in as good a shape as he was pretending. "So, are you ready to hit Susan's place?"

"Do we really have to break into these people's homes?"

"We do if I want to keep my good looks and long life."

"Funny," she scoffed. "I was thinking while you were asleep."

"Uh-oh. That could be dangerous," he commented as he pulled a sweater over his head, then raked his hands through his hair.

"We've been operating under the assumption that

whoever killed Josh was framing me. What if they were framing you, instead? This Moore person sounds like he could kill without giving it a second thought."

"Interesting theory," Jake said. "But how would he know Josh saw me with the penny?"

"I don't know," she admitted. "Maybe he was outside the Tattoo. Maybe he saw you there and figured one of us had the coin. If he came to Shelby's last night, he could just as easily have gone to Josh's that night."

Jake was shaking his head. "I'll make a few calls and see if I can find out when Moore got into town. Grayson should know."

"The gallery guy?" she asked in a surprised tone. "He knows thugs like Moore?"

"Moore is a *major* collector. Of course, he steals instead of going through legitimate channels. He has several Asian pieces Grayson would kill to acquire." Apparently seeing her reaction to that figure of speech, Jake came over and kneeled in front of her. "Sorry, I guess that was a little insensitive."

"It just doesn't seem real to me. I mean, this morning is a perfect example. Shelby tells me, over coffee no less, that she's invited my attorney to the party tonight. Which reminds me—" Ellie paused to meet his eyes "—would you please come with me this evening. It's nothing fancy, just Rose and Shelby's annual bash for friends and employees at The Rose Tattoo."

Cocking one brow, he said, "I'm a last-minute thought, am I?"

She grinned. "I was. Shelby forgot to tell me I was

invited. Then she wouldn't hear of it when I told her I didn't want to come. I felt really awkward at the memorial service and I have a feeling tonight will be about the same. It would be really nice to have a friend there.''

"Friend, huh?" he asked, stroking his chin. "Is that what I am to you?"

"Loaded question."

"Does that mean you won't answer?"

"Pretty much, yes."

"Then, just to show me that you consider me a *trusted* friend, tell me about Michael."

Clearing her throat, Ellie laced her fingers and dropped her eyes to her lap before speaking. "Michael and I have known each other since kindergarten. We both work in the same field, and a few years ago, when I was the tech on one of his cases—he's a detective—Michael asked me out. It was comfortable, he was nice. Our families got along well. We went to the same church. Everyone from the parish priest to the corner grocer just began assuming that Michael and I would get married. I guess I started to believe it, too, because when he asked, I said yes."

"But you didn't love the guy?"

"I did," she said on a sigh. "Just not the way you should love someone you're going to marry. Six months before the most elaborate wedding known to man was about to take place, I gave Michael back his ring."

"He didn't take it well?"

She chuckled sadly. "No one did. My mother was furious with me. His parents wouldn't even look at me when they saw me on the street. You'd have thought I broke an engagement to the king of England the way everyone carried on.''

"So what about the restraining order?''

"Michael wouldn't stop coming over and calling. He was disrupting my work, calling me at all hours. I begged him to stop, but when he wouldn't I had no choice but to take legal action.''

"I bet that move made you the darling of your hometown?''

"He can throw paint on my car, but I'm known around Loganville as 'the woman who broke poor Michael's heart.'''

"They'll forget in time," he said, patting her knee. "Speaking of time, if we have to go to that party tonight, let's get over to Susan's. We can't go to Beth's place until we scope out her roommate and find out what her schedule is like.''

"I don't feel right about this," she said again as they entered the yard to the small house Susan rented just over the bridge from downtown.

"Don't break any light bulbs," she told him. "Susan keeps a spare key in the garden under the bird feeder.''

"How did you get that information?''

Ellie shrugged. "I dropped her off one night and she'd forgotten her keys. She mentioned where she kept her spare. The few conversations I've had with her lead me to believe her keys aren't the only things she forgets. She's a true space cadet.''

Jake retrieved the key and they entered through the

back door, hidden by a row of high, overgrown hedges.

"Good gracious," Ellie murmured.

Jake simply whistled as he took in the odd furniture, art and objects covering every conceivable inch of the floors and walls. There was a barely discernible path between the tables, candles and other unidentifiable objects. There were also symbols painted on the hardwood floor. Some matched the symbols Ellie had seen on the deck of tarot cards Susan carried with her at all times.

There were sheer curtains over the windows and bars attached to the ceiling in front of each window. From the bars, dangling on chains of varied length and material, were hundreds of crystals in a myriad of colors, shapes and sizes.

The room smelled faintly of a mixture of incense and kitty litter. "Why doesn't it surprise me to discover that Susan has a cat?" Ellie asked in a whisper.

"You can speak in a normal tone," Jake told her. "I don't think the trolls will mind."

He pointed to the far wall. Running the distance of the wall, there was a shelf loaded with the supposedly mystical statues. They all had eerie glass eyes that gave Ellie the creeps.

"Apparently Susan has all the bases covered," he said, holding up a copy of both the Bible and the Koran.

"I told you she was weird," Ellie said. "She believes in channeling. She even claimed she spoke to Josh and that he's on his way back here for some sort of karmic restitution."

Jake laughed as he began to inspect the kitchen area. "Not much here."

"She eats at The Rose Tattoo," Ellie informed him. "Do I limit my search to any place she could hide the penny?"

"Hell no," Jake answered quickly. "Look in everything. See if she keeps a notepad. One with the duck comic on it."

"You don't think Susan—"

"Look, all I know is you didn't kill him and we've got to find out who did."

Forgetting his injured ribs, Ellie ran over to him, hugged him tightly and planted a kiss on his chin. "Thank you very much."

"For what?"

"For believing in me."

THEY WALKED out of Susan's house three-quarters of an hour later with no new information. Actually, Ellie had learned a great deal about Susan's personal habits, none of it particularly flattering. She was still thinking about the self-help sex books when she got back to Shelby's.

"Judging from that smile, I'd say you and Jake had a pretty good day together."

"It was interesting," Ellie hedged as she lifted her nephew and swung him in the air.

Chad squealed with delight and yelled "Again!" each time she tried to put him down.

"Chad, honey," Shelby intervened at the point when Ellie thought her arms would come out of their sockets. "Go up and wash your hands for dinner."

"I wanna come to the party."

Shelby inhaled deeply. "We've been over this. I'll take you out tomorrow night, but tonight you're going to stay here and guard your treasure."

"Okay," Chad said before he raced from the room.

"That was easy," Ellie observed. Normally Chad didn't give up so easily when he wanted something.

"You weren't here for the hour of arguing that led up to us striking that deal," Shelby admitted. "I still haven't reached Dylan. I hope he'll be home in time for Christmas."

Seeing the sadness in her sister-in-law's eyes, Ellie said, "I'm sure he will." When Ellie opened the cabinet, looking for a cracker or something to hold her over until the party, she discovered that she automatically began searching for evidence. Without meaning to, she slammed the door closed and jumped back.

"Is there a problem?" Shelby asked.

"No, I just thought I saw a spider coming down from the ceiling," she lied.

"I hate spiders," Shelby said with a shiver.

THE GUEST LIST for the party was very similar to the memorial service. The only additions were Ellie's attorney, Max Jennings, and the dark-haired bartender named Manetti she'd seen Jake talking to.

She had chosen a simple red dress for the occasion. It seemed appropriate for the party, and if Jake's approving once-over was any indication, it was a flattering choice.

Ice and rest had kept his face from swelling too badly, though even in the dim light of the Tattoo's main dining room, Ellie could just make out the faint outlines of his various injuries.

He looked fabulous. Like that cowboy on the cigarette ad billboards. Jeans, chambray shirt and cowboy arrogance. Half the women in the room followed his every move with blatant interest.

"Nice turnout," Manetti said to her as she angled her way up to the bar to get herself a soda.

"It looks that way," she half yelled to be heard over the combination of lively conversation and holiday music. "It's very festive the way they have it decorated," she continued as he squirted some soda into a glass for her.

"You known Jake long?"

A bit startled by the question, Ellie said, "Not really. Have you?"

Manetti smiled, though there was something artificial about the action. "We go back a ways."

"You're from Texas?"

"Sometimes," he answered as he slid the glass across the polished wood surface of the bar. "I hear he lost a rather valuable coin in here."

"That's the rumor." She watched him closely, trying to determine if she was being pumped for information, or if he was just making polite conversation. Manetti didn't strike her as the type of man to be polite about anything. His dark hair was slicked straight back from his forehead and he sported a gold cap on one of his front teeth. Half his body weight was around his neck in the form of a series of garish gold chains. No, this guy definitely wasn't the polite sort.

"Too bad you have to work tonight."

Manetti shrugged. "I'm the new kid on the block. That's how it works."

"Have you been a bartender all your life?"

"On and off," he answered before being called away to serve one of the other attendees.

Ellie added Manetti to her list of Jake's shady friends. Especially after she continued watching him for several minutes. As she stepped away from the bar, she was completely convinced Manetti was the man who had been at the gallery. But why?

Jake had disappeared somewhere into the throng of people. She looked all over the place, until she finally went up the back stairs to the offices.

"Have you seen Jake?" she asked Beth as they climbed the stairs together.

The blonde gave her an arctic stare and shook her head before ducking into the rest room. Beth obviously had her tried and convicted. Ellie could only hope the judge was a bit more open-minded.

"What do you think you're doing?" she demanded when she discovered Jake elbow-deep in Rose's desk.

"Just having a look around," he answered casually. "I figured now was a good time since our hostess is working the room."

"This is ridiculous, Jake. Rose and Shelby have both gone out of their way to scour this place for the penny. Do you really think this is necessary?"

He shrugged as he closed the drawer. "I wasn't looking for the penny," he told her in a quiet voice. "I was looking for a connection to the murder."

Ellie went to stand behind the chair facing the desk.

Her fingernails dug into the leather as she met Jake's eyes. "Were you thinking it was Rose? Or maybe Shelby?" she asked, each word dripping with sarcasm and hostility.

"I wasn't thinking anything," he said as he got to his feet and came around the desk to stand next to her. Actually, *to tower over her* was a more accurate description of his action. "Whoever killed Josh had a motive for doing so, wouldn't you think?"

"Yes. That's normally how it works."

"Rose and Shelby were his employers. Maybe he was stealing from them or something."

"So, which one of them do you think tiptoed in and strangled him? Rose or Shelby?"

"Neither."

"Then why are you going through their office?"

"They aren't the only two who work here. I was checking Josh's employment records. I thought maybe he'd replaced someone. Maybe he'd complained about one of the waitresses. Maybe he and the chef had words before the murder. Who knows?"

The anger seemed to drain from her body. "Did any of those things happen?"

He shook his head, frustration showing in his eyes. "It appears that Josh was a pretty decent employee. I found nasty letters about Beth, Susan and some other woman named Tory."

"Nasty letters?"

"Customers unhappy with the service they received."

"I guess it was worth a shot," she admitted, offering him a conciliatory smile. "Sorry I jumped down your throat."

He winked. "No problem. You're really beautiful when you're angry."

"That line is older than you are," Ellie said as she gave him a playful swat on the arm. "Let's join the others before someone comes looking for us. Beth saw me on the stairs, so we wouldn't want to have to explain ourselves."

Draping his arm around her shoulder, Jake whispered, "We could tell them we were up here fooling around?"

"That would certainly make a great impression on my sister-in-law."

They were halfway down the steps when Ellie asked Jake to get her another soda while she went to freshen up. She used the employee rest room on the second floor.

An odd sensation came over her as she stood in front of the small mirror, reapplying her lipstick. A chilling sense of déjà vu. Then she realized why. The scent. It was the same sickly sweet floral air freshener she'd smelled at Josh's apartment that night. Waving her hand in front of her face, she grimaced and said to her reflection, "This stuff is really strong. Why would anyone want to steal air freshener from their employer's bathroom?"

Ellie's face was still contorted as she lifted the angled hem of her dress to negotiate the narrow back staircase. She was a couple of steps from the bottom when she heard a familiar voice. It seemed to be coming from the back parking area. It was definitely Jake, and he was shouting at someone at the top of his lungs.

Chapter Twelve

"You can't prove a damn thing!" Jake bellowed.

"I will," Melissa fired back, here eyes blazing in the moonlight. "And this time, Devereaux, you won't get away with it."

"Get away with what?" Ellie asked as she came out into the chilly air. "And why are you out here screaming?" she added as she moved next to Jake.

"Ms. Kelly," Jake fairly spit the woman's name out, "is having another one of her hallucinations."

"Yeah, right," Melissa retorted with sheer venom in her tone.

Rubbing her bare arms against the cold night air, Ellie watched the two as if viewing a tennis match. After several more verbal volleys had been exchanged, she still had no clue what this little scene was all about.

"She'll know by tomorrow morning, Jake. I had my boss send a fax to hers," Melissa said with a sneer as she crossed her arms triumphantly.

"A fax about what?" Jake asked.

"Well, well," Melissa purred, her eyes turning on

Ellie. ''I see you're not as stupid as I gave you credit for being. He doesn't know about your phone call to the New York State Police?''

Ellie swallowed hard, almost as hard as the set of Jake's jaw when he challenged her with his angry eyes.

''I can explain,'' she stammered.

''This ought to be rich,'' Melissa said as she leaned against her car, apparently content to watch Ellie explain away her actions. ''Go ahead,'' she urged. ''Do tell Jake why you're having him investigated.''

''You're what?'' he thundered.

Cautiously touching the sleeve of his jacket, Ellie implored him with her eyes. ''Please, Jake. Let's talk about this inside.''

''And force me to miss all the fun?'' Melissa cooed.

''Go away,'' Jake said as he took Ellie's hand. ''If you make any of your crazy accusations public, I'll have lawyers swarming on you like ants to a picnic.''

''You won't get away with it, Jake,'' Melissa called after them. ''This time, I've got you.''

Jake practically dragged her through The Rose Tattoo, grabbed her coat and purse from behind the bar and yanked her out the door before she even had a chance to say good-bye to Shelby.

''I can't just walk out like that,'' she said as she struggled against his hold. ''What will Shelby think?''

''Right now,'' he began through clamped teeth, ''I don't much care what Shelby or anybody else thinks.''

They reached Jake's car and he rather unceremoniously deposited her in the passenger seat. Ellie had only the time it took him to walk around the car and slide behind the wheel to compose her explanation.

Jake tossed her purse into her lap. "So," he said as he shoved the key in the ignition. "What exactly do the New York State Police have to do with me?"

"I work for them, remember?"

"And there's some sort of background check run on men you date? Is that in the employee handbook?"

"Look," she said as she reached for the door handle. "I'm sorry you had a fight with that Melissa person, but I'm not going to sit here on the receiving end of your temper because of it."

Ellie slammed the car door hard enough to rattle the glass. In an equally childish move, Jake tore away from the curb, leaving her to breathe in the awful smell of burned rubber.

"Where's Jake?" Rose asked as Ellie reentered the Tattoo.

"Don't ask," Ellie answered as she tossed her bag over her shoulder and went to the bar.

"Jake seemed pretty upset," Manetti commented as he came over.

Ellie narrowed her eyes. "I'd like a glass of wine, not the third degree."

He raised his arms, palms forward, in mock surrender. "Fine by me. I was just making conversation."

"Sure you were," Ellie grumbled as she adjusted the strap of her purse. For some reason, it was digging into her shoulder. "Thank you," she managed as she whisked the glass off the bar and retreated to the up-stairs offices.

Sitting in Shelby's chair, she took a small sip of the wine, hoping it might calm her frazzled nerves. She couldn't decide what she was feeling. She was torn between anger and guilt. "My good Catholic up-bringing rears its ugly head," she said with a sigh.

Checking her watch, she deposited her purse on the floor and lifted the phone receiver. Dave answered on the third ring.

"Hi, it's me," she said.

"I guess you got my message," he answered. The apologetic note in his voice made her instantly alert.

"What message?"

"The one I left on the machine at your sister-in-law's place. Geez, I hope I didn't get the number wrong."

"No, Dave, I haven't been home for a while. I'm at a party and there was a woman here, her name's Melissa Kelly."

"Nice lady, isn't she?" Dave said. "Very help-ful."

Surprised, Ellie asked, "How was she helpful?"

"She sent me her entire file on Jake Devereaux."

"What kind of file?"

"She's an investigator for Southwestern Theft and Casualty. Claims and stuff."

"Has Jake been filing claims with her company?"

"Filing? No. Responsible for some, yes."

"What are you saying?"

"According to the Kelly woman, Jake Devereaux

is her prime suspect in the theft of about a dozen or so articles in the last ten years.''

''That's crazy. The guy has money coming out of his ears. Why would he be stealing things?''

''According to Miss Kelly, that's how the guy gets his jollies.''

''Well, that explains one thing.''

''What?''

''Why he doesn't mind being around a murderer.''

''Don't talk that way,'' Dave said. ''But steer clear of that Devereaux guy. Miss Kelly said she was pretty sure he was in Charleston to steal a very rare item that her company insures.''

Feeling her heart begin a slow descent into her shoes, Ellie summoned the courage to ask, ''What item?''

''Some oriental thing. A Ming something or other. All I know is, it's worth a fortune and she's sure he's there to make a move on it.''

Closing her eyes, Ellie managed to get off the line quickly, promising to be back in touch after the hearing. Her headache from the previous evening was back with a vengeance. Lifting her purse from the floor, she opened the zipper and almost let out a scream. There, nestled among her compact and her wallet, was the small, ornate box Jake had shown her at the gallery.

''Oh, God,'' she repeated over and over as she tried to think of what she should do. ''You can't walk around with this thing in your purse,'' she whispered in a panic as her eyes darted around the room. She had to get rid of it, but where? And how?

It seemed to be made of some sort of clay, so flowerpots and vases were out. It was too big to stick behind one of the frames on the wall. It was too valuable to just toss in the alley. Ellie cursed to herself and at herself for being such a fool. Well, she decided after scouring the room, the trash can was always an option. She'd rather have the priceless object go to the landfill than provide the police with another reason to arrest her.

She was half considering it, when the shape of the wastepaper basket caught her attention. The bottom of the wicker basket was dome-shaped. Turning it over, she discovered that she could tape the box to the underside and no one would be the wiser. Until, of course, she could think of a way to return it to the gallery.

"SO WHAT ARE YOU going to do?"

"Avoid him," she told Shelby the next morning. "I can't believe I fell for all that garbage about him tracking down lost and stolen stuff to nobly return it to its rightful owner."

"You had no way of knowing," Shelby said as she patted Ellie's hand.

"Mommy?" Chad asked. "Are you a thief if you find it and don't steal it?"

"No, honey."

"Then maybe Jake finded the stuff."

Ellie reached over and tousled his dark hair. "I wish it was that simple, tiger. Boy, Aunt Ellie sure can pick 'em."

"Huh?" he asked.

"Never mind," Ellie said with a wink. "I guess I thought for a while that I had a special treasure, too."

"You can't have mines," Chad announced.

"I know," she assured him. "I wouldn't dream of disturbing your treasure."

"I gonna go check," Chad said as he slipped down off the chair, abandoning the rest of his cereal.

"Even my own nephew doesn't trust me," Ellie lamented. "I do have a way with the opposite sex, don't I?"

"Well, I've got to get to work. Are you sure you won't come with me? I could find something for you to do to keep your mind occupied."

Ellie shook her head. "No thanks. I'm supposed to go see Mr. Jennings to get ready for the hearing tomorrow."

"Do you need me to come with you?"

"Nope, I'll be fine," Ellie answered, forcing a smile to her lips.

Ellie was getting dressed when the phone rang. Since Gina had taken the kids to the mall to visit Santa for the fifth time, Ellie grabbed the receiver.

"Hello?"

"Is this Eleanor Tanner?"

"Who's calling?"

"My name is Martha Cadden and I have a proposition for you."

"Like what?" Ellie asked.

"Like, you tell me where Jake's hidden the coin, and I'll give you some evidence that will probably clear you of the murder charge."

"Who are you?"

"My name is Martha Cadden. Jake and I are... business rivals, I guess you could say."

"If you're a thief, what could you possibly know about the murder?"

"You'll just have to meet me to find out."

"I have an appointment with my lawyer in an hour," Ellie explained, not sure yet how to handle this. The woman could be a total crackpot. She could be a dangerous thief like Frank Moore. Or a charming felon like Jake.

"I'll meet you at Waterfront Park in two hours. If you give me a lead on the penny, I can help you out."

"Okay. But how do I know you aren't some lunatic? How do I even know Jake is a...friend of yours?"

"I know about the box."

The line went dead and it took a part of Ellie's heart with it.

WATERFRONT PARK was aptly named, she decided as she strolled down the swing-lined pier. Every few seconds she checked her watch. The Cadden woman was more than half an hour late. Ellie was growing more and more certain that the whole thing was just a hoax. Cadden was probably one of the weirdos from the gallery who'd seen her and Jake admiring the box. There was no way she could know that the valuable piece had turned up in Ellie's purse.

"Jake obviously knew," she said to herself in a sad whisper. He hadn't called that morning, which wasn't at all like him. He must have slipped it in her purse as they were leaving the Tattoo, then planned to retrieve it later that night. Except their unexpected argument ruined his plan. He was probably back in his hotel room at that very moment, plotting a way to get it back.

"God, what a mess," she said with a sigh.

Then she felt the jab at the small of her back. It took a second for her mind to register what was happening.

"Don't make any sudden moves, Ellie."

"Manetti?"

"If you do anything to draw attention to us," he whispered against her ear, "you're dead."

Chapter Thirteen

"How long has she been gone?" Jake demanded as he stood in the kitchen of the Tanner home staring at the three stricken women.

Gina spoke up first. "She was gone when I got back from the mall with the kids around two."

Shelby spoke next. "I called Mr. Jennings at five. He said she left his office a little after noon."

Rose added, "And I found this when I kicked over the trash can."

Unwrapping a wad of tissue, Rose produced the Ming box he'd put in Ellie's purse last night. He let out a breath and raked his hands through his hair, trying to think of how to proceed.

"Is this one of yours?" Rose demanded, shaking her hand just below his chin.

"If you're asking if I took it from the gallery, the answer is yes."

He heard Shelby's startled breath and decided then and there that he would have to tell them everything if he had any hope of finding Ellie before her hearing. "It originally belonged to Dr. Charles Greenfield of

Dallas, Texas. It was stolen ten years ago, along with several other items. I was just returning it to him.''

Rose cast him a skeptical look. ''Will this Green-field verify what you've just told us?''

Jake shifted from foot to foot. ''He can verify that almost all the items stolen from his collection ten years ago have been returned to him anonymously.''

''What are you saying?'' Shelby asked.

''I've been returning Dr. Greenfield's things one or two at a time. He has no idea I'm the one that's been doing it, but I'm sure he'll be able to verify enough of what I've told you so you'll stop focusing on me and let me help find Ellie.''

''Give me his number,'' Rose said.

Jake got the number from his wallet, and as he passed it to Rose he met her eyes. ''I would appreciate it if you wouldn't mention my name when you speak to Dr. Greenfield.''

''We'll see,'' Rose said cautiously. ''It depends on what he has to say.''

Chad entered the room as Rose left. The little boy, apparently sensing something was wrong, went to his mother and tightly held her skirt. ''What's a matter?''

''Nothing, sweetie,'' Shelby said as she dropped to her knees and wrapped her arm around his waist. ''Did you see Santa?''

''Yes,'' he answered quickly. ''Where's Aunt Ellie?''

''She's not here,'' Shelby told him, her tone slightly melancholy. ''But I'm sure she'll be back.''

''Not till you give 'em my treasure,'' Chad countered, his small head dropping slightly.

"What are you talking about, sweetheart?"

"The man on the machine said I had to give up my treasure."

"Gina?" Shelby looked to the tall, slender woman for some help deciphering the child's meaning.

Gina shrugged. "We went to the arcade," she suggested.

Shelby captured Chad's face in her hands and said, "A video machine can't make you give up your secret treasure. You don't have to worry."

"Not *that* machine," Chad whined. "The one in your room. The one Chad can't never touch."

"Can't ever," Shelby corrected automatically. "My answering machine?"

Chad nodded.

"A man left a message about Aunt Ellie on the answering machine?"

"Uh-huh." Chad sniffed. "He said I had to give up one of my treasures."

"This isn't making much sense," Shelby said as Rose came back in. "Gina, did the phone ring?"

"Not since I've been home."

"Did you look at the machine when you got in?"

Gina shook her head.

"Well, he checks out," Rose announced, hooking her thumb in Jake's direction. "Greenfield seemed mighty pleased that his things were coming home to roost. He told me a rather interesting tale." She looked directly at Jake, lifting one brow toward her mound of teased hair. "Care to elaborate?"

"Maybe after we have a listen to that message. What do you say, Shelby?"

They marched up the stairs in single file with Shelby leading the way. The machine sat on the dresser, its red light blinking.

"I can't believe I didn't check this when I first got home," Shelby muttered as she smashed the play button in frustration.

The first message was from Dylan. Chad immediately identified him and went into such a fit of squeals that he woke his baby sister. Gina left to tend to Cassidy as they listened to a pitch for aluminum siding, which could be installed in time for the holidays.

Then it started. "Mrs. Tanner?"

Shelby, Rose and Jake sucked in a collective breath when they recognized Manetti's voice. Jake thought of several colorful curses, but with Chad still within earshot, he held his tongue.

"You can find Ellie, unharmed, at the Wellton's produce stand out on Main Road as soon as you convince Jake to turn over the coin. He has until midnight."

"Coin?" Rose parroted. "As in 'the famous penny'? And what would our new bartender know about your penny?"

"I've known Manetti for years, ever since he started wearing that god-awful pinkie ring with the ruby eyes. He's into acquiring collectibles. He's also a real lowlife. But I couldn't tell you about his shady past without revealing my own."

"Is Ellie in danger?" Shelby asked.

"See, Mommy," Chad began. "He said I had to give up my treasure."

The three adults stared down at the little boy.

Shelby closed her eyes and shook her head. "It isn't possible," she said. "Have you had Mr. Devereaux's penny all this time?"

Chad drew his lip into his mouth, looking as guilty as original sin, and peered up at his mother. "I finded it," he insisted.

"Well, little man," Rose piped up. "You better go and *finded* it again. Looks like we're going to need it."

"I don't want to," Chad said stubbornly. "You told me if I finded—"

"Found," Shelby corrected. "But this is different, Chad. We have to have the penny or Aunt Ellie can't come home."

"Okay," Chad agreed, then went scurrying off to get it.

"I feel like ten kinds of a fool," Rose said. "To think how long and hard we've been looking for that thing and he's had it all this time."

"I'm sorry, Jake," Shelby said.

"Do we have enough time to get to this place out on Main Road before midnight?" he asked.

"More than three hours," Shelby answered as she reached for the phone. "I'm going to call Detective Greavy and alert him to what's happening."

"I...uh..." Jake stammered.

"Don't worry," Shelby said as she touched his forearm and offered him a sweet smile. "I don't see any reason to tell the detective anything other than the fact that you lost a valuable coin in my establishment and now one of my employees is holding Ellie in some sort of extortion plan."

"Thanks."

"You going out there?" Rose asked, her hands planted firmly on her hips.

Jake nodded. "Thought I might."

"Why?" Rose asked, her head tilting off to one side.

"I feel responsible for this. I knew Manetti was scum and I didn't say anything."

Rose took him out into the hall while Shelby talked on the phone. "Is that the only reason?"

He stared at a point on the wall above a picture of Shelby, a man he assumed was Dylan and the two children. "She's got her preliminary hearing tomorrow. If she isn't there at nine, they'll probably revoke her bail and put her in jail."

Rose's stern expression told him he had not yet provided her with a satisfactory answer.

"What do you want to hear?" he asked.

"It isn't what I want to hear," Rose told him in a haughty tone, "I just don't think you ought to be leading that girl on if your only reason for meeting Manetti is to get her to the courthouse on time."

"I don't know what you're talking about."

Rose snorted just as Chad came up, holding out his hand. There, in the folds of his tiny palm, was the coin, complete with the double-strike marking that made it so rare.

"Will you give me directions to this produce stand?" Jake asked as he carefully slipped the coin into the front pocket of his jeans.

"That all depends," Rose hedged. "You look me

in the eye and tell me the real reason you're going after Ellie."

"Is it a secret?" Chad asked.

Jake looked down at the little boy. "Guess not, partner. I think Rose has my number. What do you think?"

"Do I got a number?"

He chuckled. "Not yet, but trust me, one of these days you'll get one."

"Will I ever get more treasure?" he asked.

Tapping the boy's nose with his finger, Jake said, "Count on it."

"Then I suppose I can spare a few directions," Rose relented. "Even if you can't articulate your feelings worth a damn."

JAKE IMPATIENTLY SAT in his car in the parking lot of the agreed-upon convenience store. He was in a rather unwelcoming portion of the city, the part that would never make it into any of the tourist literature. This area consisted of run-down housing and even more dilapidated pickup trucks. It was definitely the land of the Confederate flag and the gun rack. Jake knew his Mercedes stood out among all those trucks and aging sedans in various stages of decay.

"Come on, Greavy," he grumbled as yet another truckload of young boys, definitely future Klansmen of America, came over to check out his car. Donning his most intimidating look, he shifted his Stetson and checked his rearview mirror for the fiftieth time.

"Finally," he muttered as he saw the plain police vehicle pull in. As instructed, he flashed his lights twice. Greavy was out of the car and waddling over almost instantly.

"Could you have taken any more time?" Jake snapped.

"I got stuck on the bridge," Greavy answered as he struggled to get his rather rotund body into the seat. "So, there's a bartender holding Miss Tanner against her will?" Greavy asked.

His borderline bored tone set Jake's teeth on edge. Reaching into his pocket, he pulled out the Ben Franklin and passed it to Greavy.

Greavy gave it a passing inspection. "What are the shadows?"

"It's double struck," Jake explained. "That's why it's valuable."

"How valuable?"

"A few hundred."

"And this Manetti character thinks kidnapping Miss Tanner for a coin worth a couple of hundred bucks is a smart move?"

"I never said Manetti was smart. He's trying to build a rather extensive coin collection. This coin would substantially add to the value of his collection."

"Geez," Greavy groaned. "This is the flakiest case I've ever worked. I've got a stiff strangled by chilipepper lights. The perp is a frigging civilian employee of another jurisdiction. Now my perp has been kidnapped for a frigging penny."

"Interesting job you have, Detective."

"What's your angle on all this, Devereaux?"

"I posted her bond, remember. That gives me a

vested interest in seeing her show up in court tomorrow.''

"And?''

"And what?'' Jake countered.

"Miss Tanner is a pretty attractive woman. Are the two of you...you know?''

"No,'' Jake bristled. "We aren't.''

"You're doing all this for a chick you aren't even, umm, involved with? One who, according to my evidence, is probably headed for prison?''

Jake leveled his eyes on Greavy. "Ellie isn't your killer, Detective.''

"Right,'' Greavy said. "So how do you want to play this? The sister-in-law wouldn't give me all the details.''

"Manetti is expecting me to meet him at the produce stand at midnight. I give him that penny, he gives me Ellie.''

"Think it'll be that easy?''

Jake shrugged. "I've known Manetti for years and I've never known him to be violent. He may have hooked up with a guy named Frank Moore. If so, I think Ellie's life is in danger.''

Greavy checked his watch. "I can have men in position in ten minutes.''

"Won't Manetti think something is strange if the parking lot of a closed-down, roadside stand is packed with cars?''

"Give us some credit, Devereaux. He won't suspect a thing.''

"What do I do?'' Jake asked.

"You make the drop as instructed. If you see any weapons, hit the ground and stay there."

"And Ellie?"

Greavy regarded him for a long moment before saying, "We can't have her miss her prelim, now can we?"

AN HOUR AND A HALF LATER, Jake was in position, every cell in his body electrified by the adrenaline pumping through his system.

Wellton's was little more than a decaying lean-to, nearly overrun by weeds and sea grasses. Opening the window, Jake listened for any sounds. Immediately the stench of rotting vegetation and a nearby chicken coop filled the car. Aside from the sound of the occasional passing car, or the call of some animal, it was a quiet, deserted place set about five yards back from the road.

Jake waited for fifteen more minutes. He looked around for some sign of the police who were supposed to be there in force. If they were, he didn't see any, nor had he heard a car in the past few minutes. Restlessness and anticipation were making him antsy. The waiting allowed his imagination to start running wild. The thought of Manetti putting his slimy hands on Ellie turned his stomach. The thought of any man touching her made him crazy.

"What the hell is happening to me?" he whispered, longing for the days when he smoked. At least then he had a way to pass the time.

He thought of Dr. Greenfield. He thought about how difficult it had been to steal the penny from

Frank Moore's fortresslike home. Mostly, though, he thought about Ellie. For the first time in more than a decade, someone meant more to him than his quest. It was, he realized, more important for him to get Ellie back safe and sound then it was for him to finish his work.

A car, its headlights on high beam, pulled in behind him, literally coming within inches of his trunk. Jake tried shielding his eyes with his hand, but his efforts proved fruitless. He had to rely on his other senses.

The sound of two car doors being opened and closed gave him pause. He was outnumbered—unless one of the people was Ellie. But that seemed a bit unlikely.

The smell of cheap cologne, coupled with the tinkling sound of gold chains, told him Manetti had arrived and was walking up to his door. A more faint set of footsteps seemed to be coming from the other side of the car. Jake cursed, not sure how to play this out.

Reaching for the handle, he started to open the door, only to have it kicked shut.

"Stay put, Devereaux," Manetti sneered. "Lower the windows on both sides."

Jake did as instructed, trying to get a look at the man on the passenger side of the car. The lack of moonlight and the harsh glare of the headlights reflected in his mirror made that almost impossible. His gut knotted. He didn't like being blindsided.

He also didn't care much for the very big barrel of the very big gun that was shoved inside the car.

"Evening, Jake," Frank Moore greeted. "How are your ribs doing? Better, I hope."

"I'll live."

"Did you bring it?" Manetti asked, his voice revealing a nervous edge. He wasn't nearly as adept at violence as Moore was and it showed.

Jake was trying to find a way to use that to his advantage as he answered, "I know where it is."

"That's too bad, Jake," Moore said. "This was your one shot at getting your girlfriend back in one piece."

"Ellie doesn't have any idea where I put the coin," Jake told him.

"I believe that," Moore said quickly. "She was very…convincing when I talked to her."

"You son of a—" Jake didn't finish the thought. He moved with lightning speed, grabbing the barrel of the gun in one fist, while slipping the thumb of his other hand though the trigger guard.

Moore twisted and struggled, all the while barking orders to Manetti. Orders, luckily, Manetti was too much of a wimp to carry out.

"I'm not doing any killing," Manetti yelled.

"Open the bastard's door and get him!" Moore told him. "I'll do the killing!"

Suddenly Moore stopped struggling and yelling. There were at least twenty people in the parking lot. One of those people was Ellie. Obviously scared. Obviously shaken. But alive. Jake knew at that moment that he loved her.

"WHY DID YOU grab the gun?" she asked as they sat in the corridor of the police station waiting to sign their statements.

"It seemed like the right thing to do at the time. Did you call Shelby?" he asked.

"Yes," Ellie said, smiling. "She was relieved, to say the least. She got all teary and had to put Rose on the line."

Tilting her head, she looked deep into his eyes, trying to make sense of Rose's rather cryptic advice.

"What?" he asked.

"I've been told that I'm to forget all my preconceived notions about you and give you a chance."

"Great suggestion," he said. "Whose was it?"

"It was a dual thing, really. Shelby and Rose both strongly urged me to go back to your hotel with you and listen to your side of things. They seem to think you're worth hearing out."

His arm slid around her shoulders and relief was evident in his relaxed expression. "Are you going to heed this sage advice?"

"You don't know Rose. You always heed her advice, unless you want to hear about it for the rest of your natural life."

"Good," he said before brushing a light kiss across her lips. "I'll light a fire under Greavy." He gave her a lecherous grin. "I have an awful lot of explaining to do and I *really* want to get started."

BEAMS OF LIGHT cascaded down from the street lamps in front of Jake's hotel. It was nearly three-thirty by the time they arrived. In spite of her ordeal, just being with Jake was enough to make her forget the events of the day. Jake pulled his car into a spot in front of the wrought-iron staircase leading to the hotel's entrance. Her throat went inexplicably dry, in stark contrast to the sudden dampening of her palms. Every muscle in her body tensed with a sudden awareness of the man exiting the car. She sat frozen for a second, teetering on the unfamiliar brink of indecision. *Nothing has to happen,* she told herself and gathered the nerve to follow him through the door.

Once inside, she struggled to focus her attention away from her handsome host, onto something benign. The furnishings seemed like a safe bet. The room smelled of a faint mixture of industrial detergents and Jake's distinctive cologne. She heard him flip the wall switch. Light from the ceiling filled the living area.

Holding her hand, Jake led her into the bedroom, again flipping a switch as they entered the second room that made up the suite. Her pale eyes traveled no farther than the king-size bed that dominated the space. She swallowed hard.

"Make yourself comfortable," Jake said, tossing his keys on a period replica of an antique dresser. Ellie quietly studied the sharp angles of his profile.

Her eyes roamed boldly over the vast expanse of his shoulders, drinking in the sight of his shirt pulled tightly across the sculpted contours of his upper body. There were a few smudges on the back of his clothing, a vague reminder of their ordeal. Continuing her inspection, she openly admired the powerful thighs straining against the soft fabric of his jeans.

This sight produced a fluttering in the pit of her stomach.

"I'm starved!"

Ellie gave a start as the unexpected sound of his voice penetrated her thoughts.

He looked at her, head tilted questioningly to one side. A faint stain turned her cheeks a light pink.

"Is something wrong?" he asked.

"No," she said. *I was just thinking dirty thoughts and you caught me,* she added mentally.

"Do you want something from room service? I missed dinner," he said softly and pulled her to him. "Then again, I think I could simply feast on you."

Protected in the circle of his arms, Ellie closed her eyes and allowed her head to rest against his solid chest.

"I can't tell you how glad I was when I found out you were safe."

The soothing sound of his deep voice caressed her ears while his fingers danced over the outline of her spine, leaving a trail of electrifying sensation in their wake. Like a spring flower, passion flourished and blossomed from deep inside her, filling her with a frenzy of fierce desire.

"Are you going to tell me about the coin and the Ming box and the—"

He silenced her with a kiss. Jake's hand moved in a series of slow, sensual circles until it rested against her rib cage, just under the swell of her breast. He needed to see her face, needed to see the same willingness in her eyes that he felt from her body. Catching her chin between his thumb and forefinger, he tilted her head back with the intention of looking deeply into her eyes. He never made it that far.

His eyes fixed on the contours of her lips, which were slightly parted, a glistening shade of pale pink. A knot formed in his throat as he silently acknowledged his own powerful need for this woman. His eyes roamed over every delicate feature and he could feel her heart beating fast through the thin fabric of her blouse.

He lowered his head slowly until he was again able to taste her lips. Her mouth was warm, soft and pliant, much like her body where it pressed urgently against him. His hands roamed purposefully over the curves of her body, memorizing every inch of the feminine flesh beneath her clothing.

He felt his own body's response and yielded to the sudden rush of urgent desire. Her arms slid around his waist and urged him even closer. Lifting her to him, Jake marveled at the perfect way she fit against him, as if her body had been made especially for the purpose of bringing him immeasurable pleasure.

"Sweet, so sweet," he whispered against her mouth. Toying with a lock of her hair, he worked his hand up through the silken mass and gave a gentle tug, forcing her head back. Looking down into her eyes, Jake wondered if there could be another sight on earth as beautiful and inviting as the twin pools of shimmering blue reflecting up at him. His ache was constant now.

In one effortless motion, Jake carried her to the bed and carefully lowered her onto the mattress. Her dark hair fanned out, framing her face in the silhouette of a halo.

"I think you're supposed to join me," Ellie said in a husky voice.

With one finger, Jake reached out to trace the delicate outline of her mouth. Her skin, in contrast to his own, was flawless and the color of ivory, with a faint rosy glow on the cheekbones. "Are you sure?" he asked in a tight voice, not certain what he would do should she utter some form of rejection. He held his breath for her response.

"Very."

Sliding into place next to her, he began showering her face and neck with a series of light kisses. When his mouth found that sensitive place at the base of her throat, he felt her fingers working the buttons of his shirt. He waited breathlessly for the feel of her hands on his body and he wasn't disappointed when the fantasy melded into reality. He let out a pleasurable moan when she brushed away his clothing and began running her hands over the taut muscles of his stomach. His passion took control.

Capturing both her hands in one of his, Jake gently held them above her head. The position arched her back slightly, drawing his eyes to the outline of her nipples.

"This isn't fair," Ellie said pointedly as his thumb and forefinger closed around the first gold button at the top of her blouse.

"Yes it is," he assured her with a smile and a kiss. "If I let you keep touching me, I'm afraid this won't last more than fifteen seconds." He bent his head forward and planted a kiss on her slightly parted lips, quelling any further protests.

She responded by lifting her body toward him, and the round swell of her breast brushed against his arm. He removed the first barrier of her clothing and was treated to a view of her ample breasts spilling over the edges of a lacy undergarment. His eyes burned as he drank in the sight of the taut peaks straining against the lace. His hand rested first against the flatness of her stomach before inching up over the silky skin. Finally, his fingers closed over the rounded fullness.

"Jake!" Ellie expelled his name in an urgent whisper. "Please let me touch you."

"I can't. At least not yet," he told her as his fingers deftly opened the front clasp of her bra. Mesmerized, Jake stared, awed by the perfection before him. His hand flattened against the erect nipple as his lips began a sensual exploration of her beauty.

He kissed the racing pulse, felt her soft skin begin to grow warm as he worked his way lower. She gasped when his mouth closed over the rosy peak, calling his name in a voice that caused an involuntary tremor to run the full length of his body.

It could have been the sound of her voice, or possibly the way she lifted herself longingly against his mouth. It didn't really matter. Jake simply found himself overcome by the level of passion silently communicated by the urgent movements of her body.

She began to resist the hold he maintained on her wrists. "Jake, please!"

He lifted his head just long enough to speak. "Not

yet.'' He reached for the waistband of her jeans, making quick work of the snap and zipper. His fingers grazed a layer of silk and lace that threatened to send him over the edge. With Ellie's help, he pushed her pants and panties swiftly over her slender hips and legs, until she lay next to him, beautifully, gloriously naked.

"Now I can't stand it anymore," he whispered, releasing her hands and seeking her mouth. He didn't know which was more potent, the feel of her bared flesh against his, or the frantic way she worked to remove his clothing. He decided he didn't really care, the result was the same.

His body moved to partially cover hers, his tongue thrusting deeply into the warm recesses of her mouth. His hand moved downward, skimming the side of her body all the way to her thigh. Giving in to the urgent needs pulsating through him, Jake positioned himself between her legs. Every muscle in his body tensed as he looked at her face before directing his attention lower, to the point where they would join. Ellie lifted her hips toward him as her palms flattened against his hips and tugged him toward her.

"Please, Jake!" she called out just as her mouth settled over his nipple.

"Please what?" he taunted, languishing in the feel of her mouth on him.

"Make…love…to…me," she breathed between kisses.

He wasted no time responding to her request. In a single action, he thrust deeply inside her, thinking he had found heaven on earth.

He would have liked to treat her to a slow, building climax, but it wasn't to be. He caught his breath and held it. The thrill of being inside her sweet softness made him want more. Pulling back, he thrust into her again, as if trying to reach the very core of her being. Ellie moved in perfect rhythm with him, her fingernails digging into the flesh of his back as they rocked together in unison. His motions quickened, growing faster and more urgent with each successive thrust.

"I can't stop," he rasped against her ear.

"I don't want you to," she replied and wrapped her legs around his straining form just as the first explosive waves jerked through him. One after the other, ripples of pleasure poured from him into her, leaving him more satisfied than he had ever been.

With his head buried next to hers, the sweet scent of her hair filling his nostrils, Jake could not relinquish possession of her body. His breathing slowed to a steady, satiated pace.

Rolling onto his side next to her, Jake rested his head against his bent arm and looked down at her. Ellie's cheeks were flushed from unspent passion. She smiled at him and began to tug closed the wrinkled remnants of her blouse.

Reaching out, he stilled the bashful action with his hand. "What do you think you're doing?"

"Being modest," she suggested as the color in her cheeks intensified along with the smoldering in her eyes.

"What makes you think we're finished?" he asked her.

His hand left hers, and the pad of his thumb gently

began stroking one taut nipple. He watched, fascinated by the way her lips parted for the rush of breath spilling from her. Her reaction was immediate when his mouth replaced his hand at her breast, freeing him to explore other, more sensitive parts of her body.

"Jake...you...don't...know what you're doing," she gasped as he continued to stoke her body to flames.

"Want to bet?" he teased as he continued to concentrate on bringing her a pleasure to equal that which she had given him.

He succeeded.

Chapter Fourteen

"Shelby called. She wanted to make sure you weren't going to be late for court," Jake said as she emerged from the shower.

"I'll be on time," she assured him as she tucked her blouse into her jeans. "All I have to do is stop and change clothes. I have plenty of time."

Jake grabbed her around the waist, falling onto the bed and pulling her onto his lap. "How are you holding up?"

"Basically... I'm utterly and completely terrified. If the judge determines that there's enough evidence to bind me over for trial, I lose everything. My job, my life. Everything."

He nuzzled her neck. "Everything, maybe, except me."

She clung to him, wishing more than anything that what he was telling her was more than just empty words of encouragement. "We're quite a pair, huh?" she said on a sigh. "I'm a murderer and you're a thief."

"Hey." Jake held her at arm's length, holding her eyes with his. "I really am a college professor."

"Who just happens to steal rare objects for kicks."

She watched as his eyes became guarded. "It isn't like it seems, Ellie."

"Then explain it to me?" she pleaded.

Jake glanced at his watch, then back up at her. Capturing her chin between his thumb and forefinger, he said, "I'll tell you everything. I promise." He kissed her softly. "It's a long, complicated story and I can't possibly tell you everything in the short time we have before you're due in court."

Ellie stood up with her hand still lingering on his shoulder. "Will you just tell me one thing?"

"What?"

"And be honest?"

He nodded.

"Was Melissa Kelly telling the truth? Did you steal that Ming box from Grayson's gallery and put it in my purse?"

"Yes."

THE CHRISTMAS DECORATIONS lining the courthouse halls seemed obscene to Ellie as she walked with Mr. Jennings. Jake, Shelby and Rose followed. The bits and pieces of conversation Ellie could overhear annoyed her. Shelby, Rose and Jake had apparently developed some sort of camaraderie. She and Jake had barely spoken two words since his admission of guilt.

"You need to try and relax," Jennings advised when they reached the door.

Ellie read the docket posted on the door. Seeing

the caption *State v. Eleanor Tanner* wasn't exactly conducive to loosening up. Her jaw hurt from grinding her teeth and her shoulders were already sore from the tension knotting her neck.

There were a few spectators in the gallery. Some wore bright red press badges, others appeared to be there just for the fun of it. Ellie would have preferred to be anywhere but there. Especially when she saw the prosecutor, her table piled high with files, evidence bags and photographs.

Christmas was just two days away. Normally Ellie would have been dashing around picking up those last-minute things on her list. She hadn't even looked at her list since this whole thing began. And something told her she wasn't going to get to it in the next twenty-four hours. Her heart just wasn't in it.

"Remember to remain calm at all times. There isn't a jury, so it is important for you to observe the decorum of the court."

"I know," Ellie said as she took the seat next to Jennings at the table.

Rose and Shelby came up, leaned over the bar and wished her well. Jake waited until the two women had taken their seats before stepping forward. Taking both of her hands, he pulled her forward and placed a kiss on her cheek. Then, before releasing her, he said, "We made a deal, Ellie, and I plan to stick to my part of the bargain. I'll find the killer."

"But I didn't help you find your penny at Susan's, or the Tattoo, or…"

"Sure you did," he insisted. "You introduced me to Chad."

"Call to order!" came the male voice Ellie recognized from her bail review.

A few minutes later the judge was on the bench and the prosecutor had called her first witness. A patrolman described being the first officer to respond. Next came the team of detectives, including Greavy, who had investigated the murder scene and interviewed witnesses.

"Detective Greavy," the prosecutor began, "did you have occasion to interview the accused?"

"Yes," Greavy responded.

"And what, if anything, did she tell you at that initial interview."

Greavy met her eyes. He was almost apologetic before his mask of professionalism fell back into place and he answered. "Miss Tanner told me that she had not been inside the victim's apartment."

The prosecutor produced an envelope and instructed Greavy to open it. "Could you please tell the court what that item is?"

"It is a piece of fabric found on the windowsill in the victim's apartment."

"And have you identified that article?"

"Miss Tanner indicated that it was from the skirt she had on when she drove the deceased home."

"So," the prosecutor said as she retrieved the article. "Miss Tanner lied about being in the victim's apartment when she was interviewed?"

"Yes."

"No further questions, Your Honor."

"Mr. Jennings?" the judge prompted.

Jennings rose and closed the button on his jacket

before stepping up to the podium. "How did you determine that Miss Tanner had told you an untruth?" he asked.

"She told me."

"She told you that she had lied?"

"Yes."

"Was this at some later date?"

"No, sir," Greavy answered. "It was all part of the same conversation."

"Did Miss Tanner give you any explanation for her behavior?"

"She indicated that she was scared, that she knew she had been wrong to flee the scene of the crime after she discovered the victim's body."

"So Miss Tanner discovered the body?" Jennings asked.

"That was her statement."

"Thank you, Detective."

Ellie felt as if she'd just seen the first inkling of light at the end of the tunnel.

"One more question," the prosecutor said. "Detective Greavy, isn't it true that Miss Tanner only admitted to being inside the apartment—admitted to lying to you—after you showed her the piece of fabric from her clothing found at the scene?"

"Objection," Jennings yelled. "Complex and it misstates the evidence."

"I'll allow it," the judge decided.

"Yes," Greavy answered. "It was after I showed it to her."

Ellie's spirits fell again. The entire morning seemed to go that way. Every witness ended up pointing the finger at Ellie. She was so depressed by the lunch break that she declined all offers for food.

"I think I'd like to take a walk," she said.

"Be back here before one-thirty," Jennings warned.

"I'll come with you," Jake offered.

"You don't have to," she said without looking at him. Ellie was hugging her bag to her chest and staring at the floor while they waited for the elevator.

"I want to," he assured her. "I don't think you should be alone."

The brilliantly sunny day seemed a cruel irony. "They call the coroner this afternoon. Then Jennings says he'll make a decision about putting me on the stand."

"Do you want to testify?"

"Yes," she said. "I'm just afraid that woman will twist everything I say and I'll end up incriminating myself instead of exonerating myself."

Jake slipped his arm around her shoulder. "What do you want?"

"I want it all to go away," she said with a sigh. "I was listening to the testimony, Jake. Even I was starting to think I did it."

"Come on, Ellie," he pleaded, stopping and gently turning her to face him. "You've got to hang in there. I know it seems hard now, but you've got to hold on to the fact that we'll find the killer before this goes much further."

And further it did go, courtesy of the coroner. The man was in his late sixties. He made the best of what little hair he had, parting it above his ear and sweep-

ing it over the top of his shiny head in a vain attempt
to deny his encroaching baldness. He was slightly
overweight and, to Ellie's complete horror, he wasn't
a medical doctor. The coroner, she was told, was an
elected official in Charleston. Mr. Kenner was a full-
time mortician and part-time coroner.

"Great," she grumbled as he was sworn in.

Relying almost totally on the reports submitted to
him by the physician who had performed the autopsy,
Kenner explained that Josh had died as a result of
manual strangulation and he had been dead for only
a brief time prior to being discovered. And it was his
conclusion that Josh's death was a homicide.

"How did you reach this conclusion?" Jennings
asked.

The coroner looked flustered. "Huh?"

"Did you do an actual examination of the body?"

"Well..." Kenner stammered. "No."

"Your Honor," Jennings addressed the court. "I
believe when dealing with a homicide, it is incumbent
upon the state to produce credible medical testimony
as to cause of death. Failing to do so, in my opinion,
means the state has failed to meet its evidentiary obligation."

"This is a preliminary hearing, Your Honor," the
prosecutor cried.

"And my client is innocent. If you don't wish to
introduce competent medical testimony as to cause of
death, then I would respectfully request an immediate
order of dismissal from the court."

"Is this necessary, Your Honor?"

The judge shrugged. "Mr. Jennings is on solid legal ground. What will it be? Can you produce the autopsy surgeon, or do I dismiss?''

"I'll need a couple of hours," the prosecutor explained.

"That's too bad," the judge said. "You've got thirty minutes. If you can't produce the witness, I'll dismiss. You can always refile."

Ellie would have preferred it if the judge had not given that last option to the prosecutor. *Please*, she pleaded silently, *I hope the doctor went home for the holidays. I hope home is someplace in another country—one without a telephone or an extradition treaty.*

Unfortunately, her hopes were dashed quickly when Dr. Steven Becker arrived in the courthouse fifteen minutes later. The prosecutor had gotten lucky and reached him on his cellular phone, having a late lunch at a restaurant just a few blocks away.

"I can't cut a break," she mumbled as the man took the stand.

Jennings hushed her and the torture began again. Only this time, the person testifying wasn't some uneducated bozo. He was a handsome young physician with a cultured voice and a definite talent for giving testimony. He was accurate, direct and had such an affable manner, that even Ellie was having a hard time hating him. She listened intently as he described Josh's wounds. She listened even more intently as he described the ligature pattern visible on his neck.

By the time the good doctor got off the stand, Ellie had her first real glimmer of hope. Looking behind her, she met Jake's eyes, then mouthed the words, "I can't possibly be the killer."

She whispered her suspicions to Jennings.

"Are you sure?" he asked.

"Positive," Ellie said. "All you have to do is get a reputable forensic pathologist and they'll back me up."

Chapter Fifteen

Jake and Ellie decided to have dinner at The Rose Tattoo. It was the only way she would be able to tell the others of her suspicions all at once.

Susan served them, even though Rose seemed to think she'd assigned Beth to their table for the evening.

"I knew it the minute Becker started talking about the ligature marks."

"Lovely dinner conversation," Shelby observed.

Ellie was instantly contrite. "I'm sorry. I guess sometimes I forget that Josh was your friend."

"It's okay," Rose assured her. "So, tell us."

"Becker described ligature marks that were higher in the front than in the back. I got to see the photographs when they passed them to Mr. Jennings. The marks, thanks to the type of lights Josh was putting on his tree, left a very distinctive pattern."

"And that will identify the killer for you?" Jake asked.

"Not a name, but a height."

"I get it," Rose said. "Like accident reconstruction. If you know how tall Josh was, then you measure the angle of the bruises—''

''I can virtually guarantee it won't even come close to me,'' Ellie promised. ''I've seen the technique used at seminars at work, and I would guess the killer was probably around five-four.''

''You're almost six feet tall,'' Jake said, excitement creeping into his tone. ''Will Jennings be able to prove this?''

''He said he would spend all night finding an expert to do the calculations.''

''That's great!'' Rose bellowed.

''What's great?'' Beth asked.

''Ellie is working on a way to prove her innocence. She should have something substantial tomorrow. At least her attorney might have another suspect to toss some suspicion on.''

Beth sneered and said, ''Is that how you're going to do it? Try to confuse the judge into thinking someone else killed Josh.''

''Beth!'' Shelby snapped.

''Look,'' Beth said, her voice softer than before. ''I'm sorry I was nasty. If it's all the same to you, can I knock off early tonight? It's two days before Christmas and I still have some shopping to do.''

Shelby glanced around at the sparse crowd before saying, ''Sure. Maybe some holiday shopping will put you in a better mood.''

''I'll give it a try,'' Beth said. ''Good luck tomorrow, Ellie. I hope you find another suspect.''

''That's the first nice thing she's said to me since I got here,'' Ellie observed.

"She's been upset," Rose explained. "I guess all those rumors were true."

"What rumors?" Jake asked.

"The rumors about Josh and Beth. Mickey told me he used to catch them in the supply closet."

"How come you never told me?" Shelby asked.

"That explains the photo," Ellie exclaimed.

"What?" they all asked in unison.

"In the picture I brought to the memorial service, everyone was looking at the camera—except Beth. She was looking at Josh."

Rose shrugged. "I never mentioned it because I didn't think it would last. Josh wasn't exactly a long-term guy."

"True," Shelby agreed.

"I'm taking Ellie back to my place," Jake said after they'd finished coffee and agreed to all meet at the courthouse the next day for the scheduled session at one o'clock.

Ellie was absolutely horrified by his candor. As soon as they were out in the parking lot, she said, "Why didn't you just stand up and yell, 'We're having sex'! I don't think that couple by the door heard you tell everyone we were going back to your place."

Jake was smiling at her. "Why are you so touchy about this? Don't you think Rose and Shelby have figured us out already?"

"If they have," she began as she reached his car, "they're one step ahead of me. I don't have the first clue what's happening between us."

"You're starting to sound like Beth," he teased as he started the engine. "Which is okay, so long as you don't start smelling like her. I absolutely hate that woman's perfume.''

Good, she thought in a moment of possessiveness. She didn't want him liking any other woman's perfume, or anything else, for that matter.

They walked, hand in hand, up to his suite. The feel of Jake's fingers making small, sensual circles against her palm had her ready to tear his clothes off by the time they entered the room.

"Wait," she managed to get out as his mouth covered hers.

"Why?"

"I need to call my folks," she told him. "They're probably sitting on the phone, waiting to hear how it went.''

"I can understand that," he said, reluctantly letting her go. "Use the phone in the bedroom," he suggested. "I'll use the house phone to call down and have some drinks sent up. What would you like?''

"Soda," she answered as she opened the other door. Glancing at the unmade bed and dirty towels, she added, "You might want to complain about the maid service while you're at it.''

Jake leaned in, saw the room, which looked exactly as it had when they'd left for court that morning, and frowned. "I'll call and let them know we'll need fresh towels and stuff. Is there anything else madam requires for her comfort?" he teased.

"Other than peeled grapes, I can't think of a thing," she returned.

Jake left her alone to call her parents and tell them all about the proceedings. She felt fairly good when she got off the phone, knowing that she had at least given them hope.

Ellie splashed cool water on her face before she remembered that they were having a towel crisis. Hoping that the bathroom drawers might contain a cloth, or even a box of tissues, she started searching, all the time trying to keep the water from dripping all over her silk blouse.

What she found in the bottom drawer made her forget about silk and water spots. "Jake!" she yelled.

"Yes?"

"You'll never guess where I found the picture that mysteriously disappeared out of my purse."

Jake reached into the drawer and got the photograph. Apparently it didn't take him long to come to the same conclusion she had. "Someone wants you to think that I had—"

Ellie placed her finger against his lips. "I figured that part out already."

Surprise made his eyes seem larger. "You mean you don't think I had anything to do with it?"

"Nope," she said as she leaned up and kissed him. "But I'm pretty sure someone wanted me to think so."

"You're incredible," Jake said as he held her against him.

"Okay. Who hates you enough to plant this here?" Ellie asked.

"That could be a long list."

"Narrow it down to someone who would also have had access to my purse."

"Melissa Kelly?" Jake suggested.

Ellie nodded. "She's a definite front-runner. Why would she do it? And when would she have had an opportunity to pull it off?"

Jake's answer was interrupted by a knock at the door. An attractive woman with a pile of fresh towels came in, followed by a man carrying a tray with their drinks.

The woman disappeared into the bathroom and returned, carting the old towels away in a wad.

"Excuse me?" Ellie said.

The woman stopped instantly.

"Is there a reason why this room wasn't cleaned?"

The woman nodded. "We were told not to."

"By whom?" Jake asked.

"The note said the lady left word that she was going to be sleeping all day and didn't want to be disturbed."

"What lady?"

The woman's eyes lowered. "We don't ask, sir."

"What did she look like?"

"You'd have to ask Joleen. She comes on at five-thirty tomorrow morning."

"That's something," Ellie said as soon as they were alone.

"It certainly limits the suspects."

"How so?"

"Whoever put that picture in my bathroom had to be a woman and had to have access to your purse. Rose and Shelby were both in court with us all day."

"I do wish you'd stop suspecting my sister-in-law of criminal activity."

Jake came over and started kissing her neck. "Who else had access?"

"I can't think when you do that."

"Good."

"Jake," she warned, stepping away from him and selecting a chair at the small table where the gentleman had left her soda. "Before we succumb to our mutual passion, won't you *please* tell me a little bit about yourself...your past...something that would make me feel, I don't know..."

"Connected," he suggested as he came to the table and took a seat across from her. "I suppose it is time for me to tell you the whole truth."

"Go ahead," Ellie said as she reached out and gently stroked his cheek with her fingertip. "I'm completely open-minded."

"It started when I was in graduate school ten years ago."

"You've been stealing for ten years?"

"Ellie," he warned.

"Sorry."

"One of our instructors was a real stickler for accuracy. Dr. Greenfield was lucky enough to have a photographic memory. He thought nothing of giving us exams that were literally hundreds of slides of various paintings. He cost more than one of my fellow graduate students their diploma."

"You're losing me, Jake."

"Dr. Greenfield was brilliant, but tough. He also had one hell of an impressive collection of unique objects. Stamps, statues, paintings, the penny, the Ming box—a real eclectic but valuable collection.

One night I was having a few drinks with my friends. We were all pretty ticked at Greenfield because he'd failed more than seventy-five percent of the class on one of his infamous exams. Impossible questions like, 'List seven Mongolian artists active during the fifth century.'''

"So the guy made you angry back in grad school. Is that any reason to turn to a life of crime?"

"It wasn't me," he told her. "But it *was* my idea."

"What was?"

"That night when we were all sitting around drinking, I suggested a way to get even with Greenfield. I told a half-dozen people how to bypass the alarm system and gain access to Greenfield's precious collection."

"How did you know about his alarm system?"

"Greenfield sort of took me under his wing. He thought I had potential, so he had me over to his house a few times."

"And the alarm?" Ellie asked.

Jake blushed and said, "Alarms are fairly simple to get past if you have a basic understanding of wiring."

"So you did it? You robbed the man just because he was a hard teacher?"

"No," he insisted. "My so-called friends did. Unfortunately, one of the guys involved looked an awful lot like me. Campus security was all over me when it happened. I almost got thrown out of school."

"You didn't tell Dr. Greenfield that your friends had stolen his things?"

Jake shook his head. "I thought I could convince

the guys to return the stuff. By the time I got to them, they had already sold half of it on the black market. They had private collectors lined up to buy the other half. They were going to be getting enough cash to pay off their student loans the minute the heat died down. They weren't exactly open to my argument that they return the things.''

''Why didn't you turn them in?''

''Because I was stupid enough to have sketched a diagram of Greenfield's house and his alarm system. They swore that if they went to jail, I'd go with them.''

''So you steal the stuff and give it back to Greenfield. How does he feel about your methods?''

''He doesn't know about me.''

''What?''

''I do everything anonymously.''

''He doesn't know what a nice guy you are?''

''I'm the guy that planned the break-in. I don't think Greenfield would find that one of my most endearing qualities.''

''So where does Melissa Kelly fit into all this?''

''Her company insured many of the stolen objects, including the Ming box. Her fanny is on the line because her boss wants to know why they keep getting ripped off.''

''Why do they?''

''Coincidence,'' he said. ''I swear.''

''What happens when Dr. Greenfield gets an item back? Can't Melissa sue him to get it back?''

''Nope. Greenfield is the legitimate owner. He's

got all the documentation, so Melissa's company ends up paying the claim.''

''That gives her a pretty good reason for planting the picture.''

''We can go see her in the morning,'' Jake suggested. ''There's only one thing I can think for us to do tonight.''

Taking her in his arms, Jake carried her to the bedroom.

''YOU SMELL GOOD,'' Jake said. ''I'm so glad you don't smell like Beth.''

''Beth?''

''Yes,'' he said as they took the elevator down to the main floor to try to catch the housekeeper. ''She positively reeked at the Christmas party. She smells like some sort of mixture of industrial air freshener and a florist's shop.''

''Wait.'' Ellie stopped in the center of the hallway. ''Does it smell a little bit like those deodorizers in public buildings?''

Jake smiled. ''Great description. Yes, that's exactly what it smells like. Promise me you won't ever wear that—''

''She killed Josh.''

''Who? Beth?''

''I smelled her perfume in Josh's apartment the night he was killed. I smelled it again at The Rose Tattoo right after Beth had been in the bathroom.''

''Do you know where she lives?''

''No, I forgot. It was on the list with Susan's address.''

"Let's get her address from Shelby and drop by."

"Shouldn't we call Greavy?" she asked.

"Let's talk to her first. I think we need something a little more substantial then her stinky perfume."

It took a little doing, but they found the housekeeper who had been instructed not to clean the room. She remembered the event, but couldn't be very specific about the woman. Apparently she had worn a towel on her head and only allowed the housekeeper to see a small portion of her face. The general description fit Beth.

Jake relented and called Greavy while Ellie called Shelby and got Beth's address. They were on the opposite side of town from where Beth lived. Mindful that they had to be in court, Ellie and Jake left immediately.

"Why would Beth frame me for the murder?" Ellie asked.

"You're jumping the gun," he warned. "Are you sure it was her perfume you smelled at his place that night?"

"Positive," she assured him.

"Happy Christmas Eve," Jake said, placing his hand on her knee.

"It will be if I can go into court this afternoon and prove to that prosecutor that I'm not the murderer." Ellie unhooked her seat belt and scooted over so that she could rest her head against his shoulder. "Wouldn't that be the perfect Christmas gift? Getting out from under this mess?"

"It will happen, Ellie. I promise."

Closing her eyes, she sighed contentedly. She had

a good feeling about this. Somehow, everything seemed right when she was with Jake. She was in love with him. That was the only possible explanation for her feelings. Being charged with murder had given her a new perspective on things. As soon as this was resolved, she vowed as they pulled into the parking lot outside Beth's apartment, she would tell him that she loved him.

"She's not home," Ellie said, seeing no sign of Beth's blue import, which she'd seen parked outside The Rose Tattoo.

"Still, I'm glad we called Greavy before we left," Jake said, a small amount of caution evident in his voice.

"Do you really think she's dangerous? If she was a killer, she'd have been prepared like your friends Manetti and Moore. They had guns. Beth couldn't have gone to Josh's apartment *meaning* to kill him. If she had, she would have brought a weapon."

"Let's hope you're right."

Jake used a credit card to gain entry to Beth's apartment.

"That's the smell," she announced as she followed him in. The scent permeated the tiny studio. That unmistakable blend was too strong to confuse.

"It sure is," Jake agreed as he closed the door. "But I still think we need something more substantial."

Ellie went into the kitchen area and started opening drawers. "How's this?" she asked excitedly. "Come see!"

"That's substantial," Jake agreed, giving her a

hug. In the drawer, next to the collection of match-books, was a half-full pad with the duck character in the corner. It was a perfect match to the threatening note they'd found in Josh's coat pocket.

"That's mine."

Jake and Ellie looked up in unison to find a wild-eyed Beth standing in the doorway.

Chapter Sixteen

"Beth," Jake began as he protectively shoved Ellie behind him. "We've already alerted the police."

He watched as fear filtered into her wide, panicked eyes. "How did you know?" she asked.

"It was a combination of things."

"Can you prove any of them?"

"The forensic specialist will be able to prove that a person of your height strangled Josh," Ellie said.

Jake gave her hand a squeeze, afraid she might antagonize the woman. Beth looked on the verge of going off the deep end. Jake wasn't at all sure how she would react when Greavy arrived. Jake also hoped the habitually late detective would get there soon.

Beth laughed wildly and dropped a bag of groceries. Candy canes shattered as they spilled onto the hardwood floor. A lone apple rolled unevenly against the baseboard.

"It's still just one expert against another," Beth argued in a voice tinged with denial. "You may have your suspicions, but, since I took the note, you don't have anything."

Jake felt Ellie dig her fingernails into his palm. Interpreting the signal, he caught sight of Greavy standing in the shadows of the hallway behind Beth.

"Maybe you're right," Jake agreed. "But I'm sure once they do a thorough job on the lights, they'll find your prints. Those glass lights can hold fingerprints indefinitely."

Beth's smile was one of madness. Her eyes seemed to glaze over as she challenged him. "No prints," she assured him. "I had gloves on. And—" she smiled smugly "—you want to know the best part of it?"

"What?"

"I was with Josh when he bought those chili-pepper lights. They were my idea. We were going to decorate his tree together. Until I discovered he'd taken a woman home from the bar. Just like he did with you," she said, directing her rantings at Ellie.

When she took two steps toward them, Greavy made his move. He entered and came up behind her, apparently betting on the element of surprise to subdue Beth.

But Beth was not about to be subdued. She twisted viciously, bit Greavy's hand and went running from the apartment.

Jake helped Greavy to his feet. The detective cursed when he saw the trickle of blood dripping from his hand.

"You folks all right?" he asked.

"Yes," Jake answered for them both.

"Any idea what kind of car she drives?"

Ellie gave him a full description, which he radioed

in. A few minutes later word arrived that Beth had been spotted by a patrol car. In the ensuing chase she'd lost control of her car and was badly injured.

The crash was only a few miles from her apartment and Greavy allowed them to come along as he responded to the call. They found Beth's car wrapped around a tree.

"She's still inside," one of the officers said to Greavy as they arrived.

"How badly is she hurt?"

"They don't think she'll make it."

Holding Ellie's hand, Jake followed along behind the detective. Greavy apparently carried enough clout so that the uniformed officers parted and formed a path for them to reach the car.

He heard Ellie gasp in horror when she saw the extent of Beth's injuries. He felt her press against him as they stood helplessly by while Greavy moved closer.

"Miss Anderson?"

He got no response.

"Miss Anderson? I'm Detective Greavy. Do you understand?"

There was faint movement inside the twisted metal.

"Miss Anderson, did you kill Josh Richardson?"

Jake didn't see or hear anything, and it seemed like forever before Greavy backed away from the car.

"Is she going to be all right?" Ellie asked.

Greavy shook his head. "She's gone."

Jake felt Ellie bury her face against his sleeve. "Did she say anything to you before she died?"

"You're in the clear, Miss Tanner. It looked to me

like she nodded just now. Between that and what I heard in her apartment, I'll contact the D.A. and see that all the charges are dropped.''

"Really?"

"Really," Greavy answered.

Jake thought he might have detected the hint of a smile.

"Go home and have a Merry Christmas," Greavy suggested, averting his eyes.

"ARE YOU SURE you won't stay longer?" Dylan asked as he moved baby Cassidy to his shoulder and began patting her back.

"I'm all packed," Ellie said. "I'm sure you guys will be glad when I take my sour mood and go home."

"We understand," Shelby assured her.

Taking in a breath, Ellie forced a smile to her lips. Her jaw actually hurt from the days of putting on a brave front through the holidays. Jake had disappeared Christmas Eve and Ellie hadn't been the same since.

"I think it was easier being an accused murderer than this," she said in a trembling voice.

"Why don't you just call him?" Rose suggested, annoyance plain in her tone. "Tell that jackass he's ruining your life."

Ellie smiled. "This is the nineties, Rose. I lose my feminist card if I go groveling after a man who doesn't want me."

Ellie jumped and her heartbeat accelerated expectantly at the sound of the doorbell. Leaping over her suitcases, she pulled it open and quelled the urge to spit on the poor delivery man. It wasn't his fault he wasn't Jake.

"I have a delivery for a Mr. Chad Tanner?"

The adults exchanged curious expressions as Chad worked his way forward.

"Me Chad," he announced proudly.

"I, umm, guess we'll have Mom sign for you," the man suggested, holding the clipboard out. "Happy New Year," he called as he left.

"For you, maybe," Ellie grumbled. Even her nephew was getting special deliveries.

"It from Jake!" Chad cried. "It my treasure!"

Ellie went over to see what he had. "Darned if it isn't," she said, examining the penny for the short period Chad would allow. "Is there a note?"

"Here," Chad said, tossing it out of the box, not the least bit interested in anything but the penny.

"I don't suppose he mentions me?" Ellie asked.

Shelby smiled apologetically. "I'm afraid not. It says the penny is Chad's to keep. A gift from Dr. Greenfield. It's even signed by the good doctor."

"How wonderful," Ellie commented, having trouble keeping the sarcasm out of her voice. "Would someone take me to the airport, please? I would like to get home before I become suicidal. I can't run the risk of ringing in the New Year any place but in my bed, alone and lonely."

"Great attitude, Ellie," Dylan commented. "Glad to see you're taking this like an adult."

"I can't tell you how wonderful it is to have such a caring big brother."

Dylan gave her a hug and asked, "Want me to go to Tyler and beat him to a pulp?"

"Probably," she admitted. "No. I'll get over him."

After she said her good-byes, Dylan drove her to the airport. He tried to convince her to let him come in and keep her company until her plane left, but she didn't feel much like company.

Ellie handed her ticket to the perky-looking woman behind the counter. The woman read the ticket, then looked up, wearing a huge grin. "A gentleman has been looking for you. He's asked several times if you've checked in."

Her heart stopped.

"He's tall, muscular—"

"Michael?" she asked in a dejected tone.

Startled, the woman said, "I'll have to check my list for the name. He did ask me to page him when you arrived."

"I don't want Michael Avery paged, do you understand?"

The woman nodded, quickening her search. "Of course, Miss Tanner. But this gentleman gave a different name. Here it is, Devereaux."

Ellie reached across the counter and grabbed the woman's arm. "Describe him."

With some trepidation in her eyes, she stammered, "Tall, muscular, blond hair. Wears a Stetson—"

"I'm so sorry," Ellie gushed, letting go of her hold on the woman. "I've had some trouble with a former boyfriend," she whispered.

The ticket agent relaxed and said, "Shall I page him?"

"Immediately, please."

"That won't be necessary."

Ellie whirled around at the deep sound of his voice. Jake smiled down at her, then produced a huge, elaborate bouquet of white roses.

"You're a pig," she admonished as she got up on tiptoes and kissed him long and hard.

"Whatever you say," he responded as he led her away from the counter and their gawking audience.

"Where did you go? And why didn't you call?"

Jake brought her to a bench and sat them both down. He looked haggard and she secretly hoped he'd been as miserable as she had been.

"I had to work things out with Dr. Greenfield."

"What did you do?"

"I sorta bared my soul. And I threw in the Ming box for good measure."

"What did he say?"

"He was so touched by my honesty and integrity that he offered me the pick of the stolen items."

"And you took the penny for Chad?"

Jake looked puzzled and he shook his head. "I took this," he said, reaching into his pocket and taking out a small velvet box. Slowly, Jake flipped open the lid, exposing a huge ruby-and-diamond ring.

"Jake," she breathed. "Dr. Greenfield let you have this?"

"Not really," he chuckled. "It belonged to my mother. I told Dr. Greenfield I didn't want any of his stuff. I think it's about time I start my own collection. What do you think?''

Ellie didn't know how to answer, so she didn't.

''You don't like it?'' he asked.

''It's breathtaking,'' she said quickly. ''I just have a hard time picturing you as a gem collector.''

''I wasn't talking about collecting jewelry,'' Jake assured her. ''I was thinking more along the lines of collecting people. You, a few little Devereauxes... We can live on my ranch, you can—''

Ellie hugged him with so much force that she nearly knocked him backward. ''Yes.''

''Is that your final answer?'' he teased as he slipped the ring on her finger. ''I love you, Ellie.''

''I love you, too.''

He kissed her tenderly, cupped her face and said, ''I know I'm a few days late, but Merry Christmas.''

''Thanks. I had a terrible holiday. How about you?''

Jake smiled and handed her the roses. ''Pretty awful if you'd like to know the truth.''

''Where are we going?'' she asked.

''To the pay phone. I thought I'd give you the chance to call your parents and your boss.''

''To tell them I'm getting married?''

''Yes. And to tell them you're going home with me, where you belong.''

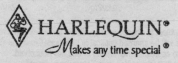

If you enjoyed what you just read,
then we've got an offer you can't resist!

Take 2
bestselling novels FREE!
Plus get a FREE surprise gift!

Where the bond of family, tradition and honor run as deep and are as vast as the great Lone Star state, that's...

TRUEBLOOD TEXAS

Texas families are at the heart of the next Harlequin 12-book continuity series.

HARLEQUIN®
INTRIGUE
is proud to launch this brand-new series of books by some of your very favorite authors.

Look for

SOMEONE'S BABY
by Dani Sinclair
On sale May 2001

SECRET BODYGUARD
by B.J. Daniels
On sale June 2001

UNCONDITIONAL SURRENDER
by Joanna Wayne
On sale July 2001

Available at your favorite retail outlet.

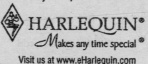

HARLEQUIN®
Makes any time special ®

Visit us at www.eHarlequin.com

HITT

HARLEQUIN *Super*ROMANCE®

To celebrate the
1000th Superromance book
We're presenting you with 3 books
from 3 of your favorite authors in

All Summer Long

Home, Hearth and Haley
by **Muriel Jensen**

Meet the men and women of Muriel's
upcoming **Men of Maple Hill** trilogy

Daddy's Girl
by **Judith Arnold**

Another **Daddy School** story!

Temperature Rising
by **Bobby Hutchinson**

Life and love at St. Joe's Hospital are as feverish
as ever in this **Emergency!** story

On sale July 2001
Available wherever Harlequin books are sold.

HARLEQUIN®
Makes any time special ®

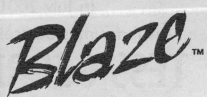

FREE Bath Spa Experience
With two proofs of purchase from specially marked Harlequin novels.

FREE Bath Spa OFFER
Proof of Purchase

Special Limited-Time Offer

<u>IN U.S., mail to:</u>
Harlequin Quiet Moments Bath Spa Offer
3010 Walden Ave.
P.O. Box 9023
Buffalo, NY 14269-9023

<u>IN CANADA, mail to:</u>
Harlequin Quiet Moments Bath Spa Offer
P.O. Box 609
Fort Erie, Ontario
L2A 5X3

YES! Please send me my FREE Introductory Bath Spa Experience Kit so I can savor Quiet Moments without cost or obligation, except for shipping and handling. Enclosed are two proofs of purchase from specially marked Harlequin novels and $3.50 shipping and handling fee.

_____

Name (PLEASE PRINT)

_____

Address   Apt. #

_____

City   State/Prov.   Zip/Postal Code

FREE SPA KIT OFFER TERMS
To receive your free Bath Spa Experience Kit, complete the above order form. Mail it to us with two proofs of purchase, one of which can be found in the upper right-hand corner of this page. Requests must be received no later than August 31, 2001. Your Quiet Moments Bath Spa Experience costs you only $3.50 for shipping and handling. The free Bath Spa Experience Kit has a retail value of $16.99 U.S./$24.99 CAN. All orders subject to approval. Products in kit illustrated on the back cover of this book are for illustrative purposes only and items may vary (retail value of items always as previously indicated). Terms and prices subject to change without notice. Sales tax applicable in N.Y. **Please allow 6-8 weeks for receipt of order. Offer good in Canada and the U.S. only.**

Offer good while quantities last. Offer limited to one per household.

425 UDN DAL9

© 2001 Harlequin Enterprises Limited
HNCPBS1

QUIET MOMENTS™

Introducing a guilt-free way to pamper yourself and restore the healthy positive balance in your life.

Indulge yourself by mailing the Free Bath Spa Experience order form. We'll send your beautiful gift box overflowing with an array of delights. It's your guilt-free reward for always being there for others.

Let Quiet Moments pamper you from head to toe. Literally!

Mail in the order form, along with two proofs of purchase from specially marked Harlequin novels (and your shipping and handling fee), and we'll send you your introductory Free Bath Spa Experience Kit.

See offer terms on previous page.